I0535632

DEATH
ON THE RUN

Book 5

The Death Card Series

By
J.S. Peck

BEJEWELED PUBLISHING
LAS VEGAS, NEVADA

Bejeweled Publishing
6480 Annie Oakley Drive
Suite 513
Las Vegas, Nevada 89120

ISBN# 978-0-9824607-9-5
First Edition: February 2021

COVER ART DESIGN: Kelly A. Martin
INTERNAL DESIGN: Jake Naylor

DEDICATION

I dedicate this book to all my beautiful readers who have picked up Death on the Run to read. It is no accident that you did, for you are the souls who know that the only choice worth making in life is to LOVE. Many blessings to you.

Table of Contents

CHAPTER 1

"Mama? I can't find my sweatshirt. It's not in my drawer!" Isabella hollered down the stairs.

"I think you left it down here. Come look."

Isabella was excited to spend her first overnight with Cal—Mike, and Brian's largest client for their detective agency. We all had referred to him as 'the mystery man' when we didn't know that he was the boss and not the chauffeur he portrayed. Cal had become part of our family, with Isabella calling him her 'grandfather.' Recently, he'd bought property close by—a large house with a separate cottage in the back where Virginia was living. Virginia was our former housekeeper and now Grandfather's girlfriend. We loved them both and were glad that they had found each other at this time in their lives.

As Isabella's foster mother, along with her Aunt Maria in Santa Fe, I was learning what it meant to be a parent to a 12-year-old daughter who was psychic. It reminded me of the time I was her age, living with my grandmother, who also had the "gift" and taught me so much about my own abilities. My grandmother's spirit still popped in with messages…sometimes at ill-timed moments.

"I've looked everywhere. I can't find it; can you help me, please?" asked Isabella in a frantic state.

"Weren't you working in the office earlier?"

"Oh, right!"

"Let's see if it's there. I'll go with you," I said.

Isabella, with Sweet Pea, our Silky Terrier, at her heels, raced to the club chair furthest from the door. Chagrined, she picked up the sweatshirt off the floor. "Got it."

We smiled at each other. "Are you all set? Grandfather should be here soon to pick you up."

My saying that seemed to make him magically appear, and as soon as Isabella heard the car pull into the driveway, she ran forward to meet him. It was a beautiful day with blue skies and warmer temperatures—typical March weather for Las Vegas. Despite that, when Cal entered, he looked upset.

"What's the matter?" I asked.

"A friend of mine called to say that his granddaughter came to Las Vegas for a stay, and now she seems to be missing. I need to talk to Mike about this and see if he'll add her to the other girl who I've hired him to find."

"It's amazing that so many girls go missing," I said despondently.

"It's easy to do here, that's for sure," he conceded.

"Do you want to wait for Mike, or will you contact him later?"

"I'll call him later. Right now, I think that this beautiful little girl and I had better not be late for Virginia's homemade pizza party. She has all sorts of things laid out so we can put on it whatever we like."

I smiled. Pizza was Isabella's favorite thing to eat. "Are you taking her to the soup kitchen tomorrow for her volunteer work?"

"Yes, and I'll pick her up afterward. We're going to spend the entire weekend together. That'll give you and Mike a chance for some alone time, too," he said with a wink.

My face warmed. "Yes, it will."

Shortly after Isabella and Cal left, Mike walked through the door. Each time I saw him, my heart lifted and beat faster. This time was no different. His handsome, dark looks drew attention, and his shy, disinterest was intriguing to women who'd like nothing better than to change that. I had been entirely unaware of his romantic interest in me when we'd worked together to bring down a drug operation. Instead of doing that, I'd broken up the auctioning off of four little girls in a sex trafficking scheme. Isabella had been one of those girls. And now, here we were a year later living like a family—the three of us—Isabella, Mike, and me.

Mike looked around. "It's mighty quiet. Did Isabella leave already?"

I laughed. "It doesn't seem possible that she's the same quiet girl who came into our lives not that long ago, does it?"

"It sure doesn't." He smiled and stepped closer. "So, we're all alone? No Sweet Pea, either?"

I nodded.

"Then, l think we should make up for lost time," he teased, grabbing my hand, pulling me toward the stairs.

I tugged against him, causing him to stop and look at me. "Before I forget to tell you, there's another missing girl

Cal wants you to find. She's the granddaughter of Cal's friend. He's going to call you later."

He breathed in deeply, shaking his head. "There's no end to all the girls who come on the run to Las Vegas looking for trouble."

"It seems to be that way."

Mike's eyes twinkled as he eyed me. "Now, *you're* a different kind of trouble."

"Me?" I protested.

"Do you know how much I love you? Come, my queen, and let me show you," he urged, grasping my hand and leading me forward.

CHAPTER 2

Later, we sat sipping wine in front of the fireplace with one of the last fires of the season. "Are the flight reservations for Isabella and me, and Sweet Pea, of course, all set?" asked Mike.

"Yup. All done," I answered. "With all the plans in place, it should be a beautiful Navajo wedding. I'm excited for Karen and Coyote; they're over-the-moon about it. And I can't wait to spend a whole week with all my sister-friends, too."

"Maybe this time, you'll be able to stay out of trouble," he said with seriousness, remembering when the girls and I'd stayed at Loews out at Lake Las Vegas and were kidnapped. At his words, a rush of goosebumps covered my body, a sign indicating that staying out of trouble might not be possible.

My thoughts turned to the phone call I'd received from Jacklyn at the Agency for Human Trafficking Services. The same Agency that had helped me become Isabella's foster mother. I was hesitant to bring the conversation up with Mike, but I thought I'd better address it.

"Mike?"

"What, baby?"

"I received a call today from Jacklyn at the Agency."

"Really? What did she want?"

My face heated. "Since the Agency's new office building is nearly complete, and they'll be moving into it at the end of June, she wanted to know if there was any change in our relationship."

"What does she mean?"

"I guess she's updating the paperwork for the state."

Mike's face turned red. "I'm not going anywhere if that's what she meant. I hope you told her that. Did you?"

I nodded and turned away to hide my disappointment that he wasn't ready to have our relationship go further. However, everything was going so well between Mike and me, and Isabella, too, that I didn't want to disturb that by forcing our relationship into something else. Yet...

The doorbell rang, and I rose to get it. When I opened the door, I was surprised to see Isabella's best friend, Sammy, standing there. His parents were in the car behind him, and they waved. "Hi Sammy, what is it?" I asked as he held out an envelope. "Ticketh for the soccer game on Sunday. There's enough for all of you, plus Grandfather and histh girlfriend," he lisped.

"How thoughtful of you! We'll be there; you can count on it," I said, hugging him.

Mike was right behind me. Good-naturedly, he lightly punched Sammy's shoulder. "Good man," he said. "We'll be there or be square."

I laughed at Mike using such an old expression. Sammy politely said, "Good. I'll call Isthabella and let her know you have them."

Before he turned away, Sammy caught my eye and whispered: "He does love you, you know."

Before I had a chance to react, Sammy was already in the car, backing out, leaving us standing in the doorway. Sammy's psychic gifts were astonishing. He seemed to know everything I was thinking, and it was a bit unnerving, to say the least. Remembering his words, I smiled and reached for Mike.

That night, we decided to dress up and go out to the fancy new restaurant in town. Now that Romano and Mimi had named their restaurant after me, I was determined to try out their competition for comparison. I thought that with Romano as the chef at Rosalie's, no other restaurant would be able to compete—he was that good.

As I backed into Mike so that he could zip up my dress, I shivered with each kiss he placed on my backbone, beginning at my lower back. When he reached the top of my spine, he nuzzled my neck, and I quivered with the remembrance of his earlier lovemaking. I was happy and turned to face him. "I love you, Mike."

"Ah, my queen, I love you too," he said, brushing back my curly, wild dark hair that insisted on being untethered, and kissed me full on the lips. I took after my grandmother with her Irish gypsy features—a look that others considered stunning—but with so many beautiful women in Las Vegas, I thought of them and myself as just one amidst many beautiful women here.

7

When we arrived at the casino, we left the car with Valet and stepped inside. The foyer was beautifully decorated with spring flower arrangements. But I was put off by the smell of stale cigarette smoke that overtook the flowers' sweet aroma. As we walked further along the path through the casino with slot machines and gambling tables on each side, I looked at the girls serving drinks to the players. They wore short outfits that did nothing to hide their intimate feminine areas. Some wore nonchalant expressions and seemed no different from the Purple Passion Lounge dancers, where I'd worked undercover the previous year with Mike and Brian.

My eyes locked with a young girl who looked unhappy and ashamed of being there. She seemed young and was different from the other girls who looked older and more experienced. The older ones appeared to dare anyone to look down on them for what they were doing. I studied the young girl for a few seconds, more to remember her face. There was something about her that was off. A man dressed to the nines approached her. He was frowning. When he got close, he leaned down and said something to her. She blanched at whatever he said and scurried away, heading toward the bar that stood toward the back. I couldn't help but wonder who the man was. As I stood there watching, he caught me staring at him. Mike, realizing I wasn't close behind him, turned and grabbed my hand to pull me away from my reflections. He'd not seen what had delayed me.

As we walked further along through the casino, I saw the same young girl standing at the bar waiting for her drink order to be filled. I stopped. "Mike, I want you to take my picture with my cell phone right now," I said, handing him my phone.

"Now? Here?"

"Yes." He looked surprised but did as I asked. "I want you to take a picture of the young girl standing at the bar, and I'll pose as if you're taking it of me."

"Whatever you say."

"Hurry. If a man in a flashy suit approaches her, take one of him too."

Several minutes later, Mike said, "I have several good ones. C'mon, let's go. People are beginning to stare… probably wondering if you're a movie star or something."

I laughed. "As if …"

"I'm serious," he said. "You could be, you know."

At the word movie star, we both became serious. Isabella's schoolmate had been kidnapped. A homeless man told her he could make her into a movie star, and she, wanting desperately to become one, had believed him. Thanks to Isabella, Sammy, and me, and our psychic abilities, she'd been lucky to escape an untimely death. I shivered at the remembrance.

When we arrived at the restaurant, a beautiful Asian lady, appearing not much older than me, greeted us. I memorized the words she used to make us feel welcomed and studied how she fussed over us as she seated us. She waved over a man standing back a few feet away. A waiter wearing a tuxedo immediately came forward and asked what kind of water we wanted—bottled or bubbly— as he unfolded our napkins and placed them in our laps. He signaled for a young boy to step forward with water choices and waited while the boy poured the bubbly water for us.

The table was beautifully set with fresh flowers displayed in a stunning, unique handcrafted glass vase placed in the center of a sparkling white, pressed tablecloth. The menus the waiter handed us were small and lighter than the awkward, larger, heavier folders usually handed out at restaurants. The waiter continued to stand by our side so he could announce the specials of the day. Afterward, he asked, "May I bring you a cocktail to begin your evening?"

Mike nodded.

"What may I bring the lady?"

"I'd like a lemon drop martini, please, with just a small amount of sugar."

"And you, sir?"

"A Scotch on the rocks, and the wine list, please."

After the waiter left, I smiled. "This is nice, huh? I'm already looking forward to my meal, aren't you?"

Mike nodded but seemed distracted. The waiter came with our drinks and the wine menu. "Take your time; I'll be back."

"Do you want red or white tonight, Rosie?" Mike asked.

"A nice red would be nice," I said.

He smiled at my double words. "Okay, red it is."

"Anything wrong, Mike? You seem preoccupied."

He covered my hand with his and looked me straight in the eye. "I've thought about Jacklyn's phone call and what she really wanted to know."

"Yes?" I asked, hopefully.

"The truth is, Rosie, that I'm not ready for marriage at this time. You know how much I love you. You mean the world to me. But marriage…"

My heart dropped. I didn't know what to say, and I promised myself I wouldn't cry. But then, my eyes filled anyway. The waiter came for our orders, and I said, "Surprise me," to the waiter, who turned to Mike in confusion. I rose. "Excuse me. Ladies' room."

I overheard Mike respond, "We'll have the filet and the salmon specials."

I knew I had to pull myself together. Mike and I'd never agreed that to love each other, we had to be married. Times today didn't dictate that. Look at my sister-friend Nancy; I scolded myself. She and her boyfriend were happy and had no intention of ever getting married. So what was my problem? I willed myself to go back into the restaurant and finish my meal with Mike and not ruin the evening, despite knowing that whatever food was placed before me would taste like cardboard no matter how tasty it appeared.

CHAPTER 3

As I lay in Mike's arms that night, things had changed between us, and it was my fault. Mike had been honest in expressing himself, and I had taken it personally instead of understanding where he was at this point in his life. This confused him because he thought I'd understand that this didn't mean he never wanted to be married. I'd taken it to mean that he didn't want to marry me.

I was embarrassed and hurt. I tried not to show it, so I put up a good front and pushed away thoughts of us merely being "friends with benefits." I wanted and needed more than that in a relationship. I'd be willing to wait it out with Mike, but he hadn't indicated anything but that he wasn't ready to commit. Where did that leave me? It was a good thing that in a few weeks, I'd be spending a week with my sister-friends in Santa Fe getting ready for our sister-friend Karen's upcoming Native American Indian wedding.

The next day, Mike stepped into the doorway of the office, where I'd kept myself busy writing another article for Women Living Well magazine. "Ready?"

I looked at my watch. It was time to watch Sammy play soccer as the star he professed to be. I grabbed the envelope with the tickets. "We're meeting Isabella, Cal, and Virginia there."

"What about Sweet Pea?" he asked.

"They're bringing her. She'll be fine."

"Okay, then. Let's hit the road."

I grabbed my jacket and followed him out to the car.

Once inside, Mike turned to me before starting the car. "Are you okay? I'm not trying to upset you, you know."

"I know," I forced out with a sigh.

"Then, let's go and have a good time, okay?"

I hated he'd said that—as if it would be my fault if he didn't have a good time. What he'd meant was that he hoped that I'd behave and not show my true feelings of being upset with him, I thought unfairly.

We met the others at the gate and headed to the bleachers where Sammy's parents were waving us over. As we walked along, Mike put his arm around me and pulled me close. "I love you, you know," he whispered.

I nodded my head and smiled sweetly, not saying a word.

True to his word, Sammy was outstanding as the lead soccer player for his team, and we cheered him on until we became hoarse. Watching him play, I sensed great things for him and saw his future as being very bright. He was exceedingly handsome, sure of himself, and emotionally healthy. He was psychically sensitive, and instead of being a handicap, he'd use his intuition for good, like Isabella. It was something I just knew.

14

"Mama, look!" said Isabella, tugging on my arm and pointing. "Tiffany!"

Tucked in between her mother and father sitting at the end of the bleacher, Tiffany saw us and waved. Her father turned and waved, smiling. Her mother sat frozen, looking unhappy. In the distance, their limo sat waiting, their chauffeur outside it, leaning against it.

There were other students from the Wilson Charter School watching the game. Interestingly enough, they sat away from Tiffany and her parents, leaving a berth of space around them. Doing so appeared to be a blatant snub to protest the times of Tiffany being a bully. Perhaps too, it was that the students didn't know how to act around someone who had been "abducted." The good thing was that since Tiffany's escape from the homeless man, she was in therapy and had become wiser in handling herself with others. There was hope for her yet, I thought as I blew her a kiss.

After the game ended, Cal and Virginia stood to wait while we talked to Sammy and his parents. Cal turned to me, "How about joining Virginia and me for an early supper at the Deli?"

I looked at Mike, who nodded. "Sounds good," I said. "It's warm enough to eat outside where Sweet Pea is allowed."

Isabella asked, "Can Sammy come too?"

Ever the doting grandfather, Cal said, "Of course."

Overhearing us, Sammy's mother, Maggie, asked, "Can we join you too? We'll make it a celebration party."

"Why not?" I said as I looped my arm through hers. "C'mon, let's go."

We sat at a large table on the restaurant's deck outside, munching our sandwiches and sipping our drinks. I felt

Mike looking my way, quietly studying me as I laughed easily at Maggie's chattering. At one point, he winked at me, and I smiled at him, happy to be with my ever-increasing family and friends.

Isabella had seen the interplay between us, and I watched her visibly relax. I knew a part of her was overly sensitive to any disruption between Mike and me. As much as I thought she was confident that the three of us would remain together, she was smart enough to realize that there were no promises that would be the case.

CHAPTER 4

Time slipped by, and before I knew it, I was packing for my trip to Santa Fe for Karen and Coyote's wedding. Mike was flying to Boston to help Brian out on a project. Then, both of them would fly into Santa Fe Thursday night to attend the wedding on Saturday. Isabella was staying with Cal and Virginia for the week, and then, they too would fly into Santa Fe Thursday night. It would be wild with everyone back together again for Karen and Coyote's celebration—including Maria's entire family. Maria, the other half of our being Isabella's foster mothers, was a joy to be around. I was looking forward to seeing her and all her family (now my family) again.

Romano and I were in charge of overseeing the construction of two buildings on the same property that used to house the Purple Passion Lounge, where Romano had been the chef, and I'd worked undercover with Brian and

Mike. All this had come about at the request of our friend and valid owner of the property, Mimi. She and Romano were in charge of the restaurant under construction and had thrilled me by naming it Rosalie's. I knew it was to honor my being instrumental in freeing the four little girls from being auctioned off in a sex trafficking scheme at the lounge—one of whom was Isabella. I was overseeing the other building, which would hold the Agency for Human Trafficking Services, a non-profit dealing with human trafficking that Jacklyn headed.

While I was away for Karen's wedding, Mimi, Romano, and Randy (Romano's life partner) would oversee some of the remaining items needed to complete the buildings' construction. The goal was to have a grand opening for the restaurant in May and the office building ready for occupation by the end of June. I hadn't realized that Mimi was crazy about gardening, and she was excited and more than willing to take on the chore of landscaping, which I was happy to hand to her.

Mike and I had pretty much renewed our loving relationship, but his unwillingness to commit was for me like a sore that wouldn't completely heal. But the fact was that I loved him, and I knew myself well enough to know that would never change, no matter what. So, I immersed myself in everyday living and keeping myself busy.

As I was putting the last item into my suitcase, Mike called up to me, "Hey, baby, can you toss down my car keys? I left them on my bureau."

"Sure, just a sec."

I hurried into the guest room to search for them in the bowl that held his loose change and several ordinary paper receipts. As I pulled his car keys from the pile, one of the keys snagged a crumbled paper receipt, which fell to the ground. Automatically, I hurriedly picked it up and stuffed it into my pocket to look at later.

"Here you go, Mike," I said as I tossed down the keys.

"Are you almost ready? I'll put my bag into the car and come back for yours."

"Yup. I just need to pack my cosmetics, and then I'm done."

When we pulled out of the driveway, my stomach swirled in excitement and nervousness. It was the first time that Isabella, Mike, and I would each be going our separate ways, and my heart already felt heavy from the loss of our connection. I realized then that a few days away from each other would be beneficial for all of us. We needed to be independent as individuals. I sighed loudly.

"What's the matter, Rosie?"

"I'm missing you and Isabella already," I said. "How silly is that?"

Mike reached over and placed his hand behind my head, stroking it. "Not silly at all. I feel that way every time I leave you."

"You do?" I asked.

"Yup." He didn't say anything more, and I didn't feel the need to ask him to explain. It was nice to know we felt the same way.

We parked the car and unloaded our bags to go into the terminal. Once inside, we stood together before going our separate ways. Mike bent his head and kissed me. "Have fun with the girls, and stay out of trouble, hear?"

"Why would we want to do that?" I teased.

His dark eyes flashed with worry. "You know what I mean. Trouble seems to follow you. Last year was a hell of a year, what with you getting hurt and almost dying so many times. We all need a break from anything more like that happening."

To hear Mike put his frustration into words made me realize how my involvement in those murders and unpleasant happenings that'd happen in the past year had affected all those in my life. I promised myself that I would be more careful and try not to get involved in anything outside my own little family.

"No worries. I promise I'll do my best to stay out of trouble. Say hello to Cowboy (my nickname for Brian, Mike's business partner) for me, and I might say to you to stay out of trouble, as well."

"Fair enough," he smiled and pulled me against him, kissing me deeply.

"Get a room," someone called out, and we both laughed.

***

On the plane, I was about to lower into my seat when someone pushed me from behind as he stretched across me to place a suitcase in the overhead bin. Annoyed, I turned to see who it was. The man scowled at me. "What's your problem?" he growled.

My problem? I thought. I ignored him and sat in my aisle seat next to an older woman. "How rude!" she said, patting my hand, consoling me. "Don't pay him any mind."

After we'd taken off, I closed my eyes to rest and relax. I was always a bit nervous until the plane got us safely up into the air. A while later, I was startled awake from a nightmare about scorpions. I must have made a sound for the man across the aisle, who'd bumped into me earlier, was staring at me. As I took him in, I was shocked to see a scorpion tattoo on the top of his hand. "What are you staring at?" he growled and pulled down the sleeve of his jacket.

I looked away but not before I'd studied him enough to be able to describe him if I ever needed to do so. When the plane landed, I remained in my seat. The same man who'd bumped into me before was now knocking into and annoying others as he grabbed his suitcase from the bin. The lady next to me and I grimaced while watching him. When most travelers had debarked, we removed our bags tucked under the seats in front of us and left.

I was arriving a day earlier than the other girls. Karen was picking me up at the airport in Albuquerque, and I was excited about seeing her and our other sister-friends and all that awaited us.

Inside the terminal, I grabbed my large bag off the luggage turnstile and turned in time to see Karen waving her arms above her head and dancing toward me like old times. Her cheeks were pink, her dark hair flowed around her pretty face, and her dancing eyes twinkled. I'd never seen her so happy. She glowed.

"Hey there, my beautiful sister-friend," I said. "Excited?"

"I can hardly wait for the big day. It's going to be so beautiful. Wait until you see my dress! It's the same Indian dress that Grandmother wore when she got married."

"Oh, my, gosh! I bet it's beautiful!"

"It is!" she answered, clasping my hands into hers. "Here! Let me take your bag."

I chuckled as I spotted my car in the crowded parking garage—an orange vehicle was hard to hide. I loved its happy color. I decided to drive the car to Santa Fe to test it out as I hadn't yet driven it since I bought it. I was glad that we'd gotten it in time for Karen to use while her car and other items were in transit to Santa Fe from Boston.

When I finally pulled into my driveway, I automatically looked to the front door. I half-expected to see a dead crow on the handle, like all the other times that'd happened to scare me away. I breathed a sigh of relief when I saw nothing there.

I grabbed my suitcase and followed Karen up the walkway. When she'd first moved to Santa Fe, I had talked Karen into staying at the house instead of renting an apartment. It would save her money, and I'd have someone here to watch over the place. Stepping inside my house always left me feeling satisfied to see its beauty and coziness and to know it was mine. Since the air was a bit chilly inside, I switched on the gas fireplace for ambiance and warmth. After I'd taken my suitcase into my bedroom, I went into the guest room where Karen was sorting through some of her things, deciding what she'd move to Coyote's house now and what she'd keep for the week ahead.

"How about a cup of fresh coffee?" I asked.

"That sounds wonderful."

"Right on," I said as I headed for the kitchen.

While the coffee dripped, I glanced through the pantry to see what I'd need to purchase at the grocery store and began to make a list. A few minutes later, Karen came into the kitchen with a suitcase.

"I'm going to take these things to Coyote's house and get them out of the way. Do you want to ride with me?"

"Why not? I'd love to see Grandmother, too."

"She's about to burst with excitement; you'll see."

"Has she said anything to you about past lives?" I asked, curious. Grandmother believed that Karen had been her sister (her bossy sister) in a past life.

"No, but she asked me if I felt anything when she fastened an antique necklace around my neck."

"Did you?"

"Not really. I've been on such a high these past weeks that I didn't pay attention to anything but how much I'm in love with Coyote."

I squeezed her. "I'm so happy for you, Karen."

Karen suddenly became shy. "So, Rosie, do you see us happy together?"

Immediately, a vision came to me of them as an older couple. They both looked happy but somewhat worn as they clutched each other and laughed. She was much heavier, and Coyote's hair was white—in stark contrast to Karen's dark hair. Yes, they'd be fine together, no doubt. But life, particularly on an Indian reservation, could be challenging, and they would have their share of ups and downs. That was life.

"I think you two are going to be very happy together," I said.

"Me, too," she agreed.

CHAPTER 5

When we got to the Tesuque Pueblo, we parked the car and got out. As we walked the path to the condominiums where Coyote and Grandmother lived, we separated— Karen heading toward Coyote's home and me to Grandmother's.

When Grandmother opened the door to let me in, she looked bright and happy, a smile stretched across her wrinkled face—unlike her sadness at Christmas time with the untimely death of her grandson. "C'mon in, my daughter."

"Thank you, Grandmother - my mother. You must be so pleased that things have worked out between Karen and Coyote, especially now that you have your sister back. Only this lifetime, I don't think she's going to get away with being so bossy," I laughed.

She smiled her toothless smile. "No… not this time."

"Karen told me about the dress she's wearing for the wedding. She said it's so beautiful."

Grandmother's face lit up. "It's ancient, handed down for many generations. It's doeskin and has held up very well."

"Can I see it?"

"Come, I'll show you."

We walked into Grandmother's bedroom, where she pulled out the dress from the back corner of the closet and laid it out on the bed. It was white leather doeskin covered with beaded designs that were breathtakingly stunning. I'd never seen anything like it before. Turquoise and red coral beaded work surrounded the neckline and trailed down the front, covering its front seam. The hem of the dress was leather fringe beaded with the same turquoise and red coral beads in different sizes, giving it a more freeform look. The sleeves of the dress were fringed as well but without the beadwork. I looked up from the dress into Grandmother's eyes.

"This is the most beautiful thing I've ever seen," I said, tears filling my eyes.

"Do you recognize it?" she asked softly.

"I think so," I nodded.

"I wore this when I was your mother in that life we shared. Back then, when my mother was dying, she told me that if I took great care of this dress and made sure to pass it down each generation, one day I would see my daughters again in a future lifetime."

"How could she know that?" I questioned.

Grandmother tenderly gathered me to her. "Everything is connected, my child. You will come to experience that more and more, especially now that the Great Spirit is showing us how to see more."

Grandmother walked closer to the bed and bent over the dress. She waved me closer. "Look here."

I turned to where she was pointing. Centered on the front of the dress toward the bottom was a scene that was part of the beaded design work that trailed down from the neckline. "What is it? What does it mean?" I asked.

"It is a mountain range. It's a symbol that means a great journey with an intended destination. So my mother was right. It was always intended for this time now." She glanced at me with a knowing look. "Maybe you'll choose to wear it on your wedding day too."

My stomach flopped at hearing her words. I'd be honored to wear the dress on that particular day, but at the moment, I had doubts if a wedding was in the cards for me anytime soon. I smiled weakly and said, "Thank you, my mother."

Karen joined us, and her eyes glowed with excitement. "Isn't that the most beautiful dress you've ever seen?"

"It truly is, and you're going to look stunning in it."

"Coyote is having a special headband made for me. Do you know what it is, Grandmother?"

She smiled and nodded her head. "I think it will be perfect for you."

We kissed Grandmother goodbye and left to go back to Santa Fe. We needed to go to Albertson's market to bring in breakfast and sandwich food, more coffee, and lots more wine. After all, we were going to be celebrating a moment we'd all waited for—to see Karen in a healthy, happy, loving relationship.

Susannah had rented a car for the week, and both she and Nancy would be with us tomorrow afternoon. We sister-friends had nearly a whole week to spend together, and we couldn't wait for it to begin.

CHAPTER 6

That night Karen and I met Coyote at the fancy restaurant at the Eldorado Hotel & Spa where we'd previously eaten together. I felt honored that Coyote was doing this as a thank you to me for introducing Karen to him.

As I watched him approach our table, it was fascinating to see the complete change in his personality when he was around Karen. Instead of the stoic sheriff he appeared to be, when his eyes spotted his soon-to-be bride, his entire stance softened. There was no question that he loved her as he absorbed her in a tender glance. Watching this, I felt that I was intruding on the intimacy that flashed between them, and my face warmed.

When Coyote lifted his eyes from Karen and turned to me, his smile was genuine. "Hi, Rosie."

"Hi, yourself, Coyote."

"Thanks for coming tonight. I want to thank you for bringing Karen and me together. You've made me a happy man. Thanks to you, I've found the woman whom Grandmother had promised me would come into my life—a true spirit of the Sun—a woman of my heart."

Upon hearing his loving words, Karen's eyes filled. I was touched by what he'd said, happy for them both.

Then the waiter stepped to the table and handed us the drinks that Karen and I'd ordered when we first arrived. I lifted my glass and touched it to theirs. "May the Sun always shine upon you both and bring you many blessings."

"Cheers," said Karen, tapping my glass once more.

"I saw the dress that Karen is wearing for the wedding. It's so beautiful! It's amazing to be in such excellent shape after all these years." I said to Coyote.

"It has quite a history in our family, that's for sure.'

"Karen said you're having a special headdress made for her. Is that right?"

"Yes," he smiled. "And no, I'm not going to tell you about it beforehand, you two, so don't ask me," he teased.

"I know it will be beautiful," I responded, "especially if it has to fit in with the dress."

"When is Mike getting here?" Coyote asked.

"He's with Brian in Boston. Both of them will get here Thursday night."

"Good, I want to make sure my best man makes it here in time." Both Mike and I had been pleased that Coyote had chosen Mike to stand up with him at the wedding. Since Mike was part Navajo himself, the ceremony's duties wouldn't be so far-fetched for him.

After a few minutes of silence, I asked, "Anything new regarding Redmond's death?"

"Still working on it," he said, avoiding any further discussion.

"Oh," I said, realizing that Coyote didn't want to upset this wedding week for Karen by bringing up that horrible time when they'd found his nephew's stiff body.

The waiter came back for our orders. We kept it simple by all three of us ordering the daily special. As we sat there enjoying our food and making small talk, I considered how life had changed drastically for all of us at the table—changed for the better in less than a year.

"Earth to Rosie," nudged Karen.

"Sorry, I was lost in my thoughts. What did you say?"

"Did you bring Isabella's wedding dress with you? I've made arrangements with Grandmother to have all the girls come for their final fitting Friday morning."

"I did. Isabella is beside herself to be included in the wedding, and I know that Nica and Angela are too."

"How could I not have them?" she smiled, pleased.

Restless, Coyote rearranged himself in his booth seat and stretched his arm out behind Karen.

"Are we boring you with all the wedding talk, Coyote?" I asked.

"I keep telling myself only a few more days, and then she'll be mine," he teased as he pulled Karen closer.

Karen looked outward, and her eyes widened. I turned to see what had caused her reaction, and I watched as a man headed our way. He was an exceptionally good-looking man—the proverbial tall, dark, and handsome type with a swagger. He walked up to the table to shake Coyote's hand. "I hear that congratulations are in order. So, you're finally tying the knot," he teased.

"Karen and Rosie, meet Tom Little Horse, an old friend whom I haven't seen in ages."

He first lifted Karen's hand, then mine, kissing the top in an old fashion way. I became a bit uncomfortable when he held my hand for what was considered a bit too long for good manners while he searched my eyes. My cheeks heated.

"What are you doing in town?" Coyote asked, tearing Tom Little Horse's attention away from me.

"Here on business. I just wanted to say hello and wish you all the best."

"It's good to see you again. If you have time, stop in the office, and we can catch up."

"Will do."

After he left, Coyote shook his head. "I sure didn't expect to see him here. We used to get in trouble together as kids. The last time I'd heard, he was a big deal in Washington, D.C. I think politics of some sort."

"He's quite something, isn't he?" mused Karen.

Considering his striking good looks, his powerful built, bright, intelligent eyes, and easy smile that drew attention, I'd have to agree. More than that, though, there was a certain arrogance about him that was undeniable. I had a feeling that we'd not seen the last of him, and goosebumps covered my body.

CHAPTER 7

The next day, Karen and I were in the kitchen preparing sandwiches for lunch when we heard the crunch of the gravel in the driveway, announcing Nancy and Susannah's arrival. We looked at each other and raced to the front door, barging out of it as if we were escaping a fire. Susannah and Nancy laughed as we raced forward. Karen ran to Nancy's side of the car while I went to Susannah's. We hugged and then gathered in the front of the rental vehicle, wrapped our arms around each other, and the four of us jumped up and down in excitement as if we were children.

Nancy was the tiny one of our group with blond curls that bounced around her usually happy face each time she moved. Her blue eyes sparkled in a face that needed no makeup with her naturally pink cheeks. She was outdoorsy, working to save any of the animals worldwide whose livelihood was threatened. Although she had allergies, she and her boyfriend lived with four dogs, among other animals.

Susannah was tall and slender with coffee-colored skin and dark eyes that shone with intelligence. She was a lawyer living and working in Boston with her husband, a lawyer, and their two Silky Terrier pups. Susannah was very proper and a bit uptight, which we teased her about. Luckily, she laughed with us, and since our college days, she was beginning to lighten up.

"Gosh, Karen, look at you! You're simply glowing!" said Nancy as she stood back from her and stared.

"You look positively beautiful, Karen. It's easy to see what love can do for you," added Susannah. "Wait! That didn't sound right. What I meant is not that you weren't beautiful before, but Nancy is right—you're glowing."

We laughed at Susannah's fumbling of words because it was so unlike her. She usually chose her words more carefully. But she'd meant well.

Nancy said, "It's okay, Susannah." She turned to Karen and me. "She went through a lot at the airport. She was hassled at the rental car agency by a very obnoxious man."

Susannah jumped in. "It was most unpleasant. That man tried to bully me, literally pushing me out of the way when he found out that I was taking the last rental car available. He demanded that I give up my car so he could have it because 'he needed it more than me.' When I told him absolutely not, he then wanted to ride with us to Santa Fe. I was furious and said to him that under no circumstance would I offer a ride to anyone as rude as he'd been," she ended in a satisfied manner.

"What a strange thing to have happened," I said.

"Almost as strange as the tattoo he had on his hand," Nancy said.

"What do you mean?" I asked.

"It was one of those bugs I'm hoping not to see here…a scorpion," replied Nancy, making a face and hunching her shoulders in disgust.

"And he wanted a ride here…to Santa Fe?" I asked.

"As if," grumbled Susannah. "Over my dead body."

Goosebumps raced across my body, and I shivered. "C'mon, let's get inside," I said.

We helped Nancy and Susannah get their luggage inside and set them up in Isabella's bedroom. They were excited about everything to do with the house and kept oohing over it.

"Anyone for lunch?" asked Karen, getting our attention.

"How about a glass of wine to go with it?" I asked.

"Yes, so we can toast Karen!" said Nancy.

"Absolutely," added Susannah.

I poured the wine while Karen doled out the sandwiches and potato chips. We sat at the island bar and munched, talking between bites about what was going on in our lives. I felt such love wash over me. My besties were the best. I didn't know where I'd be without them.

We lifted our glasses. "Here's to a long, prosperous life for you and Coyote," announced Nancy.

"Here, here," we all sang out.

"Karen, when are your parents arriving? Will your mother be here in time for the shower?" asked Susannah, curious.

"Yes, they'll arrive late Wednesday, so she'll be able to attend the shower Rosie is giving at the hotel on Thursday. They're staying right there at the Eldorado Hotel, which should make it easy for them to get around town."

"Has your mother been behaving?" asked Nancy, knowing full well that chances of her mother being supportive of Karen in any way were slim.

"You know, I've just come to accept that I'll never be good enough for her. It's her insecurities showing up, and it has nothing to do with me."

"Amen," I said. "It'll be interesting to see how your mother reacts to Grandmother. I'm looking forward to that."

"Grandmother?" Nancy asked. "Ah, yes, I remember now," she smiled.

"She's very protective of Karen," I added for clarification.

"So when are we going to meet all these wonderful people in your life now, Rosie?" Susannah asked.

"On Thursday morning, Virginia will fly here to take part in the shower. I have a limo that'll drive her to the hotel. Then, you'll see Maria, Karen's mother, and Coyote's sister, Angel, and Grandmother, of course, as well as a few others there too. Isabella arrives Thursday evening with Cal, and Mike and Brian will arrive Thursday night from Boston. On Saturday, you'll meet the rest of Maria's family and some others who I don't know." I laughed. "It's quite a crew, isn't it?"

"I remember the lonely days and nights you went through after Jeff died. I'm happy to see you surrounded by so many new 'family' members. You always said you wanted a larger family and now look at what you have!" exclaimed Susannah.

"I know," I said, pleased with myself.

"Okay, I'll eat the last sandwich if no one else wants it," Nancy broke into the silence.

We all laughed. Although Nancy was the tiniest of us four, she was the one who could pack away the food...and not gain weight. She amazed us, and the fact that she could do that annoyed Karen at times because she had to watch her weight, careful of everything she put into her mouth.

"Then let's hit the road, and Karen and I will show you downtown," I offered.

"Let's do it," agreed Susannah. "Hurry up and finish, Nancy."

CHAPTER 8

Instead of eating out as we usually did when we were together, I'd bought steaks to grill and salad makings for a simple dinner at the house. I knew Nancy and Susannah were tired... it was evident. We had walked around downtown and popped into a few of the boutiques that held high-styled clothing and displayed beautiful Native American Indian jewelry until Susannah declared, "I'm done! I can't take another step."

We returned home, and we each went our separate way to telephone our loved ones before dinner. Mike wasn't going to be available until later, so I called Isabella. She answered on the first ring. "Hi, sweetheart."

"Hi, Mama. Guess what? Last night, Virginia helped me make Lasagna for dinner. I put pepperoni in it, and Virginia said that most people didn't use that in their casserole, but when we ate it, she said that it was the best Lasagna she's ever eaten!"

"That's wonderful. You're turning into a real foodie," I laughed.

She chuckled. "I know. Are all your sister-friends there now, Mama?"

"They sure are, and they can't wait to meet you."

"I can't wait to meet them, too. When are we getting our final fitting for our dresses?"

"Friday morning."

"I'm so excited. I can't wait for the wedding."

"Well, it will be here soon enough. I called to say hello and tell you how much I love you."

"Ditto, Mama."

"Give Cal and Virginia my love."

"Okay, Mama."

I smiled. Ditto was a repeat of what I'd said to her once, and it was a very different response than her usual, more serious proclamations of love. She was becoming a teenager, all right.

Later, while I organized dinner, Karen opened up two bottles of wine to serve, and Nancy set the table. Susannah hollered from the couch that she'd clean up the dishes after dinner. It was too cold to eat outside, so we ate in the dining room, content to be together.

When we finished eating, we remained at the table to chat. "So, Karen, tell us what it's like to be here in a place that's so different from Boston… especially now that you've found a man worthy of your heart," Nancy said.

"What can I say except that it was like coming home," she smiled, then caught herself. "Not my parents' house— my spiritual home."

"Santa Fe is a beautiful place in all of its simplicity," added Susannah.

"Even though it looks simple because of its size or lack of size, its got its troubles like any big city. Just ask Coyote. As sheriff, he gets to see it all," responded Karen. "Right, Rosie?"

I nodded. After all, Santa Fe was where Coyote's nephew had kidnapped Isabella, and it is where I'd been in the proximity of two murders that had taken place here. At the time, I'd kept some of the details to myself so that I wouldn't worry my friends. Although they all knew about them, Karen had learned the more grim details of the murders because of what Coyote had shared with her. And those murders remained unresolved although presumed to be the doings of a gang from Mexico named the Scorpions.

"I think every place has much the same problems of today, no matter its size," I added.

"How are Mike and Brian doing with their new business in Las Vegas?" asked Susannah.

"Pretty good. Mike found the perfect receptionist. She's a retired, older woman who is professional, pleasant, and keeps the office organized. Mike's been busy—has another young girl to find in Las Vegas. Right now, he's with Brian back in Boston, helping him with a job. Together, they'll fly in on Thursday night, in time for the wedding festivities."

"So when do you think Mike will pop the question and ask you to marry him? Isn't it about time?" Susannah asked.

Without warning, my eyes filled. "I don't know."

"Don't you want to marry Mike?" asked Nancy.

"Of course, I do. The timing's not right, that's all," I said, sounding unconvincing. The girls looked at each other, then at me, wondering what was wrong. Just then, my phone rang, and I saw it was Mike. "Speak of the devil... excuse me while I take the call."

I went into the bedroom. "Hi, Mike."

"Hi there, Rosie. Wow, it's been hectic ever since I got here. How was your flight yesterday? All okay there?"

The man with the scorpion tattoo on my flight and the man who'd been so rude to Susannah at the car rental immediately came to my mind. Since it seemed odd to run into two men with the same tattoo, all related to the Mexican gang, I wondered if I should mention this to Mike. I decided not to worry him. Instead, I'd call Coyote in the morning about it.

"All is good here. It's so wonderful to have us girls together again. How was your flight? How is the job going with Brian?"

"It was a long flight, especially with a crying baby behind me. We're on surveillance again tonight, which is the only reason I'm still awake. I just wanted to check in and make sure you're okay and to tell you how much I love you, my queen," he said in a soft voice.

"I love you, too, handsome."

"Talk to you when I can, baby."

"I'll hold you to it," I teased.

"That's a deal," he chuckled. "Goodnight."

I walked out to the living room and found it empty. I heard the girls in the kitchen whispering. "What are you all up to?" I asked.

"Nothing," they said as one,

"C'mon, what is it?" I urged.

"We don't think you have anything to worry about with Mike. He'll come around," Nancy said. "We all think so."

"Hey, what's meant to be, will be. Now, who's ready for a nightcap?" I asked.

"Why not?" Susannah said.

"Yes," agreed Karen and Nancy separately.

It was like old times, and my heart lifted as we sat lounging before the fire, laughing, talking, and sipping our drinks.

CHAPTER 9

The next morning, I was the first one up. I decided to shower and dress so that I'd leave the bathroom free for one of the other girls to use. I shampooed my hair and blew it dry, trying to straighten out some of its mess. Once, Mike had said that it would be hard to lose me in a crowd because of my uncontrollable hair that was very noticeable. At the time, I'd laughed, but he was right. Frustrated, I pulled it back into a ponytail for now.

I reached for the jeans I'd worn on my flight to Santa Fe, and as I lifted them off the chair, I heard the crinkling of paper. I reached into the pocket and pulled out the slip that had fallen when I'd gotten Mike's car keys from his bureau. As I was about to open it to read, the door opened. "Oops, sorry," said Karen, as she saw I wasn't fully dressed.

I put the slip on the change dish on top of the dresser and turned to her. "C'mon in."

"The girls are awake. I wanted to know if you're ready for a cup of coffee."

"Heck, yeah," I answered, pulling on the day-old jeans. "I'm coming."

As we sat sipping our coffee and chewing on the Mexican donuts I'd bought yesterday, Karen said, "How about getting out the tarot cards, Rosie?"

My thoughts were topsy-turvy with Mike's not wanting to be married, and I didn't think my mind was clear enough to do four readings or even have each of us pick out a card as we'd done before. "Okay, but let's keep it simple this time. I'll shuffle the cards and spread them out on the table. Then, we'll place our hands together and choose just one card, which will be for all of us, okay?"

"How are we going to do that?" asked Nancy.

"We'll pile our hands on top of each other and hover them over the cards until we focus on a card and choose it. Deal?"

"Sounds good to me," said Susannah.

"I'm game," added Karen.

"Let's do it," agreed Nancy. "You be first, Rosie."

"Let me shuffle the cards first."

I got my cards and began to shuffle them. "Think about a question you want to ask the card, and that will help it step forward."

After several more shuffles, I spread the cards on the table. "Okay," said Nancy, "hold out your hand, Rosie, and then Susannah, you go next, then Karen, then me."

I shut my eyes and thought about my situation with Mike. I let the others guide our hands lower and then hover over a card out of alignment with the others.

"That's the one, the one sticking out of the pile, right?" asked Nancy.

"Yes, that'll do," said Karen.

"Why not?" replied Susannah.

We held our breath as they removed their hands off mine, and I bent lower toward the card we'd pick together to share. Then, I turned the card over.

"Oh, my!"

"Oh, no!"

"Why did it have to be the Death card?" moaned Karen.

"Wait! Remember, the Death card doesn't always mean death; it also means a new beginning. Look at all the changes we're going through, so it makes sense. Don't worry; this card is simply showing new beginnings," I said. "So, let's take turns to share the latest on the changes you're in the process of making. Susannah, why don't you begin?"

"Okay. As you know, Henry and I want to team up professionally with me as a probate and estate lawyer and Henry as a real estate lawyer. It makes for a nice husband-wife team, we think. We've looked at office space and have found what we want. Henry is trying to close the deal as we speak. Of course, then we have to let our law firms know what we're doing."

"How do you think that's going to work out?" asked Nancy.

"My boss and I have had several conversations this past year, and he knows I'm not happy working there. So I don't think he'll be that surprised."

"My God! How exciting! Will you be able to take Brut and Chanel into work with you?" I asked, wondering about their two Silky Terrier pups, who I'd psychically seen in their new office.

A smile spread across Susannah's face. "Yes. That's one of the benefits of our joining forces. Neither one of us will worry about the pups being alone at home." She chuckled. "They're our babies, after all."

"Maybe I'll be your first customer in your new location. I have to decide what to do with my condo in Boston. We'll talk later," Karen said.

"Speaking of babies, how about you, Nancy?" I asked.

"Well, as much fun as it is trying to get pregnant, that's not happened so far. We thought that after being together for seven years, all we'd have to say is 'Let's get pregnant,' and it'd happen. But we're not discouraged yet," declared Nancy in a positive tone.

"What changed your mind about wanting to get pregnant?" asked Susannah.

"My age. And we talked about the fact that we have so many pets and animals around that having a baby is probably not that much more work than taking care of the animals," she laughed. "And Steve said that he's had me all to himself for seven years, so he's ready to take a back seat to the baby."

We laughed. We loved Steve's open, honest, easy-going style. He and Henry would be joining us in Santa Fe on Thursday for the wedding.

"Just don't think about it or worry about getting pregnant, and it'll happen soon enough," I encouraged.

"Karen, what's new with you since our last conference call?" asked Nancy.

"Well, as you all know, I've cut all ties with my ex-boyfriend and his sister. Not that I wanted to with his sister. But she was unhappy with my decision to 'marry an Indian, of all things,' so that's a closed door. But the good news is that the school where I taught for so many years wrote a long, very complimentary letter to the pueblo school, and they are now considering me for a full-time position. I'm very excited about that."

"Congratulations, Karen! Another reason to toast you," exclaimed Susannah, lifting her coffee mug toward the rest of us.

"Hear, hear!" we cried, and I winked at Karen, knowing she'd understand I was messaging her that it was going to turn out splendidly for her.

"Alright, Rosie, your turn," urged Nancy.

"Well, where to begin, huh? You know about what happened to Isabella's friend, Tiffany. There's more to come regarding that. Other girls fell for the movie star ploy, and Mike will be helping Roberto, the Police Chief, to search for them.

"Mike and I are crazy about Sammy, Isabella's boyfriend, or rather her friend who's a boy," I laughed. "He's darling and is very psychic—eerily so. And his family is great fun."

"And you already know, I was thrilled to have Romano and Mimi name their restaurant after me. You'll come to the opening as promised, won't you?"

Each nodded with excitement. "Just make sure to send an email with the information once we get home so that we can put it into our calendar, okay?" requested Susannah.

"That's about it," I finished. "Okay, girls, let's go shopping, shall we?" I worried that they wouldn't let me off the hook without explaining more thoughts of Mike and me getting engaged. But the moment passed.

"I want to buy some Indian jewelry," said Susannah, which surprised us since her taste was strictly classic and relatively unadorned.

Karen and I looked at each other. "We know the perfect place," I said.

"The Palace of the Governors?" Karen asked.

"Yes, perfect," I said. "Go get dressed, and let's go shopping!"

I thought about the Death card we'd chosen, and I felt goosebumps across my body. Yes, we had many changes going on with each of us; yet, there were also undercurrents of something else in the works to have run into two different men with scorpion tattoos headed to Santa Fe. I was worried. I needed to make sure the girls were safe. I remembered other times I'd felt this same way, and it hadn't turned out so well.

CHAPTER 10

I went back to my bedroom to grab my purse. My car keys were on top of the dresser. Like what'd happened before getting the car keys for Mike, the same receipt snagged onto the keys and fell to the floor. This time, I picked it up and opened it. It was a jewelry receipt from the store downtown. It didn't say what it was for, and I wondered if I should check with the store to see if the ticket was no longer needed. I put it into my purse and went out to the kitchen and refilled my coffee cup. I usually had only one cup in the morning, but today I felt I needed to be alert. I could feel it in my bones.

While I waited for the girls, I called Coyote. "Do you have a minute? I have something I want to run by you. Something weird is going on, Coyote, and I don't want the girls to know what we're discussing. I don't want anything to upset Karen's special week."

"What is it?" he asked.

I told him about the two separate incidents with the men who had scorpion tattoos, and he was silent for several minutes. "Yes," he said. "It's possible since we've heard rumblings about a secret meeting here with many of the gang members. I can't see how it would affect you girls, though. But keep an eye out, and let me know right away if you notice anything—anything at all, okay?"

"Okay, I will, but I don't like it," I said. "Oops, gotta go. The girls are coming. Bye."

"You look like the cat who's swallowed the canary. What's up?" asked Susannah.

"Nothing. Just waiting on you, girls. Ready to go?" I asked.

The morning had warmed, and I wasn't sure if Grandmother would be sitting at the Palace of the Governors selling her jewelry as she usually did with the other Native American Indians from the different surrounding pueblos. We were early enough to find a parking spot a short distance away. We piled out of the car and walked across the street to face the Indians sitting on their blankets with their wares spread before them. Some were squatting, leaning forward, bartering for a sale with the few visitors already there.

Karen and I looked at each other and smiled. Grandmother was sitting in her spot, smiling, already waving us closer. Turning to Nancy and Susannah, I said, "You, my dear friends, are going to meet Grandmother, the wonderful woman whom Karen and I both talk about all the time."

Karen pushed me forward, wanting me to be the first one to greet Grandmother and to introduce her to Nancy and Susannah. "Grandmother – my mother," I said, kissing her on each cheek. "These are the two sister-friends that Karen and I have told you about. This is Nancy, and this is Susannah."

Grandmother's smile increased as she reached out and held onto each of their hands. "Welcome, my children." She turned to Karen and spoke Tewa. "They are beautiful spirits."

Karen responded in Tewa, "They are blessings to Rosie and me."

"As you are to them," she retorted.

Grandmother turned to the girls and studied them both. "You are moving, my child?" she asked Susannah.

"Yes, or I should say, our businesses are."

"Ahh. You'll be very successful and happy," stated Grandmother knowingly.

Susannah smiled. "Thank you, Grandmother," she said in reverence. Then, she backed away and went to stand beside Karen.

Grandmother patted Nancy's hand. "You have great patience, which is good. In time, your children will come— maybe more than one at a time."

"Thank you, Grandmother," smiled Nancy.

"Come, dear sister," Grandmother said to Karen, who bent and kissed each cheek. "Your special day awaits. Have you told the girls we need to rehearse their roles?"

"When do you want us to meet with you?"

"Tomorrow is soon enough. Come to the pueblo."

Susannah had walked away and was viewing the jewelry on display at the other end of the row. Nancy had picked up a piece of jewelry that Grandmother had created. "This is so beautiful." It was a simple silver band with an ornate small sun in the center and a small turquoise stone on either side. "What's the meaning of the sun, Grandmother?"

"The sun means happiness and new beginnings as with each new day."

"This is perfect, then. I'll take it," Nancy said as she placed it on her wrist.

Grandmother began to push her money away, and Nancy stood firm.

"Grandmother, I've traveled to different places in the world and have met women like you who create beautiful things. This bracelet will mean nothing to me if I can't honor you and what you've created by paying for it."

Grandmother looked pleased and took the money held out to her.

Susannah came back to where we stood, empty-handed.

"We'll be meeting with Grandmother tomorrow to go over our training for the ceremony," I told her. "Is everyone ready to move on?" I asked.

We said goodbye to Grandmother, walked to the car, and climbed back inside. "Where to?" I asked.

"Anybody for lunch?" asked Nancy.

CHAPTER 11

As we ordered our food, it was as if we were back at college. We took our time as we studied the menu, counting calories. The waitress stepped to our table for our orders, and as soon as Nancy said she was going to have the taco salad, then Susannah, Karen, and I immediately chimed in, "I'll have the same."

Nancy looked surprised. "It took you all this time to decide to have what I'm having?" she teased.

We all laughed. "Sometimes, it's just easier to go with the flow," Susannah said.

"I like to check out all the food before I decide," I said.

"Me, too," Karen said. "You never know what you might be missing unless you read the entire menu."

The food was yummy, and we were stuffed by the time we finished. No desserts—even for Nancy. We stepped outside, and Susannah pointed to a boutique across the street. "Let's go in there," she said. "It looks interesting."

A few stores down was the jewelry store listed on the receipt I had in my bag. "Sounds good," I said. "I have a quick errand to run, and I'll meet you there."

I left them at the store and walked further down the street to the jewelry store. When I walked through the door, a charming middle-aged man greeted me. "Hola. How may I help you?"

"Hola. I want to check if this receipt is still valid." I pulled it from my bag and unfolded it.

"Here, let me see," said the man, reaching for it. When he saw what it was, his face broke into a smile. "Do you need it adjusted? Do you have it with you?"

I didn't know what to say.

"I see you're not wearing it. Maybe you'd like to take more time to decide. Wear it for a while and see. You can always bring it back to be adjusted."

I looked at my wrist, which usually held the bracelet Mike had given me for Christmas. I was surprised to see it was bare. I forgot to put it on this morning. "Thank you; that's very kind of you."

"Congratulations. It's a beautiful piece," he said with a smile.

I left the store confused. I didn't want to lose this receipt should it be needed in the future. I'd have to return it to Mike's dresser, where I'd found it in the first place. Unfortunately, I wouldn't be able to do that until I was back in Las Vegas, so I stuffed it back into my purse.

Karen took one look at my face when I entered the boutique and asked, "Everything okay?"

I nodded. "Fine. Is Susannah having any luck finding anything?"

Karen smiled. "Quite a few things. Since she'll no longer have to wear boring suits, she's looking at dresses, skirts, and dress pants that are more feminine and stylish for her new office."

"Ohh, I can't wait to see them!" I exclaimed.

Susannah was shapely and tall at 5'11", and that, along with her coffee-colored skin and dark brown eyes that snapped with intelligence, drew your attention. As she tried on one outfit after another for us to vote on, she laughed and twirled around as models did on the runway. She was having a wonderful time, and we laughed with her. It ended up with her purchasing six different outfits having five of them mailed back to Boston.

"How about some jewelry to go with those outfits?" I asked. "The store where Karen and I bought our earrings is right around the corner."

"Yes, I need to do that. It's why I bought fairly simple designs that would be great as a background for beautiful Indian jewelry. I'm going to change my life around—and have fun doing it!" she exclaimed. "I need to let loose!"

The others of us looked at each other and grinned. We'd wanted Susannah to do that for a long time. Her background growing up had been rough, to say the least, and to hide her lack of positive upbringing, she was determined to do everything "by the book" and be correct. This new side of Susannah was exciting to see.

We headed to the jewelry store so Susannah could hunt for her treasures, and Nancy could look for a necklace. Once inside, Karen and I stepped back and let them take all the time they wanted to shop. We stood by the window and watched the tourists pass us by. At one point, I thought I saw the same tall man who'd met with Johnny, my former boss, at the airport a few months back—the same one

Mike, Isabella, and I had seen the last time we flew into Albuquerque. He also wore a scorpion tattoo and now was rushing down the street as if he were late for a meeting. I leaned closer to the window to continue to watch him as he turned into an alley that led to several older buildings.

"What are you looking at?" asked Karen.

"I thought I recognized someone, but I'm not sure it's the same person."

"What do you think?" asked Nancy as she approached us. "It's between these two necklaces."

One was a simple pounded silver wire about a one-quarter inch thick that could be used plain or with a slide. The other one had a silver chain that held an attachment of a sun with a turquoise stone in the center. Both were beautiful.

"Well …?" she asked.

"I think you should get them both," I laughed.

"Why did I know you'd say that? How about you, Karen?"

"It'd be hard to leave one of them behind. Sorry," Karen said, knowing she was no help, either.

"Well then, I guess I'll just have to buy them both!" exclaimed Nancy.

Susannah bought several jewelry pieces, including a necklace nearly the same as Karen's and my Indian pearls, a slide, earrings, and two bracelets. "I'm going to wait for Henry to help me pick out a few more pieces."

We ended our shopping spree and headed back to the car. As we were about to pass by the alleyway where I saw the tall man enter, I said, "Let's see what's down here, shall we?"

We headed into it, and Karen commented, "Doesn't look like there's much down here."

"Let's see where it ends up," I urged.

"Wow, look at this big house tucked in here. It looks like it could have been a small inn at one time," said Nancy, the traveler.

"It looks like one of the tiny streets in the North End in Boston," added Susannah.

As we came out the other end, we saw we weren't that far from Albertson's market. I stopped and looked around so that I would remember the location of this alleyway.

Karen eyed me and asked, "Did you find what you were looking for, Rosie?"

I shook my head. "I wanted to see what was down here, is all."

The large house in the alley would be a perfect place for the Scorpions to meet, I thought, as goosebumps covered my body. I'd have to see if Coyote knew anything about the house and check to see if he'd learned anything more about a meeting taking place in Santa Fe.

We walked a bit further and turned down another alleyway to go back to the street where we had been before. This time, small shops lined the short road, and people filled the alley. Abruptly, Nancy stopped and turned to us. "Do you think it's too early for a Margarita?"

We hooted at her and laughed as she led the way into the café at the end of the alley.

CHAPTER 12

The next morning, we were excited to find out exactly what we'd have to do in the special ceremony Grandmother was conducting as part of Karen's wedding. After leisurely sipping our coffee and relaxing in each other's company, we got dressed and headed out to the Pueblo.

Grandmother met us at the door of her townhouse with twinkling eyes. After Susannah and Nancy had admired the handiwork and art on display around the house, Grandmother gathered us into the living room. As we settled in, she handed each of us a cup of brewed spearmint tea and offered us sugar cookies that she'd made. We sat in expectation as she began to share some of the beliefs of the Navajo's celebration of marriage.

She explained that she and Coyote had received blessings from the Chief of their pueblo to modernize and shorten the "Blessingway Ceremony" to fit in the one-day wedding ceremony scheduled for Saturday. Typically, it was a two-day affair.

She continued, "The Blessingway was not intended to cure illness, but was used to invoke positive blessings and to avert misfortune. The rites and prayers in the Blessingway are concerned with healing, creation, harmony, and peace. The song cycles recount the elaborate Navajo creation story."

We looked at each other in wonderment that we were going to be involved in this. Grandmother said, "The ceremony is to honor the divine feminine as a nurturer. It is performed to bless and protect the home, to prevent complications of pregnancy, and to restore equilibrium to the cosmos."

"Wow! This is going to be something," said Susannah in awe.

"Instead of a separate ceremony, Coyote will dance with Karen to a different set of chants representing the Protectionway ceremony honoring the divine masculine as a protector provider," added Grandmother.

"How beautiful it's going to be, Grandmother," I sighed, imagining Karen and Coyote dancing together to the unique beat of the music.

"Yes," she smiled. It's going to be a beautiful ceremony from start to end. And you, my daughters, will be part of that beauty."

Grandmother then rose and left us to return with the simple dresses she had made for us to wear for the wedding ceremony. The fabric was light tan-colored fake suede that was washable and flexible—nearly impossible to distinguish from real suede. The short sleeves were fringed, as was the bottom hem of the simple A-line dress. Around the jewel neckline was sewn beadwork that'd been readymade, ordered online from a specialty store. It was mainly turquoise and a few other semi-precious stone beads, very striking against the tan fabric.

Next, Grandmother handed us store-bought moccasins that were specially ordered in our sizes. We slipped them on and laughed.

"Usually, at a wedding, I can't wait to get home to take off my shoes. Not this time, though. These are so comfortable," chuckled Nancy.

Karen, Grandmother, and I looked at each other and smiled.

"This wedding is going to be so much fun. Henry bought a new video camera so that he can record the whole thing. It's going to be historic for us sister-friends," said Susannah with a grin. "Are the younger girls going to be wearing the same style dress?"

Karen smiled and nodded.

Then Grandmother made us go through our part of the ceremony where we danced around Karen, swaying in tempo with the beat she produced from the small drum she held in her hand. I felt liberated, and my movements flowed with the beat of the music. It was hard for me to stop at the end of Grandmother's singing and pounding out her unique rhythm. When all was quiet, we looked at each other, fascinated at the sensual movements we'd made without thought.

Nancy asked, "Are the younger girls going to be dancing with us?"

Grandmother nodded. "Yes, they'll dance with you, following your movements."

"So cool. It's going to be similar to some of the native dances I saw in Africa," added Nancy.

We heard a knock at the front door, then footsteps coming our way. Coyote popped into the room. His masculine aura with his weathered cowboy boots and cowboy hat drew our attention as he immediately headed to Karen, kissing her enthusiastically on the lips. Then he turned to stand by Grandmother. "Has this old woman exhausted you with all the dancing you'll be doing at the wedding?" he asked, affectionately kissing her weathered cheek and lovingly hugging her.

We laughed and protested his idea, all in good fun. "Rosie, can I see you for a minute?" he asked.

I looked surprised.

"It'll only take a minute," he added.

"Sure," I said and followed him from the room. "What's going on?"

"Last night, we picked up a man who passed out in the park. He had a scorpion tattoo on his hand like the others we've seen. This morning, he said he'd pay whatever the fine was, but he had to get out of jail—he couldn't be late."

"Oh, my! So there *is* a meeting going on here in Santa Fe, then?"

"It appears so. We let him go, and one of my men followed him into the center of downtown. My guy lost him, though. Said, 'One minute he was there, the next he wasn't.'"

"Where did he lose him? Did he say where?" I asked, excitement growing.

"Right on Main Street, not far from that fancy clothing store. You probably know which one."

I did indeed—the one where Susannah had much luck finding her new outfits. My mind flew to the alley and the large house tucked into it. Goosebumps covered my body as my intuition said that's where he was. "I bet I know where they're meeting," I stated. I explained to Coyote my reasoning, and he agreed I might be right. He knew the owner of the house, and it made sense to him.

"However, there's nothing we can do unless the group creates a problem. We have to be careful and not jump the gun, even if we think they might be involved with the murders that'd happened last year. Or even if we think they're involved in the human trafficking going on here. We need hard evidence before we call in the FBI. So it's important to keep an eye out and watch their moves."

"Is this what you wanted to tell me?" I asked, somewhat confused.

"Actually, I wanted to ask if you'd be willing to look at some photos to see if you can recognize the man you saw on the airplane. Maybe Susannah would be willing to do the same. I don't want to upset Karen by getting her involved in this. I don't want anything to spoil our wedding."

"Certainly. I should be able to come to the office tomorrow afternoon after the shower, before Mike, Isabella, and the others fly in. I have to pick them up in Albuquerque, and Karen will be tied up with her parents then. "

"That'd be good. Thanks, Rosie."

As he began to turn around, I grabbed his arm. "Coyote, I want to make sure nothing happens to any of us."

He patted my shoulder. "Me, too."

CHAPTER 13

The next morning, we were filled with excitement. This was the day of Karen's shower. We were up early, giving us enough time to relax and chat while we sipped our coffee before starting the day.

My mind wandered to the previous night when we'd gone to eat at the little Mexican restaurant that'd become my favorite. The same one where Grandmother usually went. We had giggled and laughed, and it was only when I'd seen Maria's old neighbor pass by that I quieted to the point where Karen nudged me. "What's the matter?" she whispered.

"Nothing," I answered, pasting a smile onto my face, determined to push away the uneasiness that filled me. I'd forgotten to ask Coyote about him. I thought he was in jail for his possible involvement in one of the murders last year, as well as his harassment of me last summer when

Isabella had gone missing. Now he was out? That thought kept gnawing at me all night long, keeping me from any peaceful rest. Without my proper sleep, I was dragging the next morning as I stripped the beds and began the laundry.

Nancy and Susannah were mostly packed, ready to move into the Eldorado Hotel where they'd be staying, each with their special man. They had only to shower and get dressed, and they'd be ready for the day. Since Henry wouldn't be in until late afternoon, Susannah would have just enough time to meet with Coyote before leaving for the airport to pick him up. Steve, Nancy's boyfriend, would be in a bit later. He'd rented a car and would drive himself to Santa Fe. So tonight, each of us sister-friends would be spending time with our families. I couldn't wait to see Isabella, Mike, Brian, and, of course, Cal. Virginia was already here. I had missed them all, despite having my "besties" with me.

Karen left to have breakfast with her parents, not looking forward to it. But she said, "Duty calls." Nancy went to take her shower, leaving Susannah and me to finish the coffee before heading to do the same. I still had to pick up the flowers for the table from the florist and the shower guests' takeaway gifts. I'd taken a picture of Karen and Coyote standing together and had copies made and put inside 5"x7" silver frames that held a sculpted silver sun attached to it. The picture frames were stunning, and I was pleased to have found them as something that'd be a lasting reminder of their happy day.

"What do you think, Rosie?" asked Susannah.

"Oh, sorry. My mind was elsewhere. What is it?"

"What do you think the men we saw with the scorpion tattoos are involved in here?"

"I can't think they're here for anything good. Hopefully, you'll be able to identify the guy who gave you such a hard time at the airport. You are going to meet with Coyote after the shower, aren't you?"

"Yes, for sure." She was silent for a moment. "I know the guys are taking Coyote to the Santa Fe brewing company tomorrow night, but are we going to be doing anything for Karen?"

"Grandmother suggested that it be just the three of us sister-friends to take her out to dinner. Coyote told me of a new place that's supposed to serve the best margaritas in town, as well as having the best live dancing music. What do you think?"

"I think that sounds great," she said enthusiastically. "Does Nancy know what we're doing?"

"What are we doing?" asked Nancy as she joined us.

I filled her in. "Does Karen know?" she asked.

"No, not yet."

Looking at her watch, Nancy urged, "You guys better get going. Time is flying!"

When I saw the time, I jumped up and raced into my bedroom, tearing off my pajamas as I went. If I didn't hurry, I was going to be late for the shower. I couldn't let that happen.

THE LOVERS.

CHAPTER 14

The room where the shower was being held looked festive and beautiful. The flower arrangements were centered on the three round tables scattered casually around the small room. In total, there were 12 of us. I carefully selected the place cards and put them out on the specific tables I had in mind. At one table would be us four sister-friends; at another table would be Angel, Grandmother, Susan, and Tracy, two other teachers from the pueblo school. At the last table would be Maria, Virginia, Sunshine, and Karen's mother, Agnes. Sunshine was a soon-to-be neighbor of Karen's when Karen officially made her home at the pueblo, and they'd already become friendly. I was looking forward to acquainting myself with all three new ladies in the future.

I smiled as I turned to the multiple clacking of heels on the tile floor and waited to greet the guests. They appeared all at once, making it an uplifting, joyous, noisy party sound as the guests greeted each other and me. I immediately looked at Karen to make sure she was okay. It was difficult for her to spend any time with her parents, who were always critical of her. When I caught her eye, she winked at me, signaling me that all was okay. I breathed a sigh of relief.

Beautifully wrapped gifts began to pile onto the spare table in the corner, along with the several I'd brought with me. It was a cozy, pleasant space—small enough to make it impossible for anyone to ignore another. I walked up to Karen's mother. "Hello, Agnes, welcome to Santa Fe! Have you been here before?"

She looked at me and pursed her lips. "Oh no, dear, I've never had any desire to visit here. I suppose that'll change, but we'll have to see."

"Well, welcome. It's going to be a beautiful wedding," I added, patting her arm. "Just wait and see."

Grandmother stepped closer to us, and I sensed she was "feeling out" Agnes' energy. She took Agnes' hand in hers and said, "You have a beautiful daughter. I hope you realize she is a godsend to all of us for being here."

"Godsend? What do you mean?" she asked, confused.

"Karen is like the sun—warm, nurturing, and loving. She's forgiving too. Now that's a true blessing in itself, don't you agree?"

"I suppose," she answered, unaware of Grandmother's meaning.

Grandmother and I eyed each other. I rolled my eyes and left them to seek out the new ladies. Sunshine stood out with her light hair and blue eyes. The other two ladies had dark brown hair and eyes that twinkled with joy and mischief. They laughed at something Karen said, and it was easy to see they all enjoyed each other's company. I felt a flash of envy that I'd have to wait until the summer months before I'd be able to spend any time with them, but I was happy for Karen.

I joined Maria and Virginia, who were catching up with each other since Christmas time and all that'd happened then. How I loved them both! Maria, my partner in raising Isabella, had to be one of the greatest human gifts the Universe had given me since my besties had come into my life. And then, there was Virginia. She'd become more than paid help when I'd first stepped into the role of being Isabella's foster mother, and she'd been our housekeeper. Now, besides being my good friend, she was Cal's girlfriend. They were happy together and served as grandparents to Isabella, who had claimed Cal as her grandfather shortly after meeting him.

I kissed them both. "How are you two doing?"

They smiled. Maria put her arm around my waist, hugging me to her. I squeezed her back.

"Thank you, Virginia, for flying out early to be here in time for the shower. It's nice of Cal to wait for Isabella's school day to be through before catching the next flight here."

"He was happy to do that. They both are excited about the wedding. I don't think Isabella slept a wink last night."

I laughed. "I can just imagine."

The waitress serving my guests came to me, asking if we were ready to sit down. I nodded and said out loud, "Ladies, we're ready to sit down now. Find your places, please."

I stood with a sense of satisfaction as I watched the ladies locate their spots before joining my sister-friends at my table. I signaled the waitress over and asked her to serve the wine while waiting for the waiters to bring us our food. At the table furthest away, it was impossible not to hear Karen's mother's objection to the wine. "Don't offer that to me. I don't drink," she said, holding her hand up in protest.

"Maybe you should," whispered Nancy. "It might help the rest of us," she added, and we sister-friends laughed.

"Sorry, Karen," gasped Nancy, realizing how that had sounded.

"No worries. I couldn't agree with you more," concurred Karen as she eyed the others at her mother's table, now asking for their glasses to be filled to the top. I shook my head in wonderment that Karen and her mother were related.

The Mexican assortment of food was beyond exceptional. I'd requested the high-end restaurant chef to be in charge of our special meal, and he had surpassed my expectations. A double deep dark Mexican chocolate cake was the last to be carried in, and we oohed over it. Orders for coffee and tea were placed, and we all sat back, satisfied with our meals, except for Karen's mother, who had picked at her food with no great enthusiasm. I began to wonder how Karen had survived her younger years with a mother who seemed not to have found much joy in her life.

The waitress brought in scissors and a pink paper plate to gather the packages' ribbons to make a "shower bridal bouquet."

One of Karen's gifts that I'd bought for her was a red silk teddy with shorts to match that barely covered all the intimate parts if she stood up. I blushed as others understood what that meant, and I received their winks and teasing in a sporting way. I didn't have the nerve to look at Karen's silent mother. I didn't think she had figured it out. Karen's cheeks were red, but her smile was wide. "Ah, yes. I'm ready now for a nice evening at home, huh, Rosie?"

Next came Grandmother's gift. It was a pendant she'd made from silver of a sun. The idea of it being a sun came as no surprise since Grandmother associated Karen with the sun's meaning. But what was unusual is that she had set stones onto one-half of the sun so that it resembled the night's half-moon and was the full sun at the same time. It was stunning! Karen had tears rolling down her cheeks as she went to Grandmother to kiss her on each of her own wet, weathered cheeks. Grandmother's toothless smile illuminated her face.

We smiled at Susannah's gift when we saw Karen lift a small gift envelope from a rather large box. It was a gift certificate to the nail and spa salon right here at the hotel. What made the gift so fitting was that until Susannah had met us, she'd never had a spa experience. Now, she could afford to spoil herself regularly to get her nails done and have a pedicure. And that was her favorite gift to give.

Nancy's gift was a tall box that she'd shipped to my house in time for the shower. It was one of the treasures she'd brought back from her latest African visit—a pair of hand-carved wooden antelope resembling the deer that the Navajo Indians valued so much. They were made from ebony wood and glistened with its silkiness and dark beauty. They would be perfect by their fireplace.

Susan and Tracy had gone together and purchased a beautiful Navajo Indian Hand Drum from the now-famous local maker. An expensive but practical gift that Karen would be able to use in her classroom.

Karen couldn't stop smiling as she opened one gift after another that were wonderful and beautiful—each with a special meaning. Her mother's gift to her almost made me forgive her mother for all her cruelties toward Karen.

Almost. Not quite.

Agnes had wrapped a set of tatted placemats that had been made by her mother—Karen's grandmother—and several handkerchiefs with the same design. They were unusual, fancy, and beautiful. I could see that Karen was touched by receiving them. It appeared as if they'd never been used, which was sad in a way, I thought. Sad that Agnes had never appreciated and used them. But again, that made it all the better for Karen.

At the end of the shower, Karen stood up. "Thank you, all my beautiful friends. There was one point in my life that I believed I'd never know happiness. And now, look at me, surrounded by all of you. There is not a luckier, more happy, girl in the world than me." She spoke in Tewa, then in English, "You are my blessings, and I am grateful."

After everyone left, Nancy and I helped Karen carry the shower gifts to Angel's car, where she'd take them back to Coyote's condo at the pueblo. I watched Angel as she helped her mother into the car. Angel was sweet and caring of Grandmother, and I was looking forward to getting to know her better. She'd had a rough time of it, losing both her husband and son to alcohol and drugs. It couldn't be easy.

I hurried back to the hotel to go over the bill and make the final payment before leaving to see Coyote. I looked at my watch, and when I saw the time, my heart fluttered. Mike would be arriving within the next two hours, as would Isabella and the others. I smiled with anticipation.

CHAPTER 15

Coyote was deep in thought when I knocked on the doorframe of his office. He looked up. "Enter," he demanded with a smile.

"You seem worried, my friend," I said as I noted his furrowed brow.

"A lot on my mind. Susannah was able to identify one of the men we're watching. Let's see what you come up with, too, okay?"

"Sure. By the way, Coyote, I saw Maria's neighbor yesterday walking around in town. What's up with him? I thought he was going to jail."

A guilty expression raced across Coyote's face as he cleared his throat. "Well, there's been a change regarding him."

"What do you mean?" I asked unhappily.

Coyote looked embarrassed. "We bartered with him, and he's become our paid snitch."

I rose out of my chair and leaned toward Coyote. "You've got to be kidding!"

"Sit down and listen to me. I'm only telling you this so you won't go off on your own and mess it up. As of now, you're officially under oath to keep this between us, understand? This arrangement works to our advantage only if he's alive. That's how it is. He's helping us with the scorpion gang."

"I don't know if I'll ever be able to trust him," I muttered.

"Stranger things have happened when you give someone like him responsibility in a new way. Let's give it a try, shall we?" he asked, leaving me no choice.

My stomach dropped; I didn't like anything about the man. I sighed loudly and grimaced. "Okay, you have my word."

I turned and headed to the small conference room where the gigantic book of photos sat. I began to go through it, page after page. Toward the back, two pictures on the same page drew my attention—the man on the plane and the tall man I'd see at the airport with Mike and Isabella. Bingo!

"Coyote," I called. "I've got something. Come look."

When Coyote saw the two photos I'd chosen, he said, "Ah, yes. We know that both of them are involved with the Scorpions. We just can't prove they've done anything wrong."

"That's maddening, isn't it? They're right in front of you, and you can't do anything."

"Yes," he responded simply.

"Well, then, I guess I'll be on my way."

"Tell Mike I'll call him in the morning."

"Will do," I said as I gathered my purse and rose to leave. "Only two more days, Coyote…" I teased.

He smiled, and I turned away with a smile of my own as I headed out the door to pick up Isabella, Cal, Mike, and Brian at the airport in Albuquerque.

***

When I saw the four of them descend the escalator into the baggage claim area, my heart lifted. I waved to draw their attention and was rewarded with huge smiles from all four. It felt odd not to have Sweet Pea along. Our neighbors, Irene and Ron, were dog-sitting her. Isabella bounced off the moving stairs and raced into my waiting arms while the men made a slower path toward me. When I looked up from hugging Isabella into Mike's watchful eyes, there was a flash of intimacy between us, making me warm all over. Brian headed to the moving carousel to claim our bags with Isabella and Cal right on his tail. Mike lifted my chin and searched my eyes. "I've missed you, my queen."

I lowered his hand from my chin and said honestly, "I've missed you too, handsome."

Isabella chattered all the way into Santa Fe about her stay at Grandfather's, the meals she helped Virginia cook, her excitement about seeing her sister-friends again, and her being in the wedding. As much as we all were happy for her, I think we were relieved to reach Santa Fe and have her quiet. We dropped Cal off at the hotel where Virginia was waiting for him, and then we headed home.

Thankfully, I'd had time to make up the beds with fresh sheets and had freshly laundered towels, so all was ready for them. As we entered the house, it was plain to see that

Isabella was tired and when I suggested she go to bed, she didn't hesitate.

Mike, Brian, and I sat in the living room with our nightcaps of Amaretto and soda. "How did things go in Boston?" I asked.

Brian was quick to respond. "Great. We interviewed about a dozen people for the position we want to fill. I think we've decided on the last candidate we saw, right, Mike?"

"I guess so. She has a pretty impressive resume."

"She?" I asked, suddenly attentive. "What is she like?"

"As Mike said, pretty impressive … in all ways," Brian responded with a smirk as he emphasized "pretty."

I looked at Mike. He nodded his head in agreement. "As you can see, Cowboy here is pumped up about her."

"Me? She's got her eyes on you, buddy."

"No way! You're the one who's drooling all over the place about her."

In a moment of insecurity, a wave of relief flashed over me that she'd be working in Boston—not in Las Vegas. At this point in our relationship, the last thing I needed was to worry about a hot girl after Mike.

Mike stretched out his long legs and sighed. "It's been a long day. Time to hit the hay. Did Coyote say what time he'd be calling me in the morning?"

I shook my head. "No."

"Good, I can sleep later. Ready for bed?"

Just the way he'd asked me that in a sexy voice made me suddenly shy, and my cheeks reddened. I grabbed his outstretched hand and let him pull me to my feet. Then, I released his hand and went to check the front and back doors to make sure they were locked. Brian headed into the guest room while Mike went to our bedroom.

Something was different. I shook my head to clear away any doubts that Mike loved me, and I marched forward with purpose to be the select welcoming committee of one for the man I loved.

CHAPTER 16

I awoke with Mike's body wrapped around me in a spooning fashion. I wriggled against him, forcing my backside even closer. It felt so good to have him next to me. He held me tighter and whispered in my ear, "I've missed you, sweetheart."

Knowing what he'd said was sincere, I smiled. That was one of those special moments not to be taken lightly. Slowly, we made love that, in the end, caused both of us to lay back breathless, fully satiated. Mike wrapped his arm around my shoulders, and I snuggled closer, laying my head against his chest. "Mike?"

"What, baby?"

"Do you know what we have to do as our part in Karen and Coyote's wedding? Have you attended this type of ceremony before?"

"My mother's Navajo family was quite large, so when I was younger, I got to go to a lot of different ceremonies. Then as things got worse between my parents, that ended."

"You don't talk much about your parents. Why not?"

"There's nothing good to say," he answered. "I don't want to talk about them, Rosie," he said in a tone that halted me from asking any more questions.

I was quiet for a moment. "At least you were lucky to have your parents around," I mumbled, missing my own.

Mike heard me. He lifted my chin and looked me in the eyes. "Sometimes that can't be such a good thing, Rosie." Mike put his finger across my lips and pleaded, "Enough," before his lips closed over mine.

Aware of his distress, I pushed up and kissed him tenderly on the mouth. "I love you, Mike," I called after him as he headed into the shower.

He turned and studied me. "And I you, my queen, with all that I can give."

It was a different response from him, and I considered it. Were there limitations to what he could offer me? It sounded as if there were. Was 'not marrying me' one of them? I sighed, got up, and went into the kitchen to start the coffee.

After breakfast, Coyote came by to pick up Mike and Brian; we'd meet up with them later in the afternoon at the wedding rehearsal. Isabella and I loaded into the car with our dresses and moccasins to head to Grandmother's house. But first, we needed to pick up Angela.

As we drove into Maria's driveway, it was amazing to see the changes that had been made not only to their house with the large addition they had added. The neighbor's house next door had been repaired, painted and had all new plantings. The rest of the small houses on the street looked as if they, too, had been spiffed up a bit, making the whole area well-tended and pleasant looking.

When we got out of the car, the next-door neighbors were outside. They waved to us with a smile. When Maria came outside onto the new front porch to greet us, she smiled and waved to the neighbors. "Good morning!" she hollered to them. Then, she turned to us, "C'mon in. Angela is almost ready."

"Oh my, Maria! Your porch is beautiful; it's much bigger than I thought it was going to be. I love the swing, too."

"It's tough keeping the boys away from it. C'mon inside. Just be careful not to let the dog out ... or Rosa either," she laughed. "That girl gets into trouble quick as a wink."

Sure enough, Rosa was plopped in the kitchen with one of the lower cupboards open, feeding the dog a dog biscuit as she munched on one herself. I laughed. "I see what you mean."

In just a matter of seconds, Maria gently pushed the dog away, grabbed the box of biscuits, and placed them on the counter. Then, she swooped Rosa up into her arms, and we headed into the new addition.

It was beautiful with its soft gray walls and matching short shag carpet. Like the girls' bedroom, her furniture was white, giving the room a clean and airy feel to it that was soothing. It was easy to see Maria had turned the space into a stunning hideaway to escape the demands and responsibilities of motherhood and her role as a housekeeper.

"It couldn't be more beautiful," I gushed.

Maria's smile said it all—how excited and proud she was with it.

"Mama, we're ready," called Isabella from the hallway. As she entered Maria's bedroom with its sitting area,

Isabella's face split with a grin. "Oh, Aunt Maria, this is so beautiful!" she said as she twirled around, taking it all in.

Maria opened her arms to receive a hug from Isabella. "I'm glad you think so."

Angela stepped into the doorway and came to my side, where I hugged her close. "Hi, sweetheart. Are you all set to go?" I asked her.

"Yes. I'm so excited."

"Me, too. I can't wait to see what this ceremony is all about," I said.

"Angela, you have your cell phone with you, don't you?" asked Maria.

"Yes, Mama."

"Call me just before you go to bed so I can say goodnight. Rosie, are you sure Grandmother is okay with all three girls spending the night with her?"

"Yes," I assured her. "She has big plans for them."

"My sister is going to watch Rosa and the boys tomorrow, so we should be at the Pueblo right on time."

"Tomorrow will be fascinating. Don't forget to bring your camera," I reminded her."

I ushered the girls out of the bedroom, with Maria and Rosa following behind. At the front door, Rosa reached for me, and I kissed her outstretched hand many times. Then, Maria shooed us away before Rosa could realize we were leaving her behind.

CHAPTER 17

We arrived at the pueblo a short while later with Susannah and Nancy close behind in their rental car. It was with an exciting air that we piled out and headed to Grandmother's house. With her psychic ability, Grandmother had probably told Nica we'd arrived, for she was already racing down the pathway to meet us. We older sister-friends laughed at the younger girls as they greeted each other with squeals … we still did the same thing at our age.

Karen stood by the door, and the younger girls pushed their way inside. Then, we older ones entered and walked into the living room where Grandmother sat supervising a young Indian girl who was clearly the seamstress. One by one, the younger girls tried on their dresses and headbands, which were a simple affair of a beaded band with a few pheasant feathers in the back. They smiled at each other, pleased at how they looked.

Seeing Isabella standing there in her outfit took my breath away. I became dizzy and had to sit down to catch my balance. Isabella, looking more like my younger sister in that lifetime we shared so long ago, brought tears to my eyes. I had lost her to death then, and I was determined to make sure nothing like that happened to her this lifetime.

Isabella sensed my distress and came to my side. "Mama, what happened then is not going to happen this lifetime. We're both going to be fine; I know we will be."

Isabella's intuition and psychic abilities were growing each day, and I knew her friendship with Sammy had something to do with it. He was so sensitive psychically that his energy raised her own, and soon, as a twosome, they would be a force to be reckoned with, able to see beyond the veil of the 3rd, 4th, and 5th dimensions. They had already demonstrated that in their joint search for their schoolmate, Tiffany, who had been kidnapped.

The girls couldn't wait to see Karen's wedding dress, but she wanted it to be a surprise for them and the rest of the attendees to be seen only on her wedding day. None but Grandmother had seen the impressive wedding headdress that Coyote was having made for Karen. I knew it was going to be spectacular, and I couldn't wait to see it for myself. The unveiling of both would be spectacular.

It was Coyote who'd wanted the wedding to consist of some of the Navajo traditions, and Karen was happy to oblige him. As she told me, it all seemed very natural to her, not a bit like dress up or a costume party—rather like an easy way to express themselves in a way that meant something to both of them.

The chief of the Pueblo was the one who would give Karen away to Coyote. When Karen's father had learned of this, he seemed relieved instead of being distressed not to be the one to give his only child and daughter away. That had come as no surprise to Karen.

It was time for Mike, Brian, and Coyote to join us for a trial run of the unique wedding ceremony. In addition to Mike serving as Best Man, he would also act as an usher with Brian to seat the guests. When Mike came through the door, he strode to my side and pulled me close. I felt the eyes of my sister-friends, watching as he leaned down to kiss me. They seemed pleased to see this. They knew how much I loved Mike, and they wanted me to be happy.

We all headed out to meet with the Chief of the pueblo. The wedding was going to take place in a large round building, constructed to resemble a community-sized teepee. Inside, a large ceiling fan in the center twirled slowly, and four skylights that opened to the outside brought in light and fresh air. Chairs were placed in a semi-circle surrounding a large area where the special dances would take place.

The Chief was waiting for us inside. He was wearing jeans, a plaid shirt, moccasins, and a large feathered headpiece. My heart thudded when I saw him, for he was imposing with dark eyes that glowed with the glory and pain of the past set in a tanned, weathered face. The wise old man, indeed.

We helped Grandmother into one of the chairs to rest while we went through the expected motions during the ceremony. Tomorrow, she would be sitting next to the Chief on a raised platform representing the feminine energy to his masculine energy – both in the Blessingway and Protectionway ceremonies.

Mike and I were going to be responsible for the safekeeping of the Wedding Vase during the ceremony. The chief explained, "Unlike usual vases, this has two spouts instead of one, each representing one spouse in the dual relationship. In the middle, there is a handle that connects the two spouts. A circle, oval, or teardrop shape is present between the two spouts and the bridge, representing the new circle of life formed by marriage.

"Before the wedding ceremony begins, holy water is placed within the vase, usually put there by the medicine man. Depending on the tribal traditions, the liquid may be nectar, some tea, or purified water.

"On the day of the wedding, each spouse takes a turn drinking the holy water from the wedding vase. In the traditional ceremony, the husband offers the vase to the wife first to drink from it. Then, she returns the vase to the husband to take a drink from it as well.

"Then the bride and groom drink from the vase together as part of the ceremony." He smiled. "Some local tribal traditions suggest that if a couple can drink the holy water from the wedding vase without spilling, then they will have a long, happy life together." We all chuckled.

"After the wedding, the wedding vase becomes a representation of the couple's foundational love together. It becomes a cherished item in the home with both parties responsible for taking care of it."

The Chief was extremely patient with us, explaining the traditions and meanings and our part. After going through the motions several times, we said goodbye to the Chief and thanked him for his time.

"This isn't a simple ceremony, is it?" asked Susannah.

"No. It's not the average wedding ceremony for sure," added Nancy.

"It sure is beautiful, though, isn't it?" I said.

We nodded and smiled at Karen. "You're a lucky girl, Karen," said Susannah.

"Yes," the rest of us agreed.

***

I held onto Grandmother's arm as we headed back to her house with the others. Guiding her along, I asked, "What do you think, Grandmother? Is this wedding going to be all you dreamed about for Coyote and Karen?"

"Even more so, my daughter. The planets are aligned to protect them."

"Protect them from what, Grandmother?"

"Times are changing. There is a greater power struggle between men and women than ever before. Here on the reservation, as we separate ourselves from our traditions, it seems that our men become abusive and hide in a bottle while our women run and try to escape them. There will come a time when we connect more greatly with nature, and we become more balanced, but I won't be alive to see it," she added sadly.

"What does this have to do with Karen and Coyote?"

"They already feel a strong sense to protect those in danger, and that will bring danger to them. But that is their role this lifetime—that is what they've asked to do this time around."

"How do you know that, Grandmother?"

"The Great Spirit talks to me." She turned to look at me with her wide toothless smile. "And, sometimes, she says to mind my own business and let things be as they are meant to be."

I laughed. "Oh, Grandmother, I'm so glad we met again this lifetime. I have so much to learn from you."

By the time we got to Grandmother's house, Coyote's sister had arrived home. "Hi, Angel!" I called out as Grandmother, and I climbed together through the open door where Grandmother lived.

The men were already inside, and I made the introductions all around. It was interesting to see Brian's eyes widen in appreciation of Angel's dark beauty. I rolled my eyes at him, and he grinned. Coyote was pouring wine into goblets and handing them out to us, readying himself for a toast. "Here's to my beautiful bride-to-be and all of our friends gathered here tonight."

"Hear, hear," we hollered.

The younger girls had gone into Nica's room where they'd be spending the night together, and when they heard us, they came out to see what was going on. "We're toasting Karen and Coyote," I explained.

Mike came to stand beside me. "We're going to head out now. Don't wait up for me. I'm sure we won't be that late."

"I might say the same to you," I teased. "We're taking Karen out to the new restaurant. They're supposed to have the best Margaritas in town."

"We'll have to see who makes it home first then, won't we?" he said as he pulled me close and kissed me. "Have a good time, and stay out of trouble, hear?"

CHAPTER 18

We girls said goodbye and piled into separate cars except for Nancy and Susannah, who'd ridden together. When we pulled into the new restaurant, it was more crowded than I expected, but we were lucky. There was room for us. As we were led into the restaurant's dining area, it was easy to see that we'd want to go to the bar side later. The place was hopping with live music and dancing there.

As we gathered around our table, we smiled at each other in relief that it was just the four of us without the responsibility of entertaining others. We were quiet as we ate our dinner, thoroughly enjoying being together again. When we finished, I stood up. "C'mon, let's go dancing!"

We went into the restaurant's bar side and sat at one of the high tables, and ordered another round of Margaritas. I had my back to the restaurant, and while waiting for our drinks to arrive, I felt my chair tilt backward. I yelped. When I turned around and saw who it was, I couldn't believe my eyes. It was Maria's old neighbor who was now a snitch for Coyote.

"Hi, remember me?" he asked, leaning toward me.

I was annoyed and snapped, "Unfortunately, I do."

He leaned closer. "You don't want to make a scene now, do you?" he whispered into my ear. In a louder voice, he asked, "How about a dance?"

"I don't *think* so."

"C'mon," he urged. Quietly, he said, "I've got a message for you."

Reluctantly, I rose. He was neat and clean, nothing like the unkempt person he had been before. Maybe Coyote was right, and given his new responsibility, he had changed. "Just one dance, though."

As I stepped away, I heard Karen trying to explain to Susannah and Nancy who this man was. Thank goodness. I knew she'd make light of it.

When Maria's neighbor squeezed me tighter than necessary, I became more irritated. "What's the message?" I ordered as I loosened his hand from me.

"Don't be in such a hurry. Just enjoy the dance."

I felt as if he was toying with me, and that made me even angrier. I began to pull away.

"Okay, okay. Here's the message. Tell Coyote they're leaving tomorrow as he thought. They're planning to return this summer."

"Why did they come here now, then?" I asked, curious.

"To layout the groundwork; that's all."

The song ended much to my relief. "Thank you ..." I stood there, embarrassed. "Sorry, but I don't know your name."

"Jose," he answered with some pride.

"I'll be sure that Coyote gets the message, Jose."

Then, the music stopped completely. The band was taking a break. A DJ stepped in and, for some unknown reason, chose to pep up the crowd by playing the Chicken dance song. I joined my sister-friends as we pulled Karen from her seat. "C'mon! Let's do this!"

We eagerly got up and joined the others on the dance floor, flapping our arms and laughing joyously. Afterward, we sat back in our seats, winded and sipping the last of our drinks. Susannah nudged me. "Look, I think that's the rude man from the car rental, sitting at the bar."

"Where?" I asked, curious.

She pointed, and I saw the rude passenger who had been on my flight sitting beside the man Susannah had pointed out. "I think it's time to leave," I said.

"Yes, let's get out of here now," agreed Susannah.

Karen and Nancy weren't paying attention to us and had no idea why we suddenly stood up and grabbed our coats. But one look from us, and they gamely joined us. Once outside, it was easy to see we all were tired and ready to leave. We said goodnight, hugging each other, aware that things were about to shift with Karen becoming a bride, permanently living in Santa Fe. But this was a good thing, and we were looking forward to celebrating and being a part of Karen's big day.

Before I headed home, I texted Coyote with Jose's message. I wondered why Jose couldn't have done that himself until I realized he probably didn't want Coyote's information on his phone. That could be a mistake if he were ever accused of being a snitch by the Scorpion gang.

My mind was whirling with questions about the Scorpions and what they might be planning for the summer. Isabella and I would be back then for Isabella's summer break from school, and the last thing either one of us needed was to be entangled somehow with the Scorpions.

I was fast asleep when I heard Mike and Brian stumble in long after me. I had to hold in my laughter when I heard them scold each other in loud comical whispers, "Be quiet. Don't wake up Rosie," as only people who'd had too much to drink can do. I'd never seen Mike like this before. He was usually careful about how much he drank, but Brian could be a bad influence. He was a party goer. I pretended to be asleep when Mike came to bed, and as soon as he hit the pillow, he was snoring. He'd pay for going overboard tomorrow, as would Brian and the others, and, most likely, Coyote.

CHAPTER 19

The early morning held the night's coolness, but it wouldn't last for long. The weather was to warm up to an unusual high of the 60s later, making it a perfect day for Karen and Coyote's wedding. The festivities would start at noon and end up with the celebration wedding dinner at the hotel in town.

Sunlight streamed into the windows, making it impossible for me to sleep any longer. I got up, leaving Mike to slumber. But as I headed toward the bedroom door, I heard him groan and begin to stir. "Hang on there, handsome. I'll get some coffee brewing. You're going to need it."

He grunted and groaned some more. "Yeah, that'd be good."

I laughed as I watched him quint at the sunlight and cover his head with the covers like a kid would do. "Yeah, you're going to need lots of coffee," I laughed.

He groaned, "It's not funny."

"I agree," I replied self-righteously.

The coffee had just finished brewing when Mike and Brian stepped into the kitchen and groggily reached for the coffee mugs I stretched out to them. "What happened to you two last night?"

In unison, Mike and Brian groaned. "Coyote's friend kept buying us rounds of beer with chasers. I can't believe I tried to keep up with him," moaned Brian. "He was a big dude; held his own, though, didn't he, Mike?"

Mike rolled his eyes, saying nothing.

"Who was he?" I asked.

"Some childhood friend of Coyote. Tom Little Horse, I think or something like that." Brian chuckled and nodded toward Mike. "Mike was not impressed with him at all."

"Blowhard," mumbled Mike. "A know-it-all."

I was surprised by Mike's reaction to Tom Little Horse. When I'd met him at the restaurant with Coyote and Karen, he'd seemed nice enough. Oh well, what's that saying?— "different strokes for different folks."

I forced the guys to eat the scrambled eggs and toast I'd made for breakfast, and soon their faces began to look less peaked. After relaxing with a second cup of coffee for me, and the third one for Mike and Brian, I reminded them, "Time to get showered and dressed, guys. Noon will be here before you know it."

Coyote was wearing moccasins, dress buckskins, and his grandfather's dress suede shirt with fringe for the wedding. His shirt was fancier than the more simple suede shirts that Mike and Brian would be wearing with their blue jeans and moccasins. I was looking forward to seeing them in their casual wedding dress.

I cleaned up the kitchen while the guys went to take their showers. Isabella telephoned before I finished, and I wiped my hands on a towel to answer her call. "Hi, sweetheart."

"Hi, Mama," she said, sounding upset.

"What's the matter, Isabella?"

"Are you feeling anything, Mama? Anything bad?"

I thought about her question. I knew she wanted to know if psychically I sensed trouble. I sensed only happiness. "No, I don't, do you?"

"I guess not. It's just the last couple of times we've been here in Santa Fe, there's always been trouble. And Nica cried last night over her brother dying."

My heart squeezed with the thought of them worrying needlessly. "Sweetheart, if it will make you girls feel better, ask Grandmother to give you a special blessing. I think she'd planned to do that anyway."

"Okay, Mama, I'll ask."

"Isabella? You've had a lot of upsets happen to you in your short life. But you've also had many beautiful things happen to you as well. You'll see in time that there'll always be more wonderful things happen than not. Do you understand what I'm saying?"

"You're talking about the glass half-filled, aren't you?"

Caught off guard by her awareness of the expression, I laughed. "Exactly. And always remember that you are loved no matter what happens ... loved by me and many others."

"I love you, too, Mama."

"Now, go have fun with your sister-friends!"

Lord, help me. Her telephone call made me realize how important it was for Isabella to have *fun*. Mike and Brian accused me of drawing trouble, and now that Isabella was my responsibility, I had to do all I could to keep her safe. Luckily, with Isabella's increased psychic ability and mine, if we listened to it, we'd have a chance to be pre-warned and maybe prepare for some of the forthcoming events that may cause us concern.

I'd been lost in thought when Mike and Brian came back into the kitchen, fully dressed for the wedding. I smiled when I saw them. They were so different—Mike with his dark, Native American Indian heritage and Brian with his light-skinned, freckled Irish heritage. Each in his way was "drop dead" gorgeous. To see them dressed like many of the Indians at the Pueblo warmed my heart. They looked earthy and very masculine ... more so than usual.

Mike came to my side and kissed me thoroughly on the lips, then he rubbed the pad of his thumb across my lips. "You better hop to it, my queen," he said, pulling me off the kitchen bar stool. "Time's running out," he said as he patted my backside and lightly pushed me forward.

As I slipped my dress over my head and let it settle around me, I felt my grandmother's spirit beside me. "Hi, Gram. What do you think?"

"I think that you look beautiful, Rosie girl," she said, using her nickname for me.

"Isabella is worried that something bad might happen. Are we going to be safe today?"

"Enjoy today, for it will be a beautiful time that you will look back upon as a time to remember always. This day will change your life forever."

"What do you mean, Gram?"

"You'll see. Love you!" Her words floated through the air and then vanished.

"Thanks, Gram. I love you, too," I said to the space around me.

Knowing that, at least for today, we'd be free of worrying and not waiting for something terrible to happen, I eagerly joined the guys to head out to the Pueblo and share in Karen and Coyote's wedding festivities.

CHAPTER 20

When we arrived at the Pueblo, I headed to Grandmother's, while Mike and Brian went to Coyote's house. Nancy and Susannah had not arrived yet. As I stepped inside the house, I heard the younger girls' excited voices. I walked down the hallway to where they were. When I peeked into Nica's bedroom and saw them there, I could barely breathe. I was taken back in time. Each girl wore her moccasins, scarcely visible underneath her long fringed dress, and had her hair braided into pigtails, topped by her simple headband with feathers. With their different shades of light coffee-colored skin and dark eyes glowing in a happy face, white teeth sparkling, they were the most beautiful little girls I'd ever seen. I was overcome with emotion and held my arms wide to include all three in a hug.

"Are you crying, Mama?" asked Isabella.

"Just happy is all," I answered as I pulled them closer.

"Wait until you see Auntie Karen! She looks so beautiful. C'mon."

I followed the girls to Grandmother's room, where Karen sat in a chair while her new sister-in-law, Angel, was tying her hair into a traditional Navajo bun. I wondered how her headdress would fit around it. I looked around. "Where is it?" I asked in excitement.

"Where's what?" asked Karen.

"The headdress Coyote had made for you!"

"He hasn't brought it over yet," she answered with a nervous smile. "I can't wait to see it either."

Grandmother walked into the room with Nancy and Susannah. "Oh, my God! Stand up, Karen, so we can see your dress," ordered Susannah.

"In all my travels, I've never seen anything like it. It's beautiful," gushed Nancy.

We all jumped when we heard a knocking at the front door. "I'm looking for my bride. Is she here?" hollered Coyote.

"Yes," the three of us sister-friends called out while Karen closed her eyes and said a silent prayer before she rose from her chair.

Walking away with her head held high like a powerful princess, Karen led us to Coyote, Mike, and Brian standing in the living room. It was nearly impossible to see Coyote's face as he held up a magnificent beaded headdress filled with feathers, flowers, and ribbons. It was stunning!

We stood back as Coyote moved into the center of the room and beckoned Karen forward. He kissed her and spoke to her in Tewa with the rest of us surrounding them, and Karen's eyes immediately filled. She quietly said something in Tewa back to him. Upon hearing their words, both Grandmother and Angel teared up. Then, Coyote lifted the headdress and settled it onto Karen's head, placing a long kiss on her waiting lips.

The men left us, saying the guests had begun to arrive. We surrounded Karen and gingerly touched her headdress as she stood by, glowing in happiness. We sister-friends hugged and congratulated Karen, wishing her all the best. "Now, let's go get this gal married," I said.

***

Driving to the pueblo earlier, I'd spoken to both Mike and Brian about making sure that Karen's parents were seated by Virginia and Grandfather so it would help put Karen's mother at ease. As I peeked from behind the half-opened door where we'd enter for the ceremony, I saw Virginia leaning close to Agnes, saying something. Agnes didn't look happy, obviously uncomfortable in her new surroundings. But I didn't feel sorry for her. It was up to her whether she would be open to all that Karen's new life experiences would provide. I only hoped that Agnes would begin to appreciate Karen for the beautiful person she was. It was hard to accept that she hadn't already.

The room began to fill up even though it was a small wedding limited to family and a few close friends. My heart pounded with anticipation of what was coming. I watched Mike, who appeared comfortable in his western native clothes, as he greeted and sedately settled people into their seats. On the other hand, Brian looked pleased to be taking part in this wedding and seated his guests with more fanfare. It was interesting to note the differences between them.

"Rosie, the Chief wants to see you," said Nancy. "C'mon."

I found him standing with Karen, Grandmother, and another man wearing a headdress. I assumed he was the Medicine Man, for he held a vase with double handles—the Wedding Vase. It was made of pottery with a beautiful design all around it. Although Mike and I were going to be responsible for keeping the vase safe during the ceremony, it was up to the Medicine Man to fill it with liquid. I didn't want anything to happen to spoil Karen's special day, and I wasn't sure I could trust him. "What liquid are you going to be using?" I demanded.

"This is fresh water from the creek that we blessed," he responded.

"Is that safe?" I asked and then felt a hand around my wrist.

"Little Bird, it's fine ... it's all fine," said Grandmother with conviction, using my Indian name from the life we'd shared.

"Sorry," I said as my face reddened. I had to trust that all would be okay.

The drumbeat began, and our hearts thumped in excitement with each sound as we sister-friends entered the building, followed by Karen. We heard the rustling of people in their seats as they shifted to get the best possible view of Karen's stunning dress and headdress. Grandmother and the Chief were already seated, and Karen joined them on the platform and sat next to Grandmother while we others sat in chairs on the floor. Then the men entered, and Coyote took our attention with his beautiful headdress as large and awe-inspiring as Karen's. He mounted the platform sitting next to the Chief while Mike and Brian sat in chairs across from us. The little girls came in next, greeted by hushed appreciation, and sat on mats in front of us sister-friends. They held baskets of petals they'd use after the ceremony.

The Chief stood and took his time telling how the Navajo beliefs (like most Native American Indian ideas) were based on how they appreciated and treated nature—how it mattered to be attuned to nature's energies. "It is not one of competition to nature but one of completion with it that makes it our true foundation."

He further explained that "our music and the beat of our drums soothes the heartbeat of nature and all that's attuned to it, while our words of gratitude open our human hearts. As we strengthen our beliefs along life's journey, it draws the stars closer as we begin our dance in the heavens with the Great One, who confirms that we are all one in energy with nature and humankind."

I gasped at hearing his words, for they sounded familiar to me and were accurate enough to my personal beliefs to cause me to tear up. I bowed my head in reverence, and when I looked up, Mike was staring at me with such love that I had to catch my breath. I blushed and smiled at him, my heart happy.

The Blessingway and Protectionway ceremonies honored first the feminine energy, then the masculine. The chief explained them to the audience. As we went through the motions of each, I barely remember participating in either ceremony with their different drum beats and singing attached to them. My mind kept drifting back in time to my lifetime here at the pueblo long ago. My vision showed me that as the chief's daughter, I had been a difficult child, and as a young adult, I had lived in my own world on my own terms. I defied being tethered to the usual expectations of my gender and role as a woman, making my father unhappy with me although he loved me deeply. My sister's death flashed in front of me, and once again, I felt the sadness of that day. Isabella, my sister that lifetime, had died when I was supposed to be watching her. My heart felt heavy.

The drums changed tempo, and my daydreaming halted as I recognized the music. After listening to it for a few minutes, the music's rhythm drew me back to a happy time in my previous life when I was much older. A man, not that tall—perhaps 5'11" or so—muscular and strong, stood beside me. We were peering into a bundle of fur tucked around a small baby. The man lifted his head and stared into my eyes. The look was so intimate, and his kind eyes filled with so much love that the similarity of it to the one Mike had sent me earlier jerked me back to the present time. As I viewed the present-day surroundings, I felt light-headed. I looked across to where Mike was sitting. As if sensing me, he raised his head and looked my way. When our eyes met, he sent me the same intimate look he had before. It was such a raw emotion of love and need that I could barely breathe. I placed my hand on my heart, acknowledging my love for him. It was done without thought or expectation. I looked away, confused. Is this what my grandmother meant when she said today was a day I'd always remember?

Suddenly, Karen and Coyote stood up at the same time as Grandmother and the Chief. I shook off my thoughts and watched as Coyote reached for Karen's hand, and they stepped down together onto the floor of the building where we sat. The Chief raised his arms fully open in front of him and extended a hand over each head. He spoke in English in a commanding tone, "Coyote, do you take Karen to be

108

your lawfully wedded wife, and Karen, do you take Coyote to be your lawfully wedded husband?"

Coyote said something in Tewa, with Karen responding the same thing. Then they exchanged wedding rings. After that, the Chief reached behind him and presented the Wedding Vase. We observed the groom and bride drinking from it—first Karen, then Coyote. Not a drop spilled, and they smiled at each other, glad of its forecast of a happy life together.

Mike nodded at me, and I stepped forward to join him as we retrieved the Wedding Vase from Coyote and Karen and placed it reverently on a makeshift altar to the side of where Grandmother and the Chief had been sitting. Mike and I were responsible for ensuring that it got safely locked up in the Chief's office before we took part in the rest of the wedding celebration at the hotel.

Then, with great fanfare, the Chief announced, "Coyote and Karen, I now pronounce you man and wife. You may kiss the bride."

When Coyote finished kissing Karen, the Chief turned to the congregation. "In a traditional Indian ceremony, there is a special wedding dance that we perform after every wedding to celebrate the blending of the feminine and masculine energies. The wedding party is going to perform that for you now."

Coyote and Karen went to sit on the platform where Grandmother and the Chief had previously sat. Grandmother and the Chief took the former seats of Karen and Coyote. At the rehearsal, we were told that our dancing was performed for the bride and groom's pleasure. We gathered in the area in front of the platform. The drums' joint beat that both Grandmother and the Chief held and played was loud, fast, and uplifting. We sister-friends,

Mike, Brian, and the little girls, began to dance, our moves composed of the traditional hop, then feet kicking out in various movements, and twirling every once in a while. Grandmother and Chief began to chant in Tewa, which meant something to some but sounded guttural to the rest of us. It was a time to be free—expressive and joyful. I was in my glory, feeling at home with the dancing and connected to *everything*. I didn't remember ever feeling that way before, and I felt like what the name Little Bird represented—the freedom to fly without limits.

Isabella came to my side, and we danced together for a few minutes, both of us grinning at each other. Then she pulled me close to Mike and reached for Mike's hand, and placed it on top of mine. She began to dance around us, and we laughed at her apparent gesture. Mike held his arms wide, spread like wings, to air surround Isabella and me as we all danced together. It was a happy moment that I'd remember forever.

Soon it was time for the little girls to spread the flower petals down the aisle that Karen and Coyote would follow, leading the congregation outside where they'd stand to greet us as man and wife.

While that was taking place, Mike and I took the Wedding Vase into the Chief's office. As we placed it into the cabinet for safety, I turned to Mike, "Wasn't that the most beautiful wedding? I loved the Native American Indian part of it. Didn't you?"

"Hmm. Yes, very different, especially how the two traditions melded together."

I smiled. "Unique for sure. Did you notice Cal had tears in his eyes during the ceremony?"

"Really? No, I missed that. I wonder why?"

"Maybe it was because the ceremony was so beautiful."

Mike grabbed me close. "Nothing as beautiful as you are to me," he murmured and nuzzled my neck before his lips met mine.

CHAPTER 21

When we arrived at the Eldorado Hotel, we joined the others to stand outside the room where the dinner celebrations would take place. The doors were closed, and we waited impatiently for them to open, curious to see the inside. There was a low murmuring among us as some of us expressed the different aspects of the wedding that we'd enjoyed. I looked around to make sure that Karen's mother and father were doing okay. I didn't see them. Then I remembered that they'd be standing with Karen, Coyote, and Grandmother as hosts to welcome us into the room. Not quite the traditional way of doing things I was accustomed to, yet not much of the wedding ceremony had been.

I couldn't wait any longer. I had to make a trip to the Ladies' room before I burst. I excused myself and dashed away only to find Tom Little Horse coming out of the bar area. He was as surprised to see me as I was him. He slowed to stand in front of me, blocking my way, towering over me with his large six-foot frame. A smile crossed his handsome face. "Fancy meeting you here."

I looked into his amused dark eyes. "I could say the same to you."

Taking in my Indian garb, he asked, "How was the wedding?"

"Beautiful," I replied.

"Not as beautiful as you, I bet!" he said as he scanned me from head to toe.

My face warmed. I rolled my eyes and ignored what he'd said. "I've got to run." As I raced down the hall, I looked back over my shoulder to see him still standing where I left him, his burning gaze taking me in as I went. Annoyance flashed through me at his arrogance. I could understand now how Tom Little Horse's overconfidence would have annoyed Mike. Even more so his association with politics.

When I returned to Mike and the others, the doors were just opening. In an orderly manner, we stepped forward and took turns being greeted by the smiling faces of all but one of the hosts ... Agnes. What is it about that woman who can't seem to find joy in anything? I thought. I brushed aside her attitude and stepped into the room to join the others in celebrating the union of Karen and Coyote.

***

By 8:30 that evening, I was dragging, and others had already left. When Isabella came to sit beside me and lay her head on my shoulder, I knew it was time for us to head home, too. I'd had more to drink than I usually would have, so I was glad that Mike would be the one to drive us home. Interestingly enough, Mike hadn't had anything more to drink after the toast he gave as best man. On the other hand, Brian had downed a few more to sustain his self-confidence to keep Coyote's sister, Angel, entertained. When I looked at the two of them together, I could see that Brian's fun personality was causing Angel to smile often. She seemed to enjoy his company, and I was pleased to see her have some fun after all she'd been through lately. I didn't know if Brian would be ready to leave with us, but he could always walk or use an Uber.

Karen and Coyote had arranged to stay in the bridal suite at the hotel that night so that Karen's parents wouldn't be left on their own until their arranged limo would drive them the next afternoon to the airport in Albuquerque. When Karen had first told me her plans, I thought it was more than generous on both their parts to give up their honeymoon night, but she said they didn't want to begin their marriage with her parents any more upset than they already were.

Tomorrow was the last day before we headed back to Las Vegas later, and we sister-friends, minus Karen, would meet for breakfast at the hotel before we each went our way.

Mike headed to where Isabella and I sat. "Ready to go, babe?"

I nodded. "How about Brian? Is he coming with us?"

"Yeah, he's just saying goodbye to Angel and Grandmother."

"C'mon, then. Let's go say a quick goodbye to them, too," I urged.

I was surprised to hear the girlish tinkling of Angel's laugh as she leaned forward in her seat to listen to what Brian had to say. Grandmother was resting with her chin on her chest, snoring lightly. "Grandmother?" called Isabella, shaking her shoulder. "Are you awake?"

Grandmother stirred. "What is it, child?"

"We've come to say goodnight."

"Sleep tight, Little One. Sweet dreams. Where's Nica?" she asked as she looked around.

"She's sitting with Angela and her parents. They are planning a sleepover when I'm not going to be here," she added, a bit disgruntled.

"You can be there in spirit," said Grandmother as she received a kiss from Isabella.

"More likely be there by way of the cell phone," I added with a chuckle. I bent to kiss Grandmother goodnight, while Mike stood close behind me waiting his turn. His nearness washed over me, and I felt loved.

"Keep well until I see you in a few weeks when Isabella and I will be back for the summer break," I said as I kissed her weathered cheek. "I love you, Grandmother—my mother."

"And I you, Little Bird," she said as she grasped my hand tight. "I'm not going anywhere. I'll be here waiting for your arrival."

I stepped around the table to where Angel was sitting. I kissed her goodnight. "I'm so glad you're having a good time," I said.

"Me, too," she acknowledged with a shy smile.

"Are you coming with us?" I asked Brian. He could drag out his goodbyes, and I was exhausted, hitting that legendary wall of not being able to do anything more.

"Yeah, just give me a minute, okay?"

I nodded. "We'll meet you out front."

I headed to where Maria, Angela, Nica, and Miguel were sitting. I made the round with kisses to all, even

Miguel, who gracefully accepted it. In time, I knew that he'd forgive me for "taking Isabella away from him," but with Maria and me as her "mamas," she was in the best place.

Isabella, Mike, and I waved goodbye to all who were left and headed to the hotel's front to wait for Brian.

CHAPTER 22

When daylight seeped through the cracks of the shutters the next morning, I snuggled further down in the bedding. I had plenty of time. I wasn't meeting my sister-friends until 10 o'clock. I let my thoughts come and considered the visions I'd had during Karen and Coyote's wedding. They'd brought me understanding that love never dies; it changes partners, and form is all. I could see in my mind that baby's sweet smile and how my husband had looked at me. Then, there was the energy thing that'd happened between Mike and me. How could I forget that? I knew he loved me. Even so, what was holding Mike back from wanting to make our relationship permanent? Was it something to do with me? What was it? Disheartened, I rolled over and went back to sleep.

It was the tantalizing smell of coffee that woke me up. I stretched and groggily searched for my pup, thinking it was as it had been before, like it had been in my dream— just Sweet Pea and me during that terrible time shortly after my former fiancé's death. For a second, I wondered where I was and who'd gotten into the house. I tried to clear my foggy brain and get back to the present time. I lay back and let the past drift away. I smiled as I heard Mike, Brian, and Isabella's laughter float toward me. Pretty soon, I heard footsteps head my way. Mike peered in from the doorway. "Are you ready for your coffee, my queen?"

"You certainly know your way to a girl's heart, handsome."

He stepped forward. "I take that as a yes, then," he said as he sat on the edge of the bed and handed me a mug of hot coffee. "You were sleeping so soundly that I didn't have the heart to wake you."

"I almost wished you had; I had a weird dream about the past."

"That's too bad," he said as he kissed me tenderly on the forehead.

"Have I told you lately how much I love you?" I asked him.

"I'm always glad to hear that."

"Good to know," I said with a smile. "What time is it, anyway?"

Mike checked his watch. "Half-past nine."

"Holy cow! I've got to rush if I'm going to meet the girls on time. Here, take my coffee and set it over there, please."

"The rest of us ate breakfast earlier, but I can fix you something if you want."

"Thanks, but I'll eat with the girls." I hopped out of bed and blew him a kiss. I pulled out clean underwear, jeans, and my navy cashmere sweater and dashed into the bathroom to take a hurried shower. I didn't want to be late.

It would be the last I'd be able to spend time with my sister-friends before the opening of Rosalie's restaurant in May.

When I walked into the Eldorado Hotel's fancier restaurant where we'd agreed to meet, I didn't realize that Karen's parents might be sitting there ... alone. Susannah and Nancy waved me over to the table where they sat. I edged myself into an empty chair and faced them. I whispered, "Should we invite Karen's parents to join us?"

Susannah and Nancy looked at each other, then nodded in unison.

"I think we have no choice, really," I agreed and rose to head their way.

As I came closer to them, they looked up. "Good morning! Susannah, Nancy, and I wondered if you'd like to join us for breakfast."

Karen's father smiled. "How nice of you to ask us!"

Agnes put her hand on Karen's father's arm. "We're just going to wait for Karen and Coyote."

"Oh, okay," I responded as I received the psychic message that they weren't due to appear for a while. "What time were they going to meet you?"

Karen's father looked at his watch. "Another hour."

"Oh, my! That's too long to sit by yourselves. Come join us," I urged.

Karen's father rose and held his hand out for Agnes. She hesitated long enough to be embarrassing. "C'mon, Mother," he ordered.

After they settled in at the table, Nancy asked, "Well, what did you think of your daughter's beautiful wedding?"

Appearing uncomfortable, Karen's parents looked at each other. "Different," her father finally said.

"Didn't you just love Karen's wedding dress? Wasn't it magnificent?" asked Susannah, looking at Agnes.

"I was hoping that she'd wear the one I wore, although I don't suppose she had much choice," Agnes said.

Changing the subject, I asked, "Do you have plans to return for a visit anytime soon?"

Karen's father said, "No plans as yet."

Agnes said, "I suppose now she'll want babies, so maybe then."

"Won't that be something, huh? Are you looking forward to becoming grandparents?" asked Nancy.

"Not really," Agnes responded, "we live so far away."

"Not that far," interjected Karen's father. "The airlines make getting places pretty easy."

"Well, we'll see," Agnes said.

I turned away and rolled my eyes. I fought to hold my temper at Agnes's lack of enthusiasm for anything to do with Karen. "Are you ready to order, anyone?" I asked.

Susannah, Nancy, and I combed through the menus that the waitress had dropped off at our table. Deciding on just one thing was hard to do since everything looked delicious. "Let's each order something different, and then we can share a bite, okay?" I asked.

"Sounds good," agreed Nancy.

"Count me in," said Susannah.

"Do you girls always do that?" asked Karen's father with a chuckle.

We laughed and nodded. "If we can," I said.

After we ordered, Karen and Coyote walked into the restaurant. Looking around and spotting us together, they headed to our table, holding hands. Karen's cheeks flushed with happiness, and Coyote's eyes were soft with tenderness as he whispered something to Karen. They were such a striking couple they drew attention from the surrounding people.

"Can we join you?" Karen asked with a smile when she got close.

We shuffled our chairs around to make room for them while Karen bent and kissed each of her parents on the cheek. "I'm glad that you could make the wedding, Mom and Dad."

"We are, too," Karen's father said. "Aren't we, mother?" he said, nudging her.

Agnes said, "Yes, I didn't want to miss it. I just wish it had been back in Boston, but it's too late now."

"No worries, Mom. I'll send you pictures of the wedding so you can show your friends; then they can see what it was all about."

"Okay, dear," answered Agnes without enthusiasm.

When we all had finished eating, Karen and Coyote rose. "Time to meet the limo, Mom, and Dad. Are your bags downstairs?"

Karen's father nodded. We sister-friends rose as well and said our goodbyes to Karen's parents. Coyote graciously kissed Nancy, Susannah, and me on the cheek before guiding Karen's parents out of the restaurant. Then, we pulled Karen into a group hug, saying goodbye until we met in May in Las Vegas.

I stood with Nancy and Susannah, watching Karen rush out of the restaurant to be with her parents. We three looked at each other and shook our heads. We didn't need to say a word.

***

Cal had sprung for a limo to drive all of us to Albuquerque to catch our flight back to Las Vegas and Brian's flight to Boston. Isabella sat in the middle seat

123

between Mike and me, and she was quiet. "Are you okay?" I asked her.

"I guess. I hate leaving Nica and Angela behind. Do you feel the same way about leaving your sister-friends, Mama?"

"I do. That is why I always try to have something planned in the future, so I know I'll see them soon. Then it's not so hard."

Isabella nodded but remained quiet.

"You have a trip to Disney World coming up soon, huh?" Mike asked.

Isabella raised her eyes and smiled across to Grandfather, who was sitting next to Virginia facing her. "Yes! And we can't wait to go! When we get back home, can we set the date, Grandfather?"

"Yes, let's do that. It should probably be soon after school gets out before it gets too hot. And we'll need to make reservations to stay right there on the property."

"Good!" Isabella said. She looked at all of us sitting in the limo. "We're going to have so much fun!"

We smiled at each other, taking in Isabella's excitement. The limo pulled in close to the curb to let us out at the airport. We said goodbye to Brian and trudged our way to our terminal and gate to head home.

CHAPTER 23

Somehow, when dealing with Jacklyn at the Agency, I was able to keep our conversations strictly on the construction of the new office building and not on my personal life. I knew Jacklyn was disappointed not to have my relationship with Mike further along with a commitment of some sort. But at this time, it was what it was, and I didn't want to force the issue.

Time was flying by. Sammy and Isabella were spending a lot of time together after school and on the weekends after Sammy's soccer practice. One Saturday, they'd invited Tiffany and Deborah from school to join them at the movies to see a special showing of "Little Women." It was part of their English class requirements.

After the show, I planned to treat them to pizza at my favorite restaurant. When I saw them standing on the curb, waiting for me to pick them up, I was pleasantly surprised to see Tiffany flash a genuine smile my way. They piled into the car, and I asked, "Do you want to stop for pizza?"

Three answered, "Yes!" while Tiffany debated in silence.

"Where?" she asked.

I held my breath, not wanting to battle it out with Tiffany as we'd done in past days. "Moretti's. Is that alright with everyone?"

Tiffany eyed me and nodded. "Okay, I like that place."

I knew Tiffany was in counseling after her rough time with the homeless man, who'd hoodwinked her into believing he could make her a movie star. She'd been one of the lucky ones and hadn't experienced his wrath or her death at his hands. It was good to see that therapy seemed to be working to make her less demanding and less focused on herself and her wants only.

I was aware that Tiffany was still having trouble at school because most kids no longer allowed her to bully them. The school headmistresses had told me that my demonstrating Dr. Emoto's experiment with water, plants, and talking about the energy we create with our thoughts, words, and actions had had a positive effect on the students. It made me feel good to know that Isabella was having a much better experience at school now that Sammy was at her side and Tiffany was behaving better.

I'd already met with Mimi, Romano, and his partner, Randy, for the last walk through the restaurant before the opening scheduled in a few days. The restaurant was stunning, and I was floating on a high that Romano and Mimi had named it after me.

I hadn't seen the guest list, but Mimi and Romano said it was extensive. They wanted many of the bigwigs to be there for the celebration. I'd only invited Cal, Virginia,

Sammy's parents, and my sister-friends. I would've included my neighbors, Ron and Irene, but they insisted they were happy to stay at home with Isabella instead. I didn't want Isabella amid all the alcohol and drinking that'd be there at the opening.

Knowing that the restaurant's opening would be a huge event, I called Louie, my fashion expert. When I'd first started working at the Purple Passion Lounge, Romano introduced me to him. Louie had helped me expand my wardrobe with beautiful, sensual pieces that were stunning. "Hello, my friend. I'm wondering if you can help me pick out something special to wear for the opening of Romano's new restaurant."

"I was hoping you'd call. I just got in the perfect dress for you. Can you meet me at the store now?"

***

Excited, I stood in front of the mirror, waiting for Louie to return with what he'd picked out for me. He hung the dress on the side hook, lifted its cover, and handed the dress to me. As I let it slip over my body, I felt its coolness and shivered with the sensual feeling that silk creates. The emerald green color shimmered in the light with a richness that only dyed silk can produce. It was a dress that fit me as if it were made for me, draping my figure in all the right places, causing Louie to exclaim, "Ahhh, yes! Perfecto!"

My cheeks flushed with the excitement of knowing that this dress made me look gorgeous and "hot." It would be hard for Mike to ignore me in this. "Louie, you've outdone yourself with this one. I love it!"

"As well you should. That dress brings out all your inner beauty, making you glow. No one else at the party will be able to come close to holding a candle to you. "

My eyes softened. "Oh, Louie," I said, throwing my arms around him. "Will you be there at the opening?"

"Romano and Randy insisted I come, and I wouldn't miss it for the world."

I left Louie's with a few extra packages. He'd encouraged me to try on several casual tops and pants that'd be perfect for Santa Fe this summer.

Searching through my closet later, I was pleased to discover shoes I'd bought on sale and had never worn that'd be perfect with the new dress. I heard Sweet Pea barking, and I wondered who it was since it was too early for Isabella to be home from school. "Who is it?" I hollered down.

"It's the big bad wolf," teased Mike as he climbed the stairs.

"Oh, really?" I laughed. "What brings you home at this time?"

"I just heard from Brian, and I wanted to ask your permission before I got back to him."

"What is it?"

"He's flying in for the opening, and he's bringing Allison.

"Who's Allison?"

"Our new employee, remember?" Mike answered.

I did, indeed, remember who she was. Brian said that she'd seemed interested in Mike when they'd interviewed her for the job. "I guess so."

"Okay, then."

"Wait! Does that mean he's planning on them staying here? I don't think that's a good idea."

"Why not?"

"Think about it. Just by you asking me for permission must mean you have reservations about it too, don't you think?"

"Well, I ...."

"Are they even dating?"

"No, not really."

"Then why would I put them up in a room together?"

"I don't know. Maybe Brian could sleep on the couch."

Annoyed, I snapped, "As your employee, you and Brian should get her a room at one of the casinos if you want her to come to Las Vegas. That way, you can write it off as an expense."

"Okay. I just thought I'd ask. I'll get Allison a room at the Bellagio then."

"Mike, why would Brian think that it's okay for him to fraternize with your new employee?"

Embarrassment covered Mike's face. "Actually, it was my idea. I thought it would be nice for Allison to see the office here in Las Vegas since she'll be helping out now and then."

"Really," I said in a frosty tone. "Your idea, huh?"

"Don't make this into something it's not, Rosie," he warned.

"What reason would I have to do that?"

"Right," Mike said, ignoring my sarcasm. "Well, I'm back to work then. See you later," he said as he gave me a hurried kiss and rushed down the stairs and out the door.

Was I jealous of a woman I'd never even met? If Allison were as good at her job as both Mike and Brian had indicated, she would be a lifesaver for them at work. Maybe Brian had been exaggerating when he'd said she

was flirting with Mike. Brian was a tease and probably just
wanted to see my reaction.

CHAPTER 24

The next few days flew by. Brian and Allison arrived the day before the opening of the restaurant. After Brian dropped Allison off at the Bellagio and she settled in, Brian, Mike, Isabella, and I would meet her for dinner at one of the more excellent restaurants there.

I took an extra few minutes to fuss with my makeup and put on one of the outfits Louie had picked for me. I was pleased with how I looked, even more so when Isabella exclaimed, "Oh, Mama, you look so beautiful!"

I turned and smiled at Isabella, noting what she wore. "And just who is this beautiful young lady standing in front of me?"

"Oh, Mama," she smiled. "You're so funny."

I hugged her. "I see you're wearing your diamond earrings. How nice!"

Isabella beamed. "And I see you're wearing the diamond ring that Grandfather gave you."

I held my hand out so that both Isabella and I could marvel at the large heart-shaped diamond. It was a beautiful piece of jewelry that brought me back to the time I'd first met Cal's mother, who turned out to be his grandmother. It had been hers, and she wanted me to have it in gratitude for my grandmother's kindness to her in the past.

"That's going to be mine someday, isn't it?" asked Isabella.

"That's right. Someday in the future," I said as I pulled Isabella into a hug. "We'd better go downstairs. Mike and Brian are waiting for us."

Mike and Brian's faces lit up as they watched Isabella and me come down the stairs, followed by Sweet Pea. "Wow, Rosie and Isabella, you both look beautiful," exclaimed Brian. "You're a lucky man, Mike."

"Indeed I am," confirmed Mike, kissing Isabella on the cheek, and me a kiss on the lips but not before whispering, "And I know it." He winked at me and smiled.

We drove to the Bellagio, left the car with the valet, and entered the beautiful casino where we'd meet Allison at Olive's restaurant. Isabella had been to Bellagio's to see the stunning inside garden a few weeks earlier on a class trip and wanted me to see it. I peeked in from the main entrance area and viewed tourists flooding the garden area, stooping to take photographs. Impatient, Isabella pulled me away to catch up to Mike and Brian, who were now quite far ahead of us.

I looked around for the young girl who I'd seen a few months earlier, but I didn't see her. As soon as the restaurant came into view, I saw a beautiful woman standing by the entrance. She had long blond hair tied back into a ponytail and wore heavy makeup. She was slim with a toned figure and stood there taking in the admiring glances of several men who'd passed by, obviously enjoying their attention. So this was Allison. As soon as she saw Mike and Brian, she hollered out, "Hi there, guys! Here I am!"

Isabella and I were far enough behind the men that she didn't realize we were with them. As Mike and Brian stepped forward, they separated from each other, exposing Isabella and me as we came closer. When she understood who we were, her face fell with disappointment with the knowledge that she was not the only beautiful one in the group. She quickly recovered and greeted us in a high unnatural voice as if we were pets to be acknowledged. "Hi there, I'm Allison. You must be Isabella," nodding toward her. "And you, Rosalie, then."

"Right you are," I agreed. I looked at Mike, who seemed oblivious to any tension between Allison and me.

"Shall we go inside, ladies?" Mike asked.

Allison immediately grabbed Mike's arm, looking at him adoringly. "Why not? It's so nice to see you in person instead of just talking to you every day."

Isabella and I stood there, looking at each other. "You've got to be kidding!" I mumbled.

Brian was waiting to escort us into the restaurant. "Did you say something, Rosie?"

I shook my head. "No, nothing."

When we reached the table, Allison was standing next to Mike, waiting to be seated. She patted the chair next to her. "Sit here, Rosalie."

I ignored her and moved to sit on Mike's other side. I slid my hand across his shoulders and squeezed his arm before I lowered myself into the chair that Brian held for me.

"Everything okay?" asked Mike puzzled.

"Of course. Why wouldn't it be?" I answered with a strained smile.

Orders were taken, and when the drinks came, Allison said, "I'd like to propose a toast." She lifted her glass, "Here's to the great success that's sure to come about from us working closely together." She eyed Mike and winked. Then, she did the same with Brian.

The guys immediately raised their glass to tip it at her and each other. Meantime, Isabella and I sat with our glasses raised, waiting for any of the three to acknowledge us. Finally, good manners took over, and both Mike and Brian knocked on our drinks. "Hear, hear."

Seeing my ring flash in the light, Allison exclaimed, "What a beautiful ring! Did you pick that out, Mike?"

Mike's cheeks flushed. Silence hung in the air until I said, "No, it's a family ring."

"Oh," said Allison.

During dinner, the conversation was all about business, with Allison quickly steering it back to business each time Isabella or I tried to say something. I was becoming furious. At one point, Mike sensed my quiet. "What do you think, Rosie, about what goes on here in Las Vegas?"

"What I know is that between four and five people go missing each day here in Las Vegas."

"That seems high to me," said Allison. "It can't be that many," she said with an air of dismissal.

"I'm afraid it's true. We have many women who are on the run from the trouble they're in and think Las Vegas is the place to be. That's why Mike's main business here has been working to find these missing girls."

"Well, I think he's got more important things to do than find girls who don't want to be found. There's more money to be made in large corporations, right, Mike?"

Mike's face reddened. "True, but …"

Brian was looking between Allison and me. "If I'm not mistaken, I know there's a special chocolate fountain here in the casino. Why don't we go see what that's all about, shall we, Isabella?"

"I'll go with you. I think this business meeting is over, don't you agree, Mike?" I demanded.

"Yeah, okay. I'll get the check and be right there. You go ahead, and I'll catch up."

Brian stood. "C'mon, Allison. Let's go."

***

When we got into the car to return home, the silence was deafening. I was disappointed that Mike and Brian had hired someone who only seemed concerned about herself.

Later, when Mike and I were alone getting ready for bed, I turned to him. "Why did you invite Isabella and me to join you for dinner tonight?"

"What do you mean?" he asked.

"Think about it, Mike. We were sitting at the same table; yet, you, Brian, and Allison ignored us and never included us in your conversations or anything! How do you think your rudeness made Isabella and me feel?"

"I'm sorry," he said a little too quickly to be more than a set response that sounded trite. I didn't want him saying that to mean so little.

"I don't expect you to give me your full attention when we are with others, Mike, but I certainly don't expect you to leave me sitting there feeling foolish as I watch you and Brian all but drool over Allison."

"Hey, I was simply nice to her," he defended.

"All I'm saying is that I'm not happy with how things turned out tonight, and I want to make sure you're aware that I didn't appreciate it." I sighed heavily, and turned away, and climbed into bed.

Mike came to my side of the bed and leaned down to kiss me. "I know you're under a lot of stress, what with the opening tomorrow, and that's making you grumpy. Everything will be alright. Just relax, and look at tomorrow as just another day."

Grumpy? I was too annoyed to say anything. He doesn't get it, I thought, but he's right about one thing—tomorrow is another day.

CHAPTER 25

The next morning I awoke to find myself tangled in the sheets and one leg draped over Mike's. He was snoring softly. I stared at him and wondered why men so quickly abandoned their spouse or girlfriend when there is a new female around. The guys seem to perk up, excited to compete, like the notorious jokes about roosters in the hen house. I promised myself that I would not let things like last night happen again. I would not take a back seat to anyone, but that didn't mean I'd flaunt myself either.

I thought about what lay ahead and went over the list in my mind about what I needed to do before three o'clock. The celebration would begin at four and last until seven-thirty, at which time the restaurant would close until the following day. Romano was cooking a special dinner for Mimi, Mike, Brian, Cal and Virginia, my sister-friends and me. Now, I supposed we'd have to include Allison, I grumbled to myself.

My sister-friends were arriving mid-morning, and I was going to pick them up at the airport and drive them to Cal's house where they would be staying. None of them were bringing their better halves, so the following day, we sister-friends would have a chance to catch up. Then they'd leave the next morning.

I climbed out of bed, threw on my clothes, and went downstairs to start the coffee. This was a school day for Isabella, and I wanted to make sure she was okay with the plans of being with Irene and Ron for the night. I set the table and laid out a bowl of cut up fruit and a choice of cereals. I heard Sweet Pea coming down the stairs, her nails making music as she bounded down, followed by Isabella's softer footsteps.

"Good morning, you two!" I greeted them. "C'mon, Sweet Pea. I'll let you out."

Isabella slumped in her seat at the table, looking out-of-sorts with the world. "What's up, buttercup?" I asked.

"Nothing."

"Are you sure? What's troubling you?"

"Mama, why was that lady acting all funny last night?"

"What do you mean?"

"She acted like Tiffany did that time you got so mad at her. Remember? When she flirted with Mike?"

"Yes, I do remember. Well, that woman is Mike and Brian's new employee for their Boston office. She'll be working with them back east and sometimes here in Las Vegas."

"I don't trust her, Mama. I don't like her."

"Don't like who?" asked Mike as he quietly joined us, followed by Brian.

Isabella bowed her head for a second. Then, she lifted her chin high and faced him with determination. "That woman last night."

Mike jerked his attention my way with a questioning look. I held my hands in defense. "I didn't say anything against her. Honest."

"I want you to be nice to her, Isabella. She's going to be working with us to help find some of the girls who've gone missing here," urged Mike.

"I'll be nice to her, but I don't have to like her," she stated, allowing no rebuttal.

I handed both Mike and Brian a coffee cup before I settled next to Isabella at the table. "Are you okay with staying at Gramma Irene's tonight?"

"Yup. We're going to watch a movie tonight, and then tomorrow we're going to do some baking. She said to bring Sweet Pea too."

"Okay, then. If you're happy, I'm happy. Have fun tonight," I said, kissing her on the cheek. "Since tomorrow is Saturday, you'll be able to sleep in too."

I turned to Mike and Brian. "Guys, just to remind you. The opening starts at 4 o'clock so please be there on time. And don't forget to dress up. I have to be at the restaurant at 3 o'clock to help with the final arrangements."

Mike and Brian nodded in unison. They looked so handsome standing side by side in their wrinkled pajamas and their hair tousled. I rose, went to Mike, and leaned into him for a quick snuggle so he'd know I'd forgiven him for last night. His arm wrapped around me, and he pulled me close. "Ah, my queen. Any more orders?"

"Just one. My morning kiss," I said laughingly.

"I can handle that," he murmured as he bent and gave me a lingering kiss, making me warm inside.

The spell completely broke when Brian innocently asked, "Do you need Allison to help you get the restaurant ready for the opening?"

I felt Mike stiffen when he registered Brian's words, but he remained silent. I slid from Mike's grasp and chewed on my lower lip, struggling to hold back a retort. The air was crackling with unspoken tension.

Even Isabella was still, looking my way, waiting for my response.

Finally, I turned to Brian and spilled out, "No, thank you."

We heard the bus pull into our driveway, and I joined Isabella as she headed out the door. "Have a good day at school, sweetie. I love you."

"Love you, too, Mama."

When I returned to the kitchen, Mike and Brian were whispering back and forth. I knew they were discussing my being upset about last night. I ignored them and walked by them to go out onto the patio. The wind had pushed some debris onto it, and I wanted to clear it. I always felt better after I did any kind of exercise…even sweeping.

The guys were upstairs taking showers when I went back inside. I took my time cleaning up the kitchen, straightening up before I'd drive to the airport to pick up my sister-friends and take them to Cal's house. I was glad they were coming to share in my big event. I was curious to know what they'd think of Allison and if they thought I was over-reacting to her.

Mike and Brian came down the stairs, showered, smelling pleasant, ready for the day. "We're off," said Mike. "Catch you later, baby."

"Okay. See you then," I said as I returned his kiss and lightly punched Brian on the arm. "Behave, you two."

140

***

The girls exclaimed over Cal's house as he gallantly gave them a tour, Virginia at his side. With the pool open for swimming, it would be a nice mini-vacation for them for the few days there. I'd join them at Cal's in the morning for breakfast.

Virginia, bless her heart, had made sweet tea for us and served it with tea sandwiches and homemade cookies. We girls sat around the pool and relaxed, feeling like spoiled little girls while Virginia waited upon us.

"Heaven. This is heaven," announced Karen.

"Amen," agreed Susannah.

"What a life," remarked Nancy.

"What's going on with you, Rosie? Is everything set for tonight?" asked Susannah.

"I think we're all set. It should be a beautiful event. Romano, Randy, and Mimi have worked so hard to make it spectacular. And Romano has been fussing over a new recipe he's trying out on us for dinner tonight."

"I bet it's going to be fabulous from what you've told us about Romano's cooking," Karen said.

"I'm sure it will," I added. Looking at my watch, I jumped up. "I've got to get going. Cal and Virginia are driving you to the restaurant with them. So, I'll see you in just a couple of hours. Thanks so much for coming; I'm glad you're here."

As I drove away, I was grateful to Cal for opening his house to my friends. He loved that my friends thought of him and Virginia as part of my family—and thus theirs.

CHAPTER 26

I quickly stopped by the restaurant to see what was going on there. It was a madhouse! The florist and her helpers were fussing with the flowers. The printer had just dropped off the menus and restaurant flyers, keeping Mimi busy organizing them. Romano was shouting in the kitchen, ordering a new helper to "get with the program," and Randy was trying to calm him down. The head waitress was reviewing with her help what to do when the guests arrived. I smiled to myself. All in all, I guess it was the typical jitters before a big event.

I squeezed in next to Mimi to help her fold some of the brochures that'd be handed out as people left. It featured pictures of Romano in his chef uniform with his bio beneath. In one section, he'd written an article about how to use some of the staple herbs and spices that improved anyone's cooking. At the end of the brochure was a photo of the four of us—Romano, Randy, Mimi, and me.

When he saw me, Randy hurried out of the kitchen. "No, Rosie, that's enough. It's time for you to go home, soak in the tub, and come back and dazzle us with your new dress. Louie said it was a knockout."

"Are you sure?"

"Yes, and the same goes for you, Mimi. Go home, relax for a bit, and be back here by three."

I was utterly stress-free after my soak in the tub. I fussed with my makeup, applying a bit more than usual, and swept my hair up on one side, giving it a fresh look. Luckily, I didn't need any help slipping into my dress, although it took a few gentle tugs to pull it down over my hips. I put in my grandmother's large diamond studs I'd gotten out of the safe and slipped the heart-shaped diamond ring onto my finger. A simple diamond bangle bracelet completed my jewelry.

When I finished, I looked in the mirror and gasped. Who was that stunning woman looking back at me? I was surprised to see a young woman reflected in the mirror, much more composed with a more sophisticated air of self-confidence than she'd had a year ago. It was a sexy look that made me put a little extra swing of my hips into my movements.

I strutted into the restaurant right at three o'clock and was surprised that several guests were already there. Romano and Randy looked incredibly handsome in their tuxedos as they stood together, talking to the few special guests. I entered the large dining area to greet them, and when Romano looked up and saw me, he paused before his face split into a grin. "My God, Rosie, you took my breath away. You look stunning! Here, turn around so I can see all of you."

Randy stepped forward and kissed me and then did the same to Mimi, who'd followed me into the room. "Ladies, you have outdone yourself," he exclaimed as he turned us around. Then, the three of us surveyed the room together, pleased with the results.

Soon, people began to file into the room, and the noise level rose as people began to mingle and call out to each other. My sister-friends arrived with Cal and Virginia. Nancy and Susannah looked beautiful as always, but it was Karen who glowed. As I studied her for a moment, I saw a vision of a baby over her head. I wondered if she knew she was pregnant. I smiled as they made their way to the bar and food area. I took hold of Cal and Virginia's hands and pulled them with me to introduce them to an older couple I hadn't seen for a while. They were people I thought they'd like to socialize with in the future.

After I made the introductions, I felt a stir in the room. I turned to see Brian, Mike, and Allison enter the room. There was no doubt that Allison was an attractive woman, but her sense of knowing it spoiled it. But again, I wasn't a guy, and from what I'd seen earlier, they weren't as picky as me.

Mike searched the room, and when he saw me, his entire face lit up. Allison must have felt his energy because she looked up at him and followed his stare. When she saw I was the attraction, her eyes widened, and she pulled on Mike's arm to get his attention. Without looking at her, Mike released Allison's hand and began to walk toward me. We eyed each other with a sexual tension that was hard to deny. It was as if there were no other people in the room. But Allison wasn't having it. She stepped forward and tugged on Mike's jacket hard enough that he stopped and looked back at her. She said something, and Mike frowned. He searched around him, and when he saw Brian, he waved him forward.

That particular moment between Mike and me was broken … gone. I noticed my sister-friends watching as Allison leaned into Mike, clinging to him. They frowned and looked my way. I lifted my shoulders as if to say, "What can I say?"

I stifled a laugh as I watched Susannah march Allison's way with a determined step. When she got close to Allison, she touched her shoulder to get her attention, and she lightly pushed Mike away with her other hand. She kept talking to Allison, turned the two of them away from Mike, and led her to where Karen and Nancy stood. Allison looked too surprised to do anything but follow along.

Goosebumps covered my neck, and I turned in time to see Johnny standing in the doorway. Next to him was the tall man with the scorpion tattoo that I'd seen with Johnny in Santa Fe. He was one of the men Coyote was keeping an eye on as part of the Scorpion gang that illegally controlled getting others across Mexico's border and into the United States. There was an arrogance about the two of the men drawing attention from others in the room. One of those was Allison, who fluttered her eyes and smiled at them as they explored the room. She appeared almost desperate to escape my sister-friends, and I bit back a smile.

Mike and Brian, caught in conversation with the police chief, were oblivious to Allison's reaction. I couldn't for the life of me fathom how Allison was going to work out for them. What was wrong with Mike and Brian? Didn't they know she was nothing but trouble?

I looked Mike's way to catch his eye to make sure he was aware of the newly arrived guests. When he noticed me, I tipped my head to the front. He followed my look and nodded to me that he'd seen them. Mimi stepped to my side, and together we went to greet Johnny and his guest before they got further into the room. I let Mimi take the lead.

"Hi, Johnny, I'm surprised to see you here," she said in a no-nonsense tone of voice. Then, she turned to the tall man, "And you are?"

"Alexandro," he said, showing surprise that she didn't already know.

"I'm Mimi, and this is Rosalie," she said as she shook the man's hand. Then Alexandro turned my way. He shook my hand, taking me in. His look was curious as he held onto my hand longer than necessary. He was the man I'd seen with Johnny in New Mexico, and he was well aware that it had been me who'd upset the auctioning of the girls at the Purple Passion Lounge. A wave of goosebumps covered my body. A warning? I wondered.

"Where's Tony?" asked Johnny. "He said to meet him here."

As if simply mentioning his name was all that it took for him to appear, Tony walked in with his sidekick, Lorenzo. "Ah, this is quite a remarkable place," he said as he looked around.

Mimi was miffed to see him there. She pulled Tony aside. "What do you want, Tony? Why are you here? I didn't invite you," she whispered.

"That's not a nice way to behave. After all, we're family."

"Let me ask you again; why are you here?" she urged.

Tony glowered at Mimi. "I wanted to see what you've done with the place to see if we could get any ideas for our place. There's nothing wrong with that, is there, cuz?"

Lorenzo started forward as if to protect Tony. Mimi glowered at him. "Back off, Lorenzo," she said in a low warning. Tony held his arm out to stop Lorenzo from moving.

After staring each other down, Mimi stepped back, making room for them to enter. "C'mon in, but don't cause any trouble, understand?"

As people curiously glanced our way, it was clear that Johnny and Alexandro weren't pleased with the holdup. I couldn't decide who they were more upset with ... Mimi or Tony?

Louie and his partner arrived and headed our way. As soon as he saw me, he immediately sang out, "Rosalie, my beautiful Rosebud, you look stunning!"

All attention turned to me. My face heated at Louie's words. Mortified, I watched a bemused expression cross Johnny's face and sudden interest in Alexandro's. I pushed aside my desire to melt into the floor. Instead, I greeted Louie and his partner enthusiastically and wondered how much longer we had until the party was over.

CHAPTER 27

Looking back on the night before, I'd have to say that the restaurant's opening had been an enormous triumph despite my misgivings of having Allison with us. There was no doubt that Romano and Mimi's new restaurant would be a big success with all the celebrities and socialites who had attended. Not only was the place beautiful, but Romano's excellent, gourmet cooking couldn't be denied. The dinner he'd served us last night was a testament to that—marinated rack of lamb served with a fresh mint sauce, potatoes au gratin, and sautéed asparagus with a touch of lemon. A fluffy lemon tart that was light as a feather cleansed our palate at the end of the meal.

The conversation had flowed, and laughter abounded. The only 'fly in the ointment' had been Allison's attempts to draw herself into any conversation where Mike was involved. At one point, Cal studied Mike and raised his eyebrow in question. Mike's cheeks reddened, but he remained quiet.

After dinner, when it was time to leave, Brian got the car keys from Mike. He went to Allison's side. "Time to leave, Allison. I'll drive you to the Bellagio."

She looked at Mike in question and hesitated for just a moment when there was no response from him. "Thank you, Brian."

After they left, there seemed to be an awkward release of air coming from all of us who remained. We simply looked at each other, not saying a word. I broke the impasse.

"What a wonderful evening! Romano, Randy, and Mimi, you're going to be wildly successful; I know you are. I'm so happy for you." I rose and kissed each one around the table except for Mike. "I'll see you in the morning," I said to my sister-friends, Cal and Virginia.

***

Now, as I glanced at Mike, snoring beside me, annoyance filled me. We'd argued last night. He refused to see Allison's actions as anything more than her wanting to know Brian and him better as business partners. The funny thing was that I wasn't jealous of Allison. It was Mike's lack of boundaries with her that left me feeling like the odd man out—and an absolute disrespect toward me—unintentional or not. Allison was competing with me, and men don't always recognize the competition between women for a man's attention. It's a girl thing that only other women seem to participate in genetically.

I sighed. That seemed enough to stir Mike awake. He reached for me, and I moved away from him. "Time to get up, Mike. You promised Allison that you'd take her to *our* favorite breakfast place in old downtown."

"Shit. I didn't promise her that, did I?" he groaned.

"God only knows what else you promised her. But I've got to get going. I'm meeting the girls at Cal's house. Virginia is fixing us breakfast."

"We don't have to get up right this minute, do we? We've got a little time for ...."

"Sorry, bud, not today," I said, crawling out of bed.

Mike reached for me. "I know you're angry ..."

"I can't imagine why I would be," I said sarcastically.

"C'mon, Rosie, nothing is going on between Allison and me. So, cut it out."

"I'm not going there with you, Mike. But I'm warning you that I will not be played for a fool. We're in this relationship with no legitimate strings attached, so you're free to do what you want. Just remember, the same goes for me," I warned.

As soon as the words left my mouth, I regretted them. This was not a time for challenging each other. I was too upset to take back my words, even knowing I should if I wanted to keep things from falling apart. Instead, I went into the bathroom, stood in the shower, and let my tears of frustration fall.

I hadn't had the opportunity to follow up with Mike about Alexandro. I'd seen him speak to Alexandro, Johnny, Tony, and Lorenzo, and I was curious to know if Alexandro was going to be part of the Las Vegas new gentlemen's club. If so, I'd bet money that the club would involve human trafficking.

I arrived at Cal's house, glad to be in my sister-friends' company, and Cal and Virginia's, of course. It was a beautiful morning, hot enough to be perfect for lying about the pool where I was looking forward to spending some downtime. I'd checked in with Isabella, and she was happy to spend the day with Irene and Ron. Since their grandchildren had moved away, they were only too glad to have Isabella there. So I didn't feel as if I were simply dumping Isabella off with them.

"Good morning, all!" I called out as soon as I walked through the door.

"We're back here," Cal hollered. "Out on the patio!"

Something that smelled delicious was baking in the oven. If I weren't careful, I would be more than 10 lbs. overweight by tomorrow with all the excellent food last night and with what Virginia was cooking. I poured myself a cup of coffee and went outside.

"Hi there, sunshine," Cal said with a happy expression. "We're just enjoying this beautiful weather. Come join us."

I plopped down in a chair and smiled at everyone. "I brought my bathing suit with me. Did you all remember to bring yours?" I asked my sister-friends. They nodded. "Good."

"We were just talking about last night and how wonderful the opening was," Susannah said.

"Isn't the restaurant beautiful? Didn't Romano, Randy, and Mimi do a fabulous job?" I asked, and they all agreed.

"So, what's with that woman? Allison, that's her name, right?" asked Karen.

I nodded. "She interviewed with Mike and Brian in Boston. She came with great credentials, and they hired her. She'll be working with Brian in Boston."

"It's undeniable she's taken with Mike. She was all over him," Nancy said through a yawn.

My cheeks burned.

Seeing that, Nancy exclaimed, "Oh, my God, Rosie! I'm so sorry. I shouldn't have said that."

I put my hand out to pat hers. "No, Nancy, it's okay. It's the truth. Mike says that she's just friendly, wanting to get to know her new business partners."

"Harrumph," mumbled Susannah, "I don't think so, and I don't like her."

Virginia came out onto the deck with a carafe of coffee. "A refill, anyone?"

I held my cup out for more. I watched as the others did the same except for Karen. "Not for you, Karen?" I asked.

"No, my stomach is a bit upset. Something I ate last night hasn't settled. That's why I have tea," she said.

I bit back a smile realizing this baby was going to be a surprise to her.

"C'mon in everyone; breakfast is ready," announced Virginia.

The weekend sped by, and it was as tough as ever to say goodbye to my sister-friends on Sunday, much like Isabella had expressed when she'd left her sister-friends in Santa Fe weeks earlier.

At least I'd be able to spend some time with Karen this summer when Isabella and I returned to Santa Fe for the school break. My thoughts flashed to the first time I'd met Brian, Mike, and then Isabella. It didn't seem possible that we'd met less than a year ago! So much had happened since then that it seemed like it had been years ago when we'd first laid eyes on each other. Life with all three of them had undoubtedly positively changed my life, and I was thankful.

Before Brian and Allison flew back to Boston, they came to the house to say goodbye and pick up Brian's suitcase. As we stood together, Mike's phone went off, and we watched his face light up by what he was hearing. After he hung up, he said, "That was Roberto, the Chief of Police. He's located one of the missing girls we've been looking for!"

"Yahoo!" I said as I stood on tippy-toe and kissed Mike. "Way to go!"

Mike smiled down at me. "Cal will be pleased, too," he added as he pulled me against him.

Allison wasn't happy when she saw us nestled together. "I guess that makes *me* your lucky charm. I'm the one who told Roberto where to look next to find the girls. I think that I should work here in the Las Vegas office instead of Boston," she said, eying Mike.

I rolled my eyes at Brian. He immediately grabbed Allison's arm. "C'mon, Allison, let's get moving. We don't want to miss our plane."

"I'll drive," Mike said.

"Good riddance," I whispered to no one. I felt the air around me stir, and I knew my grandmother wasn't happy with my attitude. "You're right, Gram. I know better. Karma's a bitch."

"*Tsk, Tsk,*" my grandmother whispered. Next, I envisioned a red rose for love that she'd sent me.

"I love you, too," I called out to the air around me.

CHAPTER 28

Although Mike had assured me that he had no interest in Allison, I was too well aware that he enjoyed her attention. He was a guy, after all. However, I needed to let any worry go since I had only two more weeks before the Agency's new building would be ready for them to move in. There were lots to do before then. After that, Isabella and I would be off to Santa Fe. I didn't know how it would work out for Mike and me to be separated for that length of time. We hadn't discussed it yet.

I met with Mimi the following day to review the last-minute things to be done before the opening. We decided to have coffee at the new breakfast place in town to talk before we met with the contractor. As she approached the table where I sat, there was a glow about her that I hadn't noticed at the opening. "Hey, girl! Look at you! What's going on?"

She chuckled like a young girl. "Is it noticeable?"

"Yes, it is, so spill," I ordered.

"I've met someone new," she smiled. "A friend of Romano's, to be exact."

"How nice! I knew that you and Romano had become close lately, but I had no idea he was into matchmaking." I hesitated. "Is this friend of Romano's …."

Mimi's laughter stopped me from asking my question. "Nooo, he's not gay. He's a fellow chef that Romano has known for years, Charles Limone. He just sold his restaurant back east and is taking some time off. He heard about Romano's new restaurant and popped in to say hello."

"I'm surprised that Romano hasn't talked him into coming to work for him then."

"That might be in the works, but I don't know how that'd work out. It's not that easy for two serious chefs to share a kitchen. They'd probably have to take turns doing different days or meals."

"So, are you two serious?"

"There is definitely something between us, but we'll have to wait and see what happens," she cautioned.

"That's exciting! You'd said before that it'd been a while since you've dated anyone."

"It's been a long time, actually," Mimi responded. "Not everyone is into "the family," if you know what I mean."

She was referring to the fact that she was the daughter of a known former mafia member. "Well, I'm happy for you. I hope it works out the way you want it to, whatever that is."

"Thank you, my friend, for your support," she smiled, eyes twinkling. "Now, back to business. We have a building to open up, don't we?

"Yes, we do. Here's the list of things that need to be addressed before the opening. Plus, here's the budget showing the money we've spent and the money we have left to spend. I don't think we're going to be able to afford to do everything right now, so we'll have to pick and choose."

"Well, let me see where we stand financially and what's on the list. Then we can see what we have to do to make it all happen."

I pushed the paperwork toward her and sipped my latte as I sat quietly while Mimi reviewed the numbers. Finally, she raised her head. "It doesn't look too bad. When are we scheduled to meet with Jacklyn?"

"Tomorrow morning at 10. Does that work for you?"

"Yes, that's perfect. Are you ready to head out to talk to Red? He's been a dream to work with as our contractor ever since you were there for him when his cousin died ... no more stealing from us," she smiled.

"Yes, things have worked out better, that's for sure," I agreed, rising from my seat to join her.

Driving onto the new building site tucked back onto the property, I was pleased to see how things had turned out. Thanks to Mimi, this building was constructed as a concession to how the top management of the Purple Passion Lounge had ignored the rights of the little girls and was willing to sell them off. Mimi had had nothing to do with that and wanted to make things right by providing the Agency regarding human trafficking a new office space rent-free for one year. After that, the amount of rent would be reviewed on an annual basis. Not a bad deal for the Agency because Mimi would be more than fair about the rental amount.

As we walked through the building, I turned at the sound of steps. "Oh, here's Red now."

"Ladies," he said, nodding his head in greeting. "So what do you think?" he asked as he swept his arms wide.

"It's beautiful! Enlarging the kitchen area was the right thing to do, for sure," I said, beaming.

"I agree," added Mimi.

"Here's what we've got going forward. The carpets go down tomorrow and the next day. After that, the painter will be back to do touch up work. The plumber and electrician will come this week to finish hooking up the appliances and to install the fans. Anything else?" he asked.

"Mimi, you're all set with the landscapers?" I asked.

"Yup, they'll be here at the end of the week. Then the following week, the driveway will be completed. Right, Red?"

He nodded. "All should be set for the opening. The rest is up to you girls."

Mimi and I'd had fun poking around places to find "treasures" to decorate the fairly plain but attractive building to make it homier. "We'll need one of your crew to screw in some more hooks and help us with other accessories. Is that okay?" I asked.

"Sure, what day and time?"

"How about Friday at 10? Is that okay with you, Mimi?"

"Yes, that's fine."

"Okay, I'll send Tim to meet you," Red said. "If you're all set, I'll be off. Call me if you need anything else."

Mimi and I walked the building again, jotting down notes and slapping on post-its where we wanted hooks, etc., placed. Before Friday, we'd bring in some of the paintings and other decorative things. The furniture would be delivered and set at the beginning of the following week. We still needed to go to a toy store and purchase some new items for the younger children that came through with their mothers. That thought reminded me of Karen. I wondered if she'd figured out yet that she was pregnant. Imagine! Finally, after all these years, she'd be the first of us sister-friends to have a baby. I'd be Auntie Rose. I couldn't wait!

CHAPTER 29

I was worried about meeting with Jacklyn the next day, and I wanted to have things in place for Isabella's school break if she asked me about it. On the spur of the moment, I decided to take Sweet Pea to walk around the neighborhood. I waved to Irene and Ron as I walked by their house, but I didn't stop to talk. Sometimes, the walking helped me to clear my mind. Mike and I needed to discuss how we would handle being apart from each other this summer. We both had been so busy doing our own thing, we hadn't given it much thought.

When we finished our walk, I had enough time to take out my Tarot deck to see what the cards predicted about this summer before Isabella arrived home. I pulled three cards from the deck, laid them face down, and then turned up one after another. The first card was the Knight of Swords, representing a strong man entering my life. The second was The Lovers, meaning a choice between two attractions. The third was the Death card, representing change. For many years now, the Death card had turned into a warning of death or even murder for me. It was not something to take lightly. Although the tarot cards could have other meanings, what came to me as I turned them over was what I knew to be right for me. Before I could wallow in my thoughts, Isabella came through the door.

"Can I go to Sammy's house? He has a new video game he wants us to play."

"Let me call his mother first. Then I can drive you over if she says yes."

When we drove into Sammy's house, Maggie was already outside. Sammy's mother was a love, someone I enjoyed. I smiled as I watched her give Isabella a quick hug before Sammy grabbed Isabella and pulled her inside after waving to me. Maggie was a talker, and I bit back a chuckle as she began to talk away before she even reached my side.

"I'll bring Isabella home at 8 o'clock. Is that okay with you?"

"Sounds good. How are you doing?" I asked.

"Excellent. Thank you for inviting us to the opening the other night. It was a beautiful event, and there were so many famous people there who I would never have had the chance to meet. It was exciting, and you looked beautiful."

"Thank you, and I loved your dress—a great color for you. Yes, there were quite a few people there that I hadn't met before either. I think that Romano and Mimi did an excellent job designing the restaurant. If you haven't eaten any of Romano's creations yet, do yourself a favor and go!"

Maggie smiled. "Already done. We're going this Friday. Any chance you could watch Sammy that evening?"

"We'd love to have him for dinner and the evening. Just have Sammy come home with Isabella after school, okay?"

"Great. You're a love, Rosie. Thanks so much."

When Mike came home that night, I greeted him with a smile. "How was your day?"

He smiled and came to where I was standing in the kitchen. Tilting my chin and searching my eyes, he said, "I'm glad to see that you aren't angry with me anymore." He softly kissed my lips. Placing his hand on the small of my back, he roughly pulled me against him as he deepened his kiss with an urgency that surprised me. Coming up for air, he rested his chin on the top of my head and molded himself against me. "God, Rosie, you make me crazy!"

I tightened my arms around him and placed my head against his chest, finding comfort in our closeness. Then, I grabbed his hand and led him into the living room, where I had two glasses of wine poured, waiting for us. "What's this?" he asked.

"We need to talk about this summer. Come on, sit down, handsome." I patted the seat next to me on the couch. "We've both been so busy—you with opening your office and me with overseeing the construction of the restaurant and the office. And, we've both been making sure that Isabella is doing okay."

Mike sat beside me, and after I handed him his glass of wine, he placed his free arm across the back of the couch. "So when are you planning to leave for Santa Fe?"

"After the opening of the Agency, which I'm reminding you is in 12 days, so mark your calendar. We'll go the following week. Also, don't forget, we have that trip to Disney World with Cal and Virginia planned. You're going to go with us, aren't you?"

"I want to, but I have to see what's going on around that time, okay?"

I nodded. It was important for Mike to do what he had to do to get his company off the ground in Las Vegas. I understood that, and I wouldn't stand in his way if he couldn't make it. However, I'd be disappointed not to have him join us.

"I hope you'll be able to come to Santa Fe for the weekends," I ventured.

"I'll try to, but again, I'll have to see. Maybe we can take turns, and you can fly into Las Vegas sometimes, too." Thinking about traveling with a child and dog, I wondered how that was going to work out. Seeing my doubtful expression, Mike added, "Don't worry, we'll work it out."

I sipped my wine. "By the way, what did Johnny and Alexandro have to say when you talked with them at the opening?"

Mike chuckled. "Johnny looked as unhappy to see me as ever. I was tempted to ask him about Bambi but thought better of it, thank God."

I laughed. Johnny had gotten so upset when he'd overhead Mike tease that Brian was interested in Bambi. I wondered if Johnny and Bambi were still a couple.

"To answer your question, nothing much more than hello and goodbye," continued Mike.

"I thought I drop in to see how Tony's building is coming along. I'm curious to see it. He's hurried the construction along, and according to Mimi, he's planning on opening in another month."

"I don't like the idea of you anywhere near Tony. I don't trust that guy, or any of them," warned Mike.

"I know what you mean," I agreed.

That night, with Mike and me at peace, and with his arms around me, I slept more contently than I had in the last few weeks. It felt heavenly.

CHAPTER 30

The next morning, I dressed more carefully than usual to look my best when Mimi and I met with Jacklyn at the Agency. It helped me to know that the clothes Louie had chosen for me made me look and feel good—and more confident. I might need that extra confidence if Jacklyn wanted to discuss my relationship with Mike. I hoped that wouldn't happen today.

I sat in the Agency's reception area, waiting for Mimi to join me before our appointment with Jacklyn began. With many boxes already packed and stacked in the corner, it was easy to see how eager the employees were to move from their cramped small office space into the larger, nicer one waiting for them.

The door flew open, and in came Mimi looking even more radiant than she had the day before. Her dark eyes

J.S. Peck

sparkled, and her smile was wide when she saw me. "Ah, Rosie, life is good."

"It must be to have you look so happy," I answered.

She looked around the office and frowned. "This furniture looks so shabby. Did you order all new furniture for the new place?"

"All but a few pieces which we will use from here. I thought we'd use one of the desks I saved for the copier and file room. We can donate the rest of the pieces we're not going to use."

"Good. I think it makes sense to start with most of the things fresh and new, don't you?"

"Yes, I agree. And all that I ordered are well within the budget."

Jacklyn headed our way, and my heart began to pound. I felt nervous, just knowing she had power over me regarding Isabella, and I didn't want anything to happen not to have her support. Her smile was genuine and generous when our eyes met. I stood, and we hugged. "Jacklyn, you know Mimi …"

"I do indeed," she answered with her hand extended to Mimi. "Welcome, you two. Let's go back to my office so we can talk in peace."

We sat at the table where she'd placed bottles of water since it was a warm day. Jacklyn had a sheaf of papers before her—the agreement between the Agency and Mimi's company that Mimi needed to sign as the property owner.

Afterward, Jacklyn shuffled through them to make sure that all pages that needed signatures had them. Then, she lifted her head and smiled. "The entire Agency is grateful for what you two have made possible for us. You know, the number of clients that the Agency has served has grown to

168

an excessive number, and, as you can see, we've outgrown our space here."

I chuckled. "We saw some boxes out front already packed and ready to go."

Jacklyn smiled. "Yes, we are excited to be moving, for sure."

Mimi looked lost in thought and then turned to Jacklyn. "Do you know how many people you expect to have at the opening? Charles will need a count so that there will be enough food and drinks available."

Charles? Not Romano? I looked at Mimi, who raised an eyebrow at me and nodded.

"You told me to invite all the bigwigs involved in human trafficking, so there are quite a few coming. I'd say to plan for at least 100 people. As promised, I've lined up the media coverage for it as well."

"Sounds good," said Mimi, pleased. She began to rise from her seat.

"If that's all," said Jacklyn, "I guess we're done here then. A word with you, Rosie, before you leave, please."

"I'll wait out front," Mimi said and left the room.

My heart thudded. What now?

Jacklyn noted my worry. "Nothing to worry about right now. I wanted you to know that I passed on a six-month review of your situation with Isabella, but your first anniversary with her is coming up in the fall. That will require going before the judge if you want to make your connection with Isabella more permanent. You and Mike might want to consider changing the status of your relationship before then ... just a suggestion."

My cheeks flushed. "I understand."

"How is Isabella doing?"

My face lit up as I gushed, "She is doing just great. I'm so happy she's in my life."

Jacklyn's smile said it all. "I'm pleased you feel that way. It's not easy being the mother of a pre-teen, but it's worth the effort, isn't it? I know I feel that way about my daughters."

"I didn't realize you've been through this yourself."

"Yes, indeed," she answered while biting her lower lip and nodding.

I laughed at her expression, and she joined in. "Thanks so much, Jacklyn, for your support."

"Always," she said as we hugged goodbye.

CHAPTER 31

When I met Mimi outside, I said, "Charles, for the catering? Not Romano?"

She smiled. "I've thought that maybe Charles could take over the catering end of the business. What do you think?"

"More to the point, what will Charles and Romano think about it?" I asked.

Her face fell. "It might not work out, but we'll never know unless we approach them, right?"

"*We* approach them? I don't know, Mimi. Maybe this is something only you should take up with them since ...."

"Oh, come on," she interrupted, pulling on me. "I want you to meet Charles, anyway."

I followed along, now curious to see for myself what this Charles guy was all about. Once we reached Rosalie's, we parked our cars in the back and knocked on the back service door.

A member of the kitchen staff let us in, and we walked into the kitchen to see Romano and Charles standing together, leaning over the newspaper. The two of them looked at us in surprise. Romano's face broke into a smile. "Hi there, Rosebud. What brings you here?

At the same time, Charles looked with pleasure at Mimi. "What's new, pussycat?"

Mimi and I chuckled at our greetings. She turned to Charles, "This is Rosalie, the woman I told you about, the woman who we named the restaurant after."

Charles smiled. His handsome face was pleasant—jolly even—there was no better word to describe it. He wasn't that tall, and his body was round without being fat. He and Mimi matched like salt and pepper. I liked him immediately and could easily see why Mimi was drawn to him. After shaking his hand, I searched for Randy. He was nowhere in sight. "Where's Randy?" I asked.

Romano said, "He doesn't come in until the evening shift; why?"

Instead of answering, I turned to Mimi.

"I wanted to run an idea by the two of you and Randy if he were here. We're opening up the other building in a little more than a week. We're going to need to provide drinks and hors d'oeuvres for that night," Mimi said.

"Well, I guess we can fit that in, but we're getting swamped here. I'm not complaining, though," Romano said.

"Well, that's just it," Mimi said. "Maybe what we should do is develop our catering services. There's money to be made there, especially in a city like ours."

Romano frowned. "I dunno. I think it's best to concentrate on one or the other—the restaurant or the catering business."

"I couldn't agree more," consoled Mimi. "What if you, Charles, took over the catering end of the business? You told me that you didn't want to go back to being a full-time chef, and this would be something that would keep you busy enough right here in Las Vegas."

No one said a word. Then the three of us began to laugh, much to the embarrassment of Mimi. "What's so funny?" she asked, not realizing that what she'd said made it very clear what her real intent was regarding Charles. Yes, she wanted to set up a catering business, but she wanted Charles to be close by more than that.

Charles took Mimi's hand and kissed it. "You're something else, girl."

Romano was quiet. I knew he was mulling over the idea of having to share his kitchen and not entirely happy about it despite liking Charles as his friend.

"I have an idea," I quickly added. "Remember how we added that extra smaller kosher kitchen at the last minute. If we turned that into the catering kitchen, that would keep Charles from interfering in Romano's larger kitchen. It's set off to the side as it is anyway, so that shouldn't be a problem."

Both Romano and Charles beamed at my suggestion.

"Shall we give it a try, gentlemen?" asked Mimi. "Why don't you think about it, and we'll discuss it again when Randy is with us."

We said goodbye and left them discussing some ideas for their new venture.

I marveled at Mimi, who looked like the cat that'd swallowed the canary. I turned toward her as we walked to our cars. "You're something else, girl," repeating what Charles had said. "How you pulled that off was remarkable!"

Mimi laughed. "I did okay, didn't I?"

"Yes, ma'am, you sure did," I said, tipping an imaginary hat to her.

CHAPTER 32

The more I thought about the new catering business aspect, the more I liked the idea that in an emergency, Charles could step in as a backup to Romano should he ever get sick or something happens to him. Things seemed to have gotten lined up in Las Vegas so that when Isabella and I were in Santa Fe, I wouldn't stress out and worry about anything happening in Las Vegas. However, the fact that trouble was waiting in Santa Fe with its own set of problems involving the Scorpion gang loomed in my mind.

Now, just two days before leaving for Santa Fe, the only thing left for me to do was attend the new building's opening. Once there, I was filled with satisfaction at how lovely everything looked. As Mimi and I stood together inside and watched everything going on, we breathed a sigh of relief. All our efforts of the past week had worked out. We had fussed with arranging the new furniture and placing the decorative pieces around the building, and the look was professional yet very attractive and pretty. The employees had only two full days to unpack and set their offices in order so that they, too, were relaxing and enjoying the fruits of their labor. It turned into a spectacular event with people from all over the state attending and several government officials from Washington, D.C.

Mike popped in at the last minute and came to stand by my side. I noticed that he took care to avoid Jacklyn as much as possible other than a quick wave across the room. She smiled at him but immediately turned back to the group conversation going on around her. I swear I heard Mike breathe a sigh of relief, but I remained quiet.

It was Jacklyn's night to shine, so I felt no awkwardness about leaving a bit early. I was tired and wanted to get home. I caught Jacklyn's eye and blew her a kiss, and waved goodbye.

Exhausted from the week of preparing the new building and getting ready for Santa Fe, I crawled into bed early. Mike joined me. Something was brewing with him; I could feel it. "Mike, what's going on?"

"Brian and I are trying to work out a few things. We can talk about it when it gets more settled, okay?"

I had a feeling that I wasn't going to like whatever it was, but I didn't push. "Okay."

Both of us were tired, and there was unspoken tension between us. Isabella's and my leaving for Santa Fe for the summer were disrupting our quiet routine of living. Fortunately, Mike and I were able to push that aside as we made that lazy kind of love where it doesn't take much effort but is still satisfying. Afterward, we lay wrapped in each other's arms, and I fell into a sound sleep, despite a sense of foreboding.

The next morning, I was jarred out of my stupor when Isabella jumped on the bed, followed by Sweet Pea. Mike had gotten up earlier, and I was still lounging in bed, not ready to get up yet.

"Just one more day, Mama! I can't wait! Are you packed yet?" She had been packed for two days now and was impatient for the last 24 hours to creep by.

"Did you say goodbye to Sammy last night?" I asked.

Isabella had been upset about leaving Sammy behind until she learned that he had registered for Soccer camp for the summer. They made promises to keep in touch with each other by text or calling each day, which was nothing new because they did that now. Although Isabella had a few other friends she enjoyed, she wasn't as sad to leave them behind, knowing she'd see them at school in the fall. Leaving Cal and Virginia behind was a different story until she realized that she'd soon see them on the planned trip to Disney World.

"Yes, Mama, I did. He left for camp early this morning," she said, sadly.

I hugged her. "You'll be surprised at how quickly time flies by."

She nodded. "C'mon, get up, Mama! We've got to go and say goodbye to Grandfather and Virginia."

"Okay, let me take a shower and get dressed. Then, we'll head over there and join them for coffee."

"Good. Hurry."

"Did you say goodbye to Grammy Irene and Ron?" I called over my shoulder.

"Tonight, I'm going there for supper, remember?"

The truth was I'd forgotten. Maybe Mike and I could slip out for dinner at Rosalie's. That way, I could say goodbye to Romano and Randy.

***

Even though we had a wonderful meal at Rosalie's with Mimi and Charles joining us, Mike wasn't himself. He twitched and looked flustered when Charles asked him about his business, and he wouldn't meet my eyes when I glanced at him, questioning what was wrong. We said goodnight to them and then to Romano and Randy and left for home.

When we got into the car, I turned to Mike. "Aw right, mister, what's going on?"

He turned to me with a serious expression. "We need to talk." He hesitated, "We have a situation at work, and I've tried to work it out, but you're not going to like it."

"Tell me what it is, and I'll decide whether I like it or not. Fair enough?"

"You've never minded Brian staying with us at the condo when he's been in town, have you?"

"No," I answered, puzzled.

"Then, you wouldn't mind if he stayed at the condo this summer?"

"No..o..o," I responded. Impatient, I asked, "Where is this heading, Mike?"

"The FBI has asked Brian for his help again. With Tony's new club opening, they want Brian to go back to being a newsman like before. It'll look like he's been transferred back to the station. It'll be just for a few months until the FBI is sure nothing is going on there."

I was silent, absorbing the possibility of the same sort of trouble of human trafficking that Isabella had been involved in a while back.

"And Cindy is going to work at Tony's club again too, undercover like before," he added.

"I can't believe she's agreed to work at Tony's new place."

"Her boyfriend was called back to Afghanistan. He's military."

"Wow, this is a lot to take in." It was easy to envision trouble at Tony's place, what with Johnny and Alexandro involved. "Listen, I have no problem with Brian staying at the condo; I just hope the two of you will be able to stay out of trouble," I teased, giving Mike a light kiss on the cheek.

Mike's face turned red. "That's just it. I won't be here. I'll be in Boston taking Brian's place."

My heart fell. Had I heard it right? Was he going to be in Boston with Allison? I simply stared at Mike. No words would come. In a low toned voice, I finally asked, "Can you please repeat that?"

"This is exactly what I worried about. I knew you'd be upset even though you have no reason to be."

"Really?" I said sarcastically.

"I love you, Rosie. You know that I do. I'm not interested in Allison; she isn't even my type."

Prove it, I thought to myself angrily. "I can see it now. She'll ..." I couldn't finish. Instead, my eyes filled.

"She'll what?" Mike asked in a soft voice, using his thumbs to wipe away my unshed tears.

"She'll keep you so busy, and you'll never have time for Isabella and me. Just wait and see!"

"Then, I'll have to make sure that doesn't happen, won't I?"

Feeling foolish and completely exposed, I nodded, pushing away the same sense of loss I'd had each time my parents flew off on their acting gigs and left me behind—a lonely little girl.

"We'll make it work out, okay, Rosie?"

"Okay," I answered, plastering a forced smile onto my face. I was upset, but I swallowed my anger the best that I could. I didn't want anything to spoil our last night together. Who was I kidding? The idea of Mike in Boston with Allison, who would have no scruples about flirting with Mike and more, the evening was already spoiled. The psychic part of me knew that this summer would be a test to see if Mike and I could make it as a couple. I sensed things would not be smooth sailing for either one of us, and it saddened me.

CHAPTER 33

I was quiet in the car as we headed to the airport. Mike looked solemn as he drove us there. He gripped my hand tightly and squeezed it hard. "I'm going to miss you, girls. Be sure to keep in touch, hear?"

His cell phone buzzed, and as he reached for it, I peeked at the screen—Allison. Her voice was loud enough, so it was impossible not to hear her. "Are they off yet?"

So it's already begun, I thought, as I studied Mike.

His cheeks were pink. "What is it you want, Allison?" he demanded.

"Just wanted to tell you that I'll text you Brian's itinerary as soon as he decides which flight he's going to take. Let me know yours, and I'll be at the airport to pick you up. It'll be good to see you."

"Okay, thanks," he said, brushing her off. He turned to me. "Sorry about that."

"What exactly are you sorry about, Mike?" I challenged. He remained silent but reached for my hand again, squeezing it tightly as he kept his eyes on the road. Isabella was quiet in the backseat, and I knew she was watching us with interest. She hated any discord between Mike and me. For her sake, I let things slide. This wasn't the time or place to argue before we took off.

When we pulled up outside the kiosk for Southwest Airlines check-in, Mike got out and placed our bags on the sidewalk. One of the handlers rushed over and pulled them to the scale. In no time flat, we were set to go inside the terminal. Mike and I stood awkwardly for a moment before he swept me into his arms and held me tight. "I love you, my queen," he whispered into my ear.

"I love you too, handsome," I returned.

Isabella tugged on Mike's arm. "Bye, Mike. C'mon, Mama, we need to go inside."

Mike cupped Isabella's face and kissed her forehead. "Goodbye, Isabella. Have a great summer and take good care of Rosie for me, okay?"

She smiled. "Okay. Come on, Mama," she pleaded, heading into the terminal, dragging Sweet Pea's carrier behind her.

***

Karen was right on time to meet us at the luggage carousel. I was glad she'd agreed to pick us up, saving us the hassle of locating a shuttle. Karen was glowing despite looking a bit peaked. I sensed she was still experiencing morning sickness.

"Oh, my! You're looking good. How are you feeling?" I asked with a lilt in my voice.

"You know, don't you?"

I laughed. "Indeed, I do. Are you and Coyote happy about a baby coming so soon?"

Karen nodded. "It took us by surprise, but we're both over the moon about it now. Grandmother says that it will be a fine, healthy baby."

I raised my eyebrow in question.

"No, she won't tell us whether it's a boy or girl even though she says she knows," she said, frustrated.

I laughed. "Have you told your mother yet?"

"Heavens, no! I don't need to listen to any of her negativity."

"I agree."

The drive to Santa Fe brought my thoughts to a year ago when I'd first set foot there with Isabella to introduce her to her Mexican family. So much had happened since that day. It was then I'd met Grandmother and learned my history with her as my mother and Isabella as my sister in a past life we'd shared. Being back in Santa Fe was in some ways like coming home for me. I felt at peace more and more as we drove closer to the city.

I needed to clear my head from all the doubts I had about my relationship with Mike, and I needed to trust him. But he wasn't the one I worried about most. Mike working with Allison in Boston, gave her the perfect opportunity to pursue him. There was no question she was beautiful, and he was just a man, after all. I sighed.

"Anything wrong?" asked Karen, who knew me well.

"I'll explain later, okay?"

"Sure. Whenever you're ready," she answered.

Maybe it was a good thing that Mike and I would be tested this way. If our relationship could remain intact after this summer, I was sure we could make it together. We'd just have to wait and see.

CHAPTER 34

In a blink of an eye, four days went by. Brian had made it into Las Vegas and had begun his stint at the radio station. Mike had packed up, ready to go on his flight to Boston scheduled for that night. He'd be staying at Brian's condo in the North End—Boston's Italian section. It was a great location, accessible to all modes of transportation to get around the city. Mike's fabulous administrative assistant, Patricia Newheart, was set to run Las Vegas's office while he was away. Of course, Brian would be available to check on things daily.

Isabella, Nica, and Angela had been inseparable since we'd arrived. They spent their time having sleepovers among the three families … mostly at Angela's house or here. I made sure that when Isabella stayed at either Nica's or Angela's home, I sent food with her to share. The girls were growing, and so were their appetites.

Coyote asked me if I would help him review some of his unsolved murder cases and see if I got any psychic information. He still was convinced that his nephew didn't die of an overdose but had been murdered. After settling in for the summer stretch, I began to relax and let my psychic abilities expand. Interestingly enough, the opposite had happened for Isabella. Her gift took a backseat to her being busy with her sister-friends. She felt safe and was not so "on guard," worrying about my safety or hers. I was delighted to see her so relaxed, peaceful, and happy.

Karen had invited me to join her and Coyote that night for a casual dinner at the new restaurant where we sister-friends had taken her before her wedding. I was looking forward to it. Since I was out of their way to pick me up, I decided to meet them there.

When I stepped inside the restaurant, I searched the dining room for Karen's smiling face and Coyote's tall physique. When I saw them already seated, I waved and bypassed the receptionist to join them. "Howdy."

"Hi there, yourself," Karen said.

"Rosie," acknowledged Coyote as he stood to seat me.

"Gosh, Karen, you look wonderful! No more morning sickness?"

She laughed. "No, thank God. That's why I wanted to go out tonight, so I could gorge on something wonderful and keep it down for a change."

I chuckled. I turned to Coyote, who seemed to glow as well. His happiness shone on his face. "Anything new happening, Coyote?"

"Not much. Are you going to be able to give me some time tomorrow to look over some of my files?"

"Absolutely. I'll be by in the morning." Both Mike and I had promised Coyote we'd take a look at some of his files to see if we could spot something he might have missed. He was hoping with my psychic abilities that I would be able to help him. I felt a stir in the room, and conversation ceased among the tables around us. I turned in my seat to look behind me. "Is that who I think it is?" I whispered to Karen.

"Yup, Mr. Handsome has arrived," she said.

I shook my head. "Too bad, he knows it," I said and watched as Karen's eyes widened with surprise.

I shivered when I felt a warm hand on my shoulder. "Is this seat taken? Do you mind if I join you?" Tom Little Horse asked Coyote.

Coyote chuckled. "You're just as smooth as you were in the old days. It's alright with me. Ladies?"

Karen and I both nodded as Coyote extended his hand in a welcoming gesture.

Tom Little Horse squeezed my shoulder before he pulled out his chair and sat down. "So what are you doing back in town, beautiful?"

Not prepared for his question, I faltered. "Summer school break."

"Ah, so you'll be here for a while. Good." He smiled with satisfaction.

Coyote eyed him. "What are you doing back in town yourself?"

"A few weeks off. Things need tending to at the ranch. Hey, do you want to see my place? Why don't the three of you join me for dinner tomorrow, say around six o'clock?"

Karen was already nodding in agreement while Coyote studied him. Finally, he said, "Sounds good. I'll drive you there, Rosie," he said to me, cutting off any chance for Tom Little Horse to be more than the host for dinner.

We chatted, ate, and laughed. Although Coyote had used the word smooth to describe Tom Little Horse, I thought the phrase slick would be a better description. He asked us not to use his full name, instead simply call him Tom. I was aware that I was acting a bit stiff around him because Karen gave me a 'what's up with you' look.

When my cell phone beeped, I opened my purse and read Mike's text message: *"Made it. Will call tomorrow."* My heart fell. No, *I love you*, or *I miss you* or anything else. Was this how it was going to be all summer? I swallowed my disappointment and joined the ongoing conversation.

At the end of the meal, I was ready to call it a night. Tom had a different idea. He wanted to continue with a nightcap and dance to the DJ's music in the bar area. Cutting him off, I turned to the others. "Not for me tonight. Thanks for a wonderful meal and time together. I enjoyed it."

"I hope that includes me, too," Tom said as he stood by my side.

"Of course, it does," I said, a bit annoyed at his obvious ploy for a compliment.

Tom just smiled. "Good. Let me walk you to your car, then."

"No, don't bother," I said, holding up my hand in protest. "Karen and Coyote can see me out. I'm parked next to them anyway. Let me know if you change your mind and want me to bring something for dinner tomorrow."

He took my hand and bent to kiss it in an old-fashioned way. Then, he did the same for Karen as I rolled my eyes. His performance was drawing attention from the surrounding people. What is it with this guy? I thought. Then, he shook Coyote's hand and patted him on the back. "Good to see you again, my friend," he said before he turned and headed into the bar area.

As we made our way through the maze of tables, all eyes were on us. I'm sure they were curious to know our connection to such a man. Many of the ladies looked longingly after him as Tom walked away.

Once outside, Karen nudged my shoulder. "Oh, my! That man is into you!"

"I doubt that very much. He just likes playing up to any female he finds attractive."

Karen hugged me. "I'm not so sure about that, my dear friend."

Coyote stood by my car. "Ready, or are you two ladies going to talk all night?"

I smiled. I knew Coyote was in a hurry to get Karen home for his pleasure. Who could blame him? It was evident that Karen adored him as he did her.

Pulling into my driveway, I found the house dark and silent. I was more aware than ever of being alone— not lonely, necessarily but alone. What a difference a year makes. For the three years after Jeff's death, I lived by myself, not socializing much at all. Although I had Sweet Pea with me, of course, it wasn't the same as being in a relationship with another human being. I chuckled. Sweet Pea might have something to say about that, I thought. Now, I had enough people who I loved in my life that I felt alone without them near me.

CHAPTER 35

The next day, Coyote brought out the files on the men that he and Jose, as his new informant, kept an eye on. The Scorpion gang was set up by one of the Mexican cartels and served as border commandos for it. When they started just a few years ago, the Scorpions set up their own sting operation to eliminate the former group's members. That's how they got their name—the Scorpions—and they were as deadly as any living one. Some of the members had become brazen and entered the United States to get rid of anyone who used to be in the former group because they felt immense amounts of drug money had been withheld from them.

It was known that there was a war going on between the Scorpions and several other gangs currently involved in human trafficking, which is where I thought Johnny and Alexandro came in. The more I thought about what'd happened to Isabella and the other little girls ready to be auctioned off, I didn't believe that Mama had the smarts or finesse to set it up by herself. And Tony was nothing more than a braggart about being part of the "Family" despite Mimi's father (Tony's uncle) no longer active in it. I believe the brains behind that particular operation at the time had been Johnny, who'd been smart enough to use both Tony and the Police Chief as a shield to hide behind. Johnny was clever that way. I'd seen it for myself when I'd worked undercover at the Purple Passion Lounge.

I opened the files and began to flip through them. When I did, I started to see visions of the men in the files dying. It was bloody and horrible to witness. Some of the men were crying out, pleading for their life, sounding like women do when fighting to save themselves from an abuser. Some of the men were moaning and groaning as they flopped on the floor, blood pooling all around them. Blood spatters were flying through the air covering the walls as brains and organs scattered. Their screams were chilling, still resounding in my mind. I saw Coyote's pale face in the background and was unsure if he was part of the raid or not. I felt sick and put my head between my legs to clear my vision. I was confused. Had they already died, or was what I'd see was what lay ahead for them?

"Coyote?"

"Yeah, Rosie?" he answered from his office.

"Are these men in the file folders still alive?"

"Yup, as far as I know. Why?"

"I think there's going to be a terrible bloody battle soon." I stared at him, shaken. "You may be involved. Are you aware of that?"

"Grandmother has already warned me to be careful."

"It doesn't look good, Coyote. When's the meeting going to take place? Do you know?"

"No. Jose says we should know soon. Did you see anything else?"

"No, I'll keep going and see if anything more comes to me." I flipped through the files with my eyes closed, and no new visions came. I left the office and headed home to change for dinner at Tom's ranch. I chose a bottle of Pinot from Oregon to take with me as my donation toward dinner.

Isabella was at Nica's house for the night along with Angela. Tomorrow it was going to be my turn to have the girls. Sweet Pea would be happy since she was missing Isabella, and I felt sorry to leave her home alone again.

When we pulled into the long dirt road that led to Tom's ranch, I was impressed at its elegance. It was a newly built typical ranch house made of brick with a wraparound porch with white pillars supporting the overhanging roof. An attached three-car garage was almost as long as the house. Alongside the house was a white-painted wooden fenced-in pasture that held two horses—Arabians, if I wasn't mistaken. A newly constructed wooden barn could be seen in the back. I didn't realize politicians made this kind of money.

Tom came out onto the porch when he heard us drive up. He was dressed casually in blue jeans that hugged him in all the right places and a black t-shirt that showed off his muscular body. His black hair was swept back and hung a bit long in the back, and his dark eyes looked black from a distance, matching the color of his hair. He exuded confidence, well aware that his stunning good looks were exceptional.

"My God, Rosie! Look at the man. Could he be more handsome?" asked Karen.

Coyote turned to her. "Looks aren't everything, you know."

Was Coyote serious? I bit my lip so that I wouldn't laugh, but when Karen began to chuckle, I joined in. "Says one man to another—never," Karen declared.

As Tom headed our way, a Golden Retriever lumbered after him. Tom seemed more relaxed and much different than he'd acted out in public. "Welcome to my humble abode," he said, spreading his arms wide.

I handed him the bottle of wine I'd brought with me, and he wrapped his arm around my shoulders and led us inside. "C'mon in. My cook is making a wonderful meal for us. I hope you like Mexican food," he asked me.

I nodded.

"Good," he said.

The house's interior had a very masculine feel to it. The living room had a large stone fireplace in the center of the room, a pair of brown leather couches facing each other in front of it, and various club chairs scattered around covered with Native American Indian designs. It was a beautiful, warm room. I was impressed.

As we began to head outside, I peeked around the fireplace to see the dining room located right behind it, and further back was the open kitchen. A small, squat woman was standing over the stainless steel range, stirring something in a pot. She was humming and looked content to be cooking.

The sliding glass doors were opened wide, folding inside the walls as if they didn't exist and outside was simply a part of the house. The huge paver-stoned patio lined the entire back of the house. In an area off to the left rested a beautiful handcrafted metal table and two chairs near a sliding glass door that opened into what I presumed was the master bedroom.

As I reclined in my chair, I sighed with pleasure at being able to relax with a glass of wine and take in the view of a beautiful but simple ranch tucked in against one of the hills surrounding Santa Fe. I turned to Karen, "Pretty nice, huh?"

Karen smiled. "It sure is."

Coyote and Tom returned; they'd gone inside to get a special fruit drink for Karen, who was abstaining from alcohol because of her pregnancy. They joined us where we sat at a large round table and could see the horses hanging their heads over the fence, eying us.

"Tom, are those Arabian horses?" I asked.

"Yes, beautiful, aren't they? Do you like horses?"

"I do, although I have had minimal experience with them."

"Why don't we take a closer look at them? Are you all game to do that?"

The four of us left our drinks and, along with the dog, walked to where the horses stood against the fence, watching us with interest as we came near. When Tom got closer, the horses whinnied in greeting, nodding their heads up and down.

"They sure know who their boss is, don't they?" I laughed.

Tom smiled and puffed out his chest a bit. "As well, they should."

"Should?" I questioned.

"I'm the one who pays for their food and all their luxurious living," Tom said.

"How are they supposed to know that?" I asked, surprised at his expectation.

Coyote laughed. "Typical of you, Tom. Always thinking someone owes you."

Tom scowled. "And you're different? I haven't forgotten our younger days."

"But things are different now," declared Coyote. "Let it go."

Karen and I looked at each other. Neither of us had any idea what the two of them were talking about, so we remained quiet. Coyote and Tom eyed each other in a challenging way until Karen took Coyote's arm, "Let's go back, okay? I'm thirsty."

Coyote wrapped his arm around Karen's growing waist and led her to the table while I followed. Tom had turned back to the horse nearest him and patted him, talking to him in whispers. He soon caught up with me. "That's my favorite horse, Scout."

"He's beautiful. They all are."

"I love beautiful things around me," he said honestly. "Especially a woman as beautiful as you."

Tom's words made me uncomfortable. It's always flattering to have someone think you're beautiful, but not as an object to be owned. I kept on walking, and he followed, grabbing my elbow at the last minute to assist me up the stairs to the patio.

As we gathered around the table, the dog sat at Tom's feet until he patted him on the head. "Go lay down, Chief."

Then, Tom's cook brought out several appetizers and another bottle of wine. She'd already filled Karen's glass with juice. While we dug into the chili nachos with cheese stretching from one nacho to another, the tension between the guys drifted away, and we girls relaxed, enjoying the conversation. Tom brought up a story about Grandmother finding the two of them as kids hiding in what they thought was a safe place. "I swear that woman had eyes in the back of her head," he laughed.

"She's still got that gift," announced Coyote. "She knows things before they happen. She knew our baby was on the way long before we did. So did you, Rosie."

"When Karen wasn't feeling well, it wasn't that hard to think she might be pregnant," I chuckled.

"We're delighted to be expecting our little one at the end of the year," confirmed Karen.

"You said that you're here for the summer break, right? So tell me about your child, Rosie," said Tom.

"Isabella is my twelve-year-old daughter. She's quite something. Besides her Mexican family here, Karen and Coyote are her aunt and uncle."

"Twelve is such a great age. Do you think she'd like to come here and ride one of the horses?" Karen and I both smiled at the thought of Isabella coming without her sister-friends.

"I can't answer for her, but I'm afraid if she's interested, it would be only if she could bring her two friends with her."

"That's okay by me," he said.

"And if Auntie Karen will come as well," I added, making the point that I wasn't interested in being here by myself on a more intimate level.

"We'll make it a party then," exclaimed Tom. "How does tomorrow sound?"

"Not tomorrow, but the next day?" Karen asked.

"That'll be fine," said Tom with a smile. "Come around 10 o'clock and then stay for lunch. I'll have my cook make something special for them."

As we sat with the light beginning to fade, Tom's cook announced that dinner was served in the dining room. With the sliding glass doors opened wide, it felt as if we were still outside while eating a wonderful meal of a variety of Mexican dishes that were the best I'd ever eaten.

After we finished eating and had a nightcap, it was time to leave. As we all walked toward Coyote's truck, Tom pulled me back. I looked at his handsome face close to mine, and my stomach churned with nervousness.

"It was nice to have you here, Rosie. I'm glad that you're coming out to the ranch with the girls."

"Thank you, Tom. It's generous of you to have them here to ride your horses."

"You can ride, too, you know."

"I'll have to see about that," I returned.

"Goodnight, beautiful," he said as he leaned in for a kiss.

"Goodnight, Tom," I said, moving my head to avoid a kiss on the lips.

Seeing that, he cupped my face and held it tenderly as he leaned down and kissed the tip of my nose. My cheeks warmed at the unexpected placement of his kiss. Tom just smiled.

"Goodnight, my beautiful Rosie."

"Goodnight, Tom Little Horse."

Tom opened the truck door for me to climb into the back seat.

"Goodnight, all," he said as he knocked twice on the hood of Coyote's truck and backed away to let it pull forward.

"What did I tell you, Rosie," proclaimed Karen, "that man is definitely into you."

I was quiet. I wasn't sure what it all meant, but there was indeed a strong connection between us. There was no denying it. And I was glad to see how different Tom was in an everyday situation. Yes, it was hard not to be drawn into his handsome looks and sexy ways, but I was determined not to respond to it.

CHAPTER 36

The next morning, I rose with a smile remembering the lovely time I'd had the night before, relaxing in the beautiful surroundings of Tom's ranch with him, Karen, and Coyote. But the person I was missing and wanted to hear from was Mike. His two-hour time difference meant his day had already begun, and I wouldn't be disturbing his sleep if I called him. With anticipation, I picked up my cell phone and pressed his number.

"Hello," came a female voice.

I pulled the phone away from me to check if I'd called the right number. I had.

"Who's this?" I asked.

"Who are you calling?" came an annoyed voice.

Recognizing it, I demanded, "For God's sake, Allison, is that you?"

"Yes. Mike is busy right now."

"Who is it?" came Mike's voice from a distance. "Whoever it is, tell them I'll be right with them."

After a few scuffling sounds, Mike's voice came through the phone. "Hello?"

"Mike, it's me. What's going on?"

"Oh, hi there, Rosie! I'm here fixing the leak under Allison's sink. How are things there?"

"Okay. Any chance of you getting away and coming to Santa Fe?"

"I don't see how. We've got a new case and several others we're trying to finish up. We have more corporate cases now than ever before, which is a good thing, although they can take longer. But they pay better, so …"

"Does that mean you're not interested in locating missing young girls anymore?" I interrupted.

"Of course not. Back in Las Vegas, we'll still do that. We're getting a reputation for it. But I think Allison is on to something with bringing in more corporate work because there's more money to be had."

"I see," I said in a cool tone. "I hope all your work doesn't boil down to how much money there is to be made. I liked the idea of you helping families who are frantic to locate their missing children."

"Rosie, there's room for both," he said in an irritated manner.

"I guess so," I responded, annoyed. "Listen, I'll let you go so that you can finish fixing Allison's leak."

"We'll talk later," Mike said as I heard Allison whispering in the background to hurry up and end the call.

"Later," I agreed and disconnected the call.

I didn't know who I was more annoyed with—Allison or myself. Allison for toying with me or me for responding like a worried, jealous woman, which played right into Allison's hand.

Sweet Pea stirred beside me, and I got up to take a shower, leaving her behind to stretch and take her time to ready herself for the day. I would drive up to the Pueblo and pick up the girls and then give Grandmother a ride to town to sell her items if she wanted.

When Sweet Pea and I arrived at Grandmother's house, the girls squealed at seeing the dog. Giggles abounded as the girls ran away from her in their game of 'catch me if you can' that they played with Sweet Pea. The expression I wore had Grandmother turning to me with a questioning look.

"Are you finding things not to your liking, my daughter?"

I shook my head at my silliness. "Oh, Grandmother, I guess all my insecurities are rearing their ugly heads these days, what with Mike being in Boston with Allison."

"Hmm," she said, studying me.

"What do you think is going to happen?" I asked, hopefully.

Her eyes were kind as she answered, "Karma is at play. You will make choices that will lead you on and off the right path for you. Just know and believe that it will work out as it's meant to … whatever that is."

"Why does everything have to be so difficult? Why can't everything run smoothly?"

Grandmother chuckled. "That is the question, isn't it? We'd all like to have that answer."

"Girls?" I called out. "Are you packed up and ready to go to Santa Fe? And you, Grandmother—my mother, are you going into town today?"

We all piled into the car with the three girls and the dog in the back and Grandmother riding shotgun. As we drove closer to the city, my mood lightened. I glimpsed the girls through the rear-view mirror. They were so beautiful.

"I have something for the three of you to consider. Coyote's childhood friend has offered the three of you, Auntie Karen, and me to go to his ranch tomorrow so that you can ride his horses and then have lunch. Is that something you'd like to do?"

The three girls looked at each other and squealed "Yes!" in unison.

"Okay, I'll confirm it."

Grandmother eyed me but said nothing.

I pulled into the Palace of the Governors and helped Grandmother out of the car while the girls carried her items for sale to her reserved spot as "the ancient one." I smiled at the other women and one man who were regulars there. I kissed Grandmother on both cheeks, as did the girls, and then we left.

Back at my house, the girls piled out and went inside. I went to call Tom to confirm our visit and realized I had no way to contact him. Instead, I called Karen.

"Good morning, Karen! The girls want to ride the horses at Tom's tomorrow. I have no way to contact him. Do you mind calling him?"

"I'll have to get the number from Coyote, and then I'll forward his contact information to you. I think you should be the one to confirm with him."

"Oh, okay," I said, somewhat surprised. "So, how are you feeling?"

"I'm feeling great. Even all that glorious food I stuffed myself with last night stayed down. Lord, that food was certainly delicious!"

"Indeed, it was. My tummy was happy too. Oh, oh. I hear the girls calling me. I've got to run. I'll pick you up around a quarter to ten tomorrow, okay?"

"Sounds good. See you then!" Karen ended.

The girls wanted to go to the dollar store to find some treasures. It was fine with me. We piled back into the car, Sweet Pea too, and headed out. Just as we parked in front of the store, my cell phone rang. The girls rushed out of the car and into the store, giving me privacy to answer it.

"Hello."

"Hi, beautiful," came Tom's deep voice. "I got your message. I'm glad that you'll be coming out to the ranch tomorrow."

"Thank you. It's very kind of you to have us all. Is there anything you want me to bring for lunch?"

"No, just yourselves. See you then," Tom ended.

I thought about Tom. He certainly was extremely handsome—there was no doubt about that—and any woman would be flattered to draw his attention. I was aware that he found me attractive, and so far, he'd acted in a gentlemanly manner. Being Coyote's friend, I didn't think he would step out of line. Yet, I couldn't seem to relax around him and acted more like a teenager on a first date.

Then I thought about Mike back in Boston with Allison. As much time as he was spending with Allison, he insisted that he had no love interest in her. I needed to trust him. And if I wanted a friendship with Tom, then Mike would have to trust me as well. Fair was fair.

My conversation with Mike that night was short. Soon, he and Allison would meet with a potential client for dinner, so that didn't give us a chance to talk other than to wish each other a good night. Although Mike had wanted to be sure to check in with me before the day ended, this call was disappointing. It felt more like a 'duty' call. I had a feeling Allison had been close by, and it had stifled Mike's normal conversation with me.

CHAPTER 37

The next morning, the girls in the back seat chattered like a flock of crows. As they laughed at each other, egging each other on, it was the first time I saw Isabella as a young girl merely having fun without her troubled past showing on her face. She was happy, and I felt proud that maybe I'd played a small part in helping her lighten her way of living.

After picking up Karen, we drove out to the ranch. As we pulled up to Tom's house, my car crunched on the gravel, making enough noise to let him know we'd arrived. When he stepped outside to greet us, I had to bit my lip so I wouldn't laugh out loud when I heard the girls suck in their breath when they saw Tom. It seemed his good looks affected women of all ages. Karen looked at me and winked.

Tom came forward and shook the hand of each little girl as they exited the car. He leaned across the car to say hello to Karen before turning to me. With smoldering eyes, he simply said, "Hi, beautiful."

"Hi ..." I paused. I'd almost said, 'Hi, handsome' like I did for Mike. My cheeks warmed at the near mistake.

He didn't seem to notice as he turned and led us inside with his hand on the small of my back. He kept glancing down at me with a smile. He leaned closer. "I'm glad you're here, Rosie."

"Me, too," I responded honestly.

The girls were excited to see the dog who'd come outside. "What's the dog's name?" asked Nica, patting him.

"His name is Chief," said Tom, smiling at the three girls as they hovered around the dog, petting him and telling him he was a good dog.

"C'mon in," Tom urged us.

The girls stood in the doorway and took in the large living room.

"How come there are no doors?" Angela asked the other girls in a small voice as she pointed to where the patio doors would typically be.

The three of us adults chuckled.

"Here, I'll show you," said Tom, walking closer and pushing the button on the wall that controlled the doors.

The girls laughed. "That's super cool," said Isabella, turning to me with a smile.

Tom's cook stepped forward with a plate of cookies. She spoke in Spanish, and all of the little girls nodded and reached for a cookie. I heard Isabella ask her name.

"Ana."

"Gracias, Ana," Isabella said, which was repeated by Nica and Angela.

Ana looked pleased and held the plate out again, tempting them to take another cookie. Each of them did.

Then, Nica stepped out onto the patio and pointed to the horses outside. "Look!"

"Here," said Tom. "Let's go out and walk down to the barn. Juan is waiting for us there. Have you girls ridden a horse before?"

Isabella and Angela shook their heads. Nica piped up, "I have."

"Well then, for the first time with the horses, I'm going to have Juan lift you onto the saddle and walk you around the corral. Is that okay with you, girls?"

The girls nodded and rushed forward to where a horse stood in a pasture next to the barn. Juan came outside from the barn, leading another horse already saddled. He greeted the girls, calling out good morning to them in Spanish. I still could not speak fluent Spanish, but I could make out what he said. I was still trying to learn it with an app on my phone.

Each girl took a turn riding the horse, and then Juan put all three of them on the back of the horse so Karen and I could take several photos with our cell phones. Afterward, we headed back to the house for lunch. Ana had set up a special table on the patio for the little girls and had lunch for us adults arranged inside. When Tom asked Ana about the arrangements, she said. "Sun not good for the ladies."

No one argued with her, so we ended up eating inside with more wonderful Mexican food prepared by her, ending with flan for dessert. "Tom, you are one lucky man to have a cook like Ana," I said, wiping my mouth with my napkin. "That was delicious."

"Ana has been with me for quite a few years now. She's a good woman who keeps me in my place. She doesn't let me get away with anything," he laughed good-naturedly.

"Good to know," chuckled Karen.

It was the first time I'd heard Tom be even a little bit disapproving about himself, and I liked the idea that he could laugh about it. Several minutes later, the house phone rang, and Ana came to Tom and whispered to him in Spanish. The change in him was astounding. His face reddened with anger, and he abruptly left the table, saying, "Excuse me, ladies. This will only take a minute. I'll be right back."

He looked fierce as he strode across the room and entered the bedroom wing of the house. Although he was some distance away, we heard his muffled voice raised in anger. At one point, I saw Isabella hush the other girls as she tried to listen in on his conversation. Then we heard a loud bang from a door being slammed shut. Tom's footsteps soon came our way. Karen and I looked at each other with raised brows, not knowing what to expect.

Tom entered the room with an embarrassed look. "I'm sorry, ladies, but business calls." He then went out to where the girls were waiting.

"Little ladies, would you like to come back to ride the horse again?"

"Yes," they said in unison.

"Good. I'll make arrangements with Rosie, and we can set up another time soon."

Karen and I rose from the table, gathered our purses, and waited for the girls to come inside. Then we headed to the front door. As we walked to the car, Tom asked me, "Have you ever hiked in the Santa Fe National Forest Park? Its land runs into mine."

"No, I don't know anything about it. I'm not that familiar with much outside of Santa Fe and Chimayo."

"Well, we'll have to do something about that then, won't we? New Mexico is a beautiful area. I'll be your tour guide. I'll call you in a day or two," he said as he grabbed my hand and squeezed it.

Before I got behind the wheel, Tom lifted my hand to his lips and kissed it. "Until then, beautiful Rosie."

I drove off with mixed feelings. It was hard to deny that I didn't enjoy the attention Tom was giving me. But even more so, I felt special in that I sensed that I saw a side of him that few people saw—a kinder, more authentic side. In public, he was glib with his words and strutted and drew attention to himself. His whole demeanor was one of arrogance. With Coyote, Karen, and me, Tom was relaxed and more natural. He seemed to be genuinely interested in what we had to say, and he was able to laugh at himself. As well, it was evident that both he and Coyote were enjoying their renewed relationship.

Tom was a large man, and today it'd touched my heart to see him squat down to speak tenderly to the small girls as they sat eating lunch. And there were other tender moments when he fussed with his animals, calling them endearing Indian names. Tom was an interesting man—a man at odds with himself—and I was curious to know more about him. I mostly wanted to learn how he got to be a politician. When Coyote had begun to talk about it the other night, Tom had pushed it aside, saying it was a night to relax without business.

I loved Mike; there was no doubt about that. Yet, I had taken for granted that he felt the same about me until the moment Mike had said he wasn't up to taking our relationship further. What exactly did that mean? It had been almost a week since I'd last seen Mike, and in the meantime, he had given me only a few hurried minutes of conversation over the phone. It seemed that he was always in the middle of something with Allison at his side. I sighed.

The more I thought about it, the more I liked the idea of Tom being my tour guide and seeing through his eyes the beauty of New Mexico that I'd been missing. I hoped that he'd followed through, and I'd hear from him. I wasn't going to feel guilty about spending time with him, either, I told myself.

CHAPTER 38

The following evening, I was pleasantly surprised to receive a telephone call from Tom. "Hello, beautiful. Do you have plans tomorrow? I thought we'd take my three-wheel motorcycle, and I'll show you some of the National Forest."

"That sounds wonderful. What time were you thinking?" I asked.

"Why not make a day of it? I can pick you up at nine o'clock, and we can grab breakfast in town before we head out. I'll have Ana pack us a picnic for lunch."

"That works for me. I'll have time to drop the girls off at Maria's and be back home by nine." I gave him my address and said goodnight.

"Okay, my beautiful Rosie, I'll see you tomorrow."

I was sitting outside on the patio in the fading light that splashed with the sunset's stunning orange and purple colors. Earlier, I'd had a chance to speak with Mike, and, once again, it'd been a disappointing call. He never asked how I was doing. Instead, with Allison by his side, he talked on and on about how they'd worked together to solve a client's issue. Although he'd told me that he loved me when he said goodbye, it'd sounded stilted, not anything like when we were alone, eye to eye. I missed that intimacy from him.

I leaned back in my chair and thought about my plans for tomorrow. It'd be a new experience for me to be on a large motorcycle like the one Tom described. I had a feeling that spending any amount of time with Tom was going to be filled with many new experiences, and I was ready for them. I decided to enjoy my freedom and not worry about my relationship with Mike. Things would work out as they were meant to—isn't that what Grandmother said?

Inside, I could hear the girls laughing as they played a game together. I wandered in. "It sounds like you girls are having a good time."

They nodded, and Isabella held up her playing cards and pointed to the pile in front of her. "I'm winning."

"Yeah, but I won the game last time," announced Nica. Angela sat quietly.

"Angela won a few games, too," interjected Isabella.

"As far as I'm concerned, you're all winners!" I laughed.

The girls giggled.

"I'm going to drop you off at Angela's house a bit early tomorrow morning, so be ready, okay?"

"What are you doing, Mama?" Isabella asked.

"Tom is going to show me around Santa Fe National Park. I've never been there."

"It's cool," Nica said.

"I'll see what it's like, and maybe we all can go there for a picnic or something," I suggested.

Isabella studied me but didn't say a word. Then, she said, "I bet that's something Mike would like."

"I bet you're right," I agreed.

I took out my computer and looked up the Santa Fe National Park. I learned it was established in 1915 and covered 1,558,452 acres with elevations from 5,300 to 13,103 feet at Truchas Peak's summit. Its address was Los Alamos in New Mexico, and although I was aware that Tom's ranch was located there, I wondered what part of the park abutted his land. I'd have to wait until tomorrow to see for myself.

The next morning, I dropped off the girls at Maria's and made it back to the house in time to see a man standing in front of it. During the spring, we had gone ahead and had a garage built that was separate from the house in the fashion of many older homes. Karen had overseen that part of the project. During the garage's construction, I decided to build a breezeway between it and the house. As I pulled into the driveway, I wasn't that surprised to see that my contractor was waiting for me. He wanted an okay to begin.

A few minutes later, as the contractor was backing away, Tom pulled up to the house in his fancy sports car. He climbed out and came my way. "Ready?"

"Not quite. I need to let Sweet Pea out to do her thing. She's also the reason I'll need to get back home by 5 o'clock."

"Okay, then. Let's let her out."

Sweet Pea was waiting right by the door when I opened it. When she saw me, she wiggled around in delight but became even more excited when she saw Tom and began to dance at his feet. Instead of being annoyed, he scooped her up and held her in his arms. "Ah, a dog with a spirit like her mama," he said as the dog squirmed against him.

Sweet Pea licked his face, and Tom allowed her several kisses before he carefully placed the small dog back down. Both the man and the dog wore smiles. I laughed at the sight.

"C'mon, Sweet Pea, time to go outside," I urged.

***

As we sat eating breakfast at the restaurant Tom had chosen, I watched him stiffen as he looked outside. I turned and looked in the same direction. I watched the Chief of the Tesuque Pueblo enter the restaurant. When he was inside and saw Tom, he scowled and marched to our table.

"What are you doing here, Tom Little Horse? I'm surprised you're not back in Washington taking bribes from the oil companies to use our land for fracking or some such outlandish thing!"

His angry words drew attention from some sitting near us, and the din in the restaurant lowered to hear what was happening. Tom's eyes hardened. "You've turned into a bitter old man, Chief."

"Is it any wonder when I see that my own flesh and blood is more interested in money than protecting his heritage?"

"Do you not understand that it could be financially beneficial for our people?" Tom asked, angry.

"Again, it's about money for you. Once an outsider enters our land, it becomes blighted, and nothing can save it," he said in disgust.

The chief suddenly noticed me. "Sorry about this. My apologies," he said and turned away to join others at a table in the corner."

"Wow," I said, "he certainly was angry."

216

"Yeah, he doesn't understand that we have to change with the times. That or get run over."

"So you're not a politician?" I asked.

"I'm a lobbyist," he stated as he signaled the waitress for the bill.

Once outside, Tom seemed to mentally shake himself before putting his hand on the small of my back and leading me to his car to head out to the ranch.

CHAPTER 39

Driving closer to the ranch, Tom visually relaxed, and his mood lightened. "Ah, what a beautiful morning! There's nothing like being here in the hills of New Mexico. You can practically feel the heartbeat of Mother Nature here, can't you?"

I smiled. "Yes."

When we got to the ranch, Chief greeted us, and then the dog lumbered back inside with us. I heard Ana humming in the background, and I went to say hello while Tom went to change into leather riding pants.

"Good morning, Ana!"

"Good morning, Rosie. Your lunch is here," she said, pointing to the basket resting on the counter.

"Thank you. May I look?" I asked, curious to see what she'd prepared for us.

"Si," she said, opening the lid of the picnic basket.

"Oh, Ana, it all looks so good!"

"Si, you will like," she said with a smile.

"How long have you worked for Tom?" I asked, curious.

"Many years. He, not a bad man." I thought her wording a bit strange until she patted my hand. "Good man. He a good man."

Steps bounded our way. We stood and waited for Tom to join us. When he came through the doorway, smiling at the two of us, he stole my breath away. My God, he was handsome! I tried to see beyond his good looks to get a better sense of what he was about. He seemed to have so many sides to him—rough and tough, arrogant and smug, mild and sensitive, insightful and aware, kind and loving. He was engaging, all right, and I found myself intrigued by him.

"Ready?" Tom asked as he stepped forward and grabbed the picnic basket. "We better get going if we're going to get back in time for Sweet Pea."

"Okay, let's go! Thanks, Ana, for the wonderful lunch."

Tom looked at me with a brow raised.

"I peeked," I laughed. "And you're going to like it, too."

Mounting the large motorcycle was like climbing on a nostril-steaming, pawing, ready-to-go stead. I was intimidated by it, and I clung to Tom as we drove away. He drew my arms around him even more. "Tighter," he said.

We took off across his land and followed a well-worn path to enter the tree-filled National Park. I laid my head against his broad back and hung on for dear life. As we neared the park, he slowed down enough so that we could easily talk. He pointed out some of the different trees, naming them. We continued forward until we came to a clearing near a small waterfall and pond, several miles in from where his land ended. It was a whole new world. It smelled of damp wood, giving off a pleasant pine odor, and the quiet was deafening. The light made it through the trees, and the sun felt like a heavenly blessing as it kissed our shoulders.

"We'll stop here. Is this okay with you?" Tom asked.

"It's beautiful," I said, looking around. "Yes, this is perfect."

I laughed in embarrassment as I began to get down off the bike. My body was stiff and sore, and I wasn't sure that I'd be able to make it without falling. Tom caught on right away and came to my aid.

"Here, let me help you off," he offered. He steadied me until I had both feet on the ground. "There," he said with a smile.

"Thanks for the help," I said, my cheeks reddening.

"You are so beautiful," Tom said as he pushed a loose clump of hair behind my ear. He looked at me with a quizzical look. "I feel as if I've known you before."

I was too stunned to say anything. The vision I'd seen at Karen's wedding of the man next to me peering at the bundled baby flashed before me. I felt a connection between us, too. Could that be it? A lifetime we'd shared?

"Quite a line, isn't it?" he scolded himself. "But it's true."

Without awareness of what I was doing, I stretched my hand up and placed it against his cheek. He bent and kissed me on my waiting lips, and if it was correct that we'd shared a lifetime, it was as if no time had passed at all. It felt right.

He pulled me against the length of him, and I melted into him, aware of the pleasure erupting from the center of my being. It was a soul-searching, deep kiss that took both of us by surprise. I stepped back, and we studied each other. After several seconds of absorbing each other, we parted, both shaken. Tom walked to the bike to retrieve the blanket and picnic basket while I tried to pretend that nothing extraordinary had happened. I helped to spread the blanket on a soft spot on the ground, and we sat down. Tom was quiet as he opened the basket and poured the wine that Ana had packed. He handed me a glass of wine and raised his filled glass to tap against mine. "Here's to a life worth living."

"My, that's quite a toast," I said as I tapped his glass once more. "Here, here."

Tom sprawled across the blanket, resting his back against the tree closest to us.

"Tom, I'm curious. What is your relationship with the Chief? He said you were his flesh and blood."

"Him? He was my mother's first cousin. So an uncle of sorts, I guess."

"Do you still have any family at the Pueblo? Is your mother still alive?"

Tom squirmed, uncomfortable. "Coyote can probably tell you better than me about my family growing up because I was always running away from them. They got caught up in addictions, and I escaped and got attention the only way I knew how—by becoming a trouble maker." He chuckled and shook his head. "Coyote and I were all that and then some."

"Coyote mentioned that the two of you got into trouble a lot."

"Yeah," he said as he stood up. He held his hand out, and I grabbed onto it so that he could pull me up. "I want to show you something."

He led me to the pond. "As a kid, we'd hitchhike and come here to get away from the pueblo. And when it was hot, we'd come here to take a swim."

"I can see why. The water is so clean and pure that it makes me want to dive right in." Seeing Tom's amused expression, I added, "But I'm not going to."

He smiled, and still holding my hand, led me back to the blanket. We sat together with his arm around my shoulders, leaning against the tree there. We talked about everything as we sipped wine and nibbled on the food that Ana had packed for us. I was comfortable with him, no longer tense as I had been before. Something had changed for me. It felt right to be with him. I told him about Isabella, and then I told him about Mike.

"If Mike is the man in your life, why isn't he here?" he asked, confused.

I blushed. "He's back in Boston working in their office there."

"I can tell you're upset by that. Am I right?"

My cheeks reddened even more. "Maybe."

Tom reached across and lifted my chin to stare into my eyes. "A man should never leave his woman unhappy."

His hand brushed my face, and his eyes searched mine. He pushed a lock of hair beyond my ear and bent forward to kiss me. Just then, we heard crashing sounds coming through the trees, headed our way. We rose in alarm and saw an Indian woman stumbling forward, out of breath.

"Please, help me. He's going to kill me."

"Who?" I asked in fright. "Who's going to kill you?"

Then a large Indian man burst through the brush and stood looking at us in surprise as the woman hid behind Tom. "Who are *you*?" demanded the man.

"More to the point, who are you?" ordered Tom.

"It don't matter. Just give me my woman," he commanded.

The woman tugged on Tom. "NO! Please, no."

"Hold on. What's going on here?" demanded Tom looking between them. Then he raised the woman's arm covered with bruises. "Did you do this to her?" he asked the man.

"I wouldn't need to teach her a lesson if she'd obey me, but she won't!"

Tom flung Tewa words at him. The man hung his head down for a few seconds and then raised it in defiance. "Give her back! She's mine!"

"Listen, you son of a bitch, get outta here!" Tom threatened as he stepped toward the man. "Go home and sleep it off. She's coming with me so that she can get some help for all the damage you've done to her."

The man raced forward, and being unsteady on his feet, he lost his balance, and with the added punch that Tom gave him, the man landed on his back, out cold.

"C'mon, he can sleep it off here. We need to get you some medical attention," he said to the woman. "Rosie, let's load up everything."

The woman came to my side and tried to help me fold the blanket, but she was too weak to do much. She was shy, and I knew she was embarrassed by her circumstance. I put my arm around her and said, "Don't worry. We'll make sure you're safe."

CHAPTER 40

The woman was exhausted and in pain. It was hard to see any of her injuries under the long house dress hanging limp from her shoulders, but she winced as we tucked her into the bike's seat in front of Tom. With a helping hand from Tom, I hoisted myself up behind him. Sensing the woman's discomfort, Tom drove more slowly out of the park. On the way, Tom had me call for an ambulance to meet us at the house.

When we got back to the ranch, the ambulance was waiting there for us to arrive. I knew the woman was afraid, but she was in too much pain to resist. I held her hand. "Do you want me to go with you?"

She looked at me with pleading eyes. Finally, she nodded as tears slid down her cheeks.

Tom said, "I'm coming with you."

The ambulance attendant held up his arm. "Only the women, sir."

"Okay, I'll follow in my car. I'll meet you there, Rosie."

I nodded. "Okay."

Later, sitting in the waiting room, Tom and I held hands—he reassuring me that everything would turn out all right. "Does this happen all the time?" I asked.

"Enough so that it's not unique, I'm sorry to say."

"Do you have safe houses for women and children who need to escape?"

"A few, of course. I don't really know."

I shivered. "That was scary. That poor woman looked like death on the run. And it's scarier still to know that she's not alone ... that there are others."

Tom picked up our locked hands and kissed the top of mine. As I watched him do this, I wondered how we had gotten to this point so quickly. It seemed surreal. Suddenly self-conscious, I pulled my hand away and rose to get a drink of water.

The doctor came out and told us that the woman would be spending a few days in the hospital. She had several broken ribs and some burn marks that looked like they were from cigarettes. He'd reported all this to the police, and they were going to provide protective custody until they could find a safe place for her.

I felt sick to my stomach. I'd had such a protected life. The more I was exposed to the reality of how many people lived, the more I knew how blessed I was to have had my parents and, most of all, my grandmother to raise me. Before this past year, I had been very naïve, and it hurt me to see how many people were suffering.

"Ready to go home? Sweet Pea will be waiting for you."

"Yeah, I'm ready."

We were silent in the car. Today had brought about unexpected experiences, and I felt drained. I looked at Tom and saw a man saddened by what'd happened to the woman. He pulled at my heartstrings. I would never have guessed a few days ago that I'd feel this way about anyone other than Mike. Perhaps it boiled down to something as simple as having shared a previous lifetime. I wasn't sure. I knew, though, how I felt about Isabella and Grandmother and that my feeling of love for them today was as deep as anything I'd ever experienced with them before. My unspoken thoughts caused him to reach for my hand. I didn't fight it and let our energies mesh.

When we arrived home, Sweet Pea was excited to see us and, once again, danced at Tom's feet. I called her, and we went to the sliding glass door. Tom's cell phone rang. He took it from his pocket, looked at it, and then at me. "I have to take this call. Excuse me."

He went outside, and I heard mumbled words. Then I heard him clearly say, "Okay, then. I'll see you tomorrow," as he walked back inside.

I fed Sweet Pea and asked, "Would you like a drink, Tom?"

"Do you have a beer?"

"Yes. Here you go," I said as I handed him a cold bottle. "Here's a glass."

"I'll drink from the bottle if you don't mind. Here, let me pour you your glass of wine."

We sat on the couch in the living room. Tom rested his head against the back of it and took several deep breaths. He reached for my hand and squeezed it. After a minute, he turned to me. "I don't know exactly what's happening between us, but I realize that you are someone special to me. You are a once in a lifetime happening for me. I sense

227

that you feel something too. I don't know where this is going, so if you're not interested in pursuing a relationship with me, tell me now."

I thought of Mike—my beautiful, handsome man who'd stuck by me through my trials of making Isabella my daughter. I loved him and wanted him in my life. After all, he was someone who I'd been ready to commit to for the rest of my life not that long ago. However, he'd been the one to decide the timing wasn't right, if at all, leaving me unsure if our relationship was the right one for me.

Then fate had stepped in and placed Tom in my life. It was apparent that I'd never be able to fully commit to Mike unless I settled my feelings for Tom. It was almost as if it were all out of my control … unfinished business of sorts. And now, all our futures were left for fate to decide.

I turned to Tom and, as before, laid my palm against his cheek, searching his eyes. "I think we have uncompleted business to take care of, don't you?"

His worried eyes cleared, and he pulled me against him, crushing my lips with his, arousing my deep feelings of need. His hand wandered down to my breast, and I moaned. He pulled back, raking me in with his dark sexual gaze. Unexpectedly, his eyes filled. "You are so beautiful, my little bird."

I stilled. Tom had said my name Little Bird from lifetimes ago. Had I heard him correctly? "What did you call me?"

"I said you are so beautiful," he smiled as he traced my mouth with his thumb.

"What else?"

Tom looked stumped. "I don't remember. Does it matter?"

I shook my head. "No." I put my arms around his neck and pulled him close to me. He kissed me again, and it deepened as both of our hearts pounded with passion. Suddenly, I pushed myself upright. "Not like this," I said.

He leaned back against the couch and took several deep breaths. I nestled against him until we both calmed.

"I have to fly back to Washington tomorrow. I'll be gone for a couple of weeks or so," he said.

"Is everything all right?"

"Yeah, it's just business. Will you miss me?" he teased.

I laughed at his leading question and pushed him away, teasing him. "I'll be away too. I'll be in Florida with the kids at Disney World for a few days."

"Is it okay for me to call you?"

"Of course," I answered.

He reached for me and brought me close, holding me tight. He leaned down and tenderly gave me a long, searching kiss that made me want more. He looked at me with longing and sighed. Finally, he hauled himself to his feet. "I better get going, or I'll never leave."

I rose and walked him to the door. He said something to me in Tewa—something similar to what Coyote had said to Karen. I knew it was special. My eyes filled. One kiss and he was gone.

"Take care, Tom Little Horse," I whispered as I watched him walk away. It was a good thing that Tom would be gone. That would give me time to get my life back on track.

CHAPTER 41

The next morning, I awoke early and called Mike, knowing I'd catch him before his day started. I was hoping his schedule had cleared where he could join us in Florida.

"Hi there, handsome. How's it going?"

"Oh, hi there, Rosie. What's up?" he asked.

"I'm missing you! I'm hoping you're going to be able to join us at Disney World."

"I'm sorry, but we have a heavy load of business here, and I'm not going to be able to make it. I wish I could, though. It sounds like fun."

"Are you certain you can't shift things around?" I pleaded. "I'm missing you, and I know Isabella is too."

"And I'm missing you as well, but as you can ..." I heard knocking. "Wait a minute, hold on. Allison is here. Coming!" he called out. "C'mon in, Allison. I'm almost done here."

"What time is it there?" I asked, puzzled.

"Seven o'clock. Why?"

"Isn't it early to start your day?" I asked.

"Not really. We like starting early. Listen, can I call you later?"

"Sure, if you want to. I should be here," I said with disappointment. "Well, have a good day then."

"Hey, you too."

And that was it … the conversation was over. I was dumbfounded. Our love relationship was slipping away, or was I making too much of things? After all, Mike was busy in Boston for business, and if Allison was a part of that, there was nothing I could do about it.

I nudged Sweet Pea to move over, and I slipped under the covers again, wanting more sleep. But the phone rang, and this time, it was Tom.

"Good morning, beautiful lady. I'm at the airport, ready to fly out. I'll be thinking of you every minute I'm gone until I can return and be with you again," he said in a husky voice.

My heart pounded, and I felt my face warm. "I'll look forward to your return then," I said with a smile in my voice.

He said something in Tewa.

"What did you say, Tom?"

"Well, the closest I can translate it is, "You fill me with knowing you are all I desire."

I was speechless for a moment. "That's beautiful, Tom. Thank you." I chuckled. "Is that something you say to all the ladies?" I teased.

He was silent for a moment. "I'm surprised that you'd think that of me. When I get back, I'll make sure to acquaint you with all of what that saying means," he whispered seductively.

I shivered with anticipation. What had I gotten myself into? Mike and Brian were always teasing me about getting in trouble, and this time I was in it knee-deep for sure. I thought about what Tom had said and realized I'd like to explore the ways he might desire me.

We said goodbye, and I leaned back in bed, letting my thoughts wander. Finally, I rose and took a shower. I was meeting with Coyote, and then I was picking up the girls and heading to Grandmother's, where they had another sleepover with her. Sleepovers with her meant that she was teaching them some of the Indian ways and stories. The girls were like sponges soaking it all up, fascinated about times long ago. I loved to hear them talking about what she'd shared with them.

The station was buzzing when I arrived. Jose was speaking with Coyote, which was unusual. Usually, Jose avoided being seen with the sheriff, especially now in his role of an informant.

"What's going on?" I asked, surprising them both.

"Just got a call from the FBI. They picked up several of the men we've been watching," Coyote said.

"Where?"

"At the border in San Ysidro that crosses into Tijuana, Mexico. When they tried to cross the border, they didn't realize we had warrants out for their arrest," smiled Coyote.

"That must've surprised them," I chuckled. "Well, that's good to have them out of the way."

"Not quite," added Coyote. "With a good lawyer, they'll return with a vengeance, like their moniker—the Scorpion, or have replacements for them."

"That's not so good, then," I said. "Any news on the upcoming meeting?" I asked, looking at Jose.

"It's still a go," he responded with a shrug, "just not sure when. Well, I'd better get out of here."

"Okay. Thanks, Jose, for the update," Coyote said.

I plopped down in the chair in front of his desk. "I don't know how you're going to be able to find the specific people who are responsible for the killings last year. The psychic message I keep getting is that they're part of the Scorpion gang, and unless someone is willing to defect from it, there's not a chance in hell of you finding out anything. Especially since it's a life or death thing."

"I know," Coyote said.

"I studied the file you gave me regarding your nephew. I believe he was murdered, too. It's all part of the drug scene going on here. I don't know how you can prove it, though. Won't you have to pursue it through the reservation anyway, since he was killed there?"

He nodded. "I want to put away his killer. I want to see justice done. I hate to think anyone deserves to die the way Redmond did."

"I know exactly how you feel. I was so angry after Jeff's death, knowing he was murdered and I had no power to bring down his killers. Eventually, things right themselves, and I think they will work out for you and your nephew, too."

"Well, thanks for taking the time to look through the files," Coyote said, reaching for his nephew's file to take back.

"Don't forget the vision I *did* have, Coyote. That bloody scene was real and horrible. I think it has something to do with a raid at the meeting of the Scorpions. You need to be careful."

"The FBI is handling it now. I don't even know if I'll be involved."

"It would be nice for Karen if you weren't."

"I have to do what I have to do," Coyote replied, brushing aside my worry.

I looked at Coyote. He had shared more of himself with me than ever before. That made me further aware of how tough his job was with all that was going on in the city.

"Just take care and keep safe, my friend," I urged as I rose. "The girls are going to Grandmother's for another sleepover tonight."

Coyote chuckled. "Grandmother's determined that she's going to make well-schooled Indians out of them yet."

I laughed. "I think you're right."

"Karen tells me you are sight-seeing with Tom....?"

I blushed. "He showed me Santa Fe National Park yesterday. I'd never been there before, and the spot where you used to go with him as a boy is simply beautiful."

"We went through a lot together as kids. Tom's okay … just got caught up in lousy politics. And that's a jungle for sure with no one agreeing to disagree, and, pretty much, that ends up with everyone pissed off."

"Yes, I have to agree with what you said. It's hard to have everyone happy in that arena. I'm glad not to be a part of it."

Coyote studied me for a moment but remained quiet.

"See you later, Coyote," I said and left thinking about Tom and his working with the oil companies. I disagreed with what the oil companies wanted to do regarding fracking. It didn't seem right to force Mother Nature to give up her resources in that way. But there was little I could do about it.

CHAPTER 42

The girls were dawdling and not yet packed when I arrived at Maria's to pick them up. I sat sipping a cup of herbal tea with Maria while the girls got moving.

"How are things with you, Maria?"

"Better and better. Miguel is becoming a changed man, more like his old self. His having to go to anger management classes was the best thing to happen to him. He got another promotion at work last week, too."

"That's wonderful!"

"He said something the other day that I wasn't sure I'd heard him right. He said, 'Isabella and Angela are not only lucky to have each other but to have two mothers, too.'"

"Are you kidding?" I asked, surprised.

"No, he actually said that," she chuckled.

"Imagine that," I laughed. "Now we're talking *miracles*."

Maria laughed. "I know, right?"

Miguel had wanted nothing to do with me or have me anywhere near his niece. To scare me away, he'd paid Coyote's nephew to put dead crows on the door handle of the house I was renting. When that came to light, and his odd involvement with Isabella's abduction, instead of arresting Miguel, Coyote had arranged for him to attend anger management classes. And it was working.

"We leave in a few days for Disney World. Mike isn't going to be able to get away, so it'll be the girls, Cal, Virginia, and me."

"Are you alright with that? Mike, not going with you?" Maria asked. She knew I wasn't happy having Allison in the picture.

"I was hoping he could go with us, but it should be fine without him. The girls will be easy enough to handle, and Cal and Virginia will be there. Four days will pass quickly. Just enough time to wear them out," I grinned.

Maria smiled. "Karen's taking Sweet Pea?"

"Yes, she's happy to have her." I looked at Maria's worried eyes. "And I don't want you to concern yourself about Angela. I'll take good care of her, I promise," I said as I patted Maria's hand.

I knew how hard it could be to allow your child to explore the world without you. It'd taken me time to adjust to Isabella spending those first few overnights with Irene, my next-door neighbor. Or, to be honest, her attending those early few days at school without me.

"I know you will," Maria assured me.

The girls came into the room, packed and ready to leave.

"You're spending tonight with Grandmother, and then you'll each spend tomorrow night at your home. That will give you time to pack for Disney World, and then the following day, we're off to Florida."

The girls looked at each other and smiled.

"We can't wait!" Nica said, and the other two girls chimed in.

"Well then, say goodbye, and let's get going to Grandmother's house."

I heard the boys in their room, playing and having a good time. Maria was lucky that they seemed to get along so well. Then I heard Rosa calling from her crib. "Up, Mama, up."

Her naptime was over. "Hurry, so Rosa doesn't see you here," Maria urged. And we quietly left.

At the pueblo, Grandmother was there to greet us. "Children, come in. My daughter, are you sure you won't join us?"

"No, Grandmother—my mother. Thank you, but no. Karen is expecting me."

She eyed me. "You're different, child. Trust yourself and your feelings. Life is nothing more than a journey."

My face burned with embarrassment. I had been thinking about Tom. "Thank you, Grandmother."

Karen greeted me, smiling and glowing. Once inside, she reached for my hand and placed it against her belly. "She's moving now. See if you can feel her."

"Her?" I laughed. My eyes widened as I felt a flutter, and then it was still. "I felt her!"

Placing her hand atop mine, Karen stated, "This is your Auntie Rose." Together we felt another little flutter.

My eyes filled. "How beautiful, Karen."

"I'm so happy, Rosie. I can't begin to tell you how happy I am," Karen said.

"I'm so glad for you, my dear friend."

"Enough about me. Come sit down. I want to hear how your sightseeing went with Mr. Handsome."

After I told her about what had happened yesterday, she lit up with mischief. "So Mike is going to have to fight for his woman, huh? That's as it should be after he allows all of Allison's shenanigans."

"You know how I feel about Mike. I love him. But, I have to be honest, there's also something about Tom that pulls at my heart, too. I'm torn, Karen."

"There's no right or wrong in this, Rosie. Without Mike committing, you're free to do what's right for you. Things will work out as they're meant to—you're the one who taught me that," she said, coming to me with a hug.

"I know. I've decided not to lock myself into thinking about what I should or shouldn't do. I think I'm just going to enjoy my time with Tom."

Karen nodded in agreement.

I became lost in thought. "Tom says that it's not that rare to have a husband beat up his Indian wife or girlfriend. Honestly, Karen, if you had seen the woman yesterday, it was pathetic. I felt so sorry for her. I want to find out about the resources available here in Santa Fe for women like her. Maybe I'll volunteer or something."

"That's hard to do when you are going back and forth between here and Las Vegas."

"That's true, but maybe there's something I can do."

"Are you ready for lunch?" Karen asked.

"Yes, that sounds wonderful. What did you make? Whatever it is, I know it's going to be good because you are a great cook."

"That's why I'm always a bit overweight. I can't seem to help myself," Karen laughed, "I do love to eat. C'mon, and see for yourself."

I hurried behind her, salivating at the thought of something extraordinary to eat waiting for me.

THE LOVERS.

CHAPTER 43

That night, I was happy to hear from Mike. Although he seemed rushed, he asked in a tender voice, "How are things with you?"

"All is good, although I wish you were here. We miss you—all three of us."

Mike chuckled. "Are you including Sweet Pea?"

I laughed. "Yes, even her."

"Things are crazy here, Rosie. I'm looking to hire another person because Allison has brought so much work our way. It makes for long days."

"Well, I hope that you find someone soon then. How is Brian doing in Las Vegas? Anything new going on at Tony and Johnny's place?"

"I think they're going back to their old ways. Brian has become no stranger to their men's club, and working with Cindy is like old times for him. I'm just hoping to get things set up here so that I can get back to my own office in Las Vegas. I want to build that business up."

"You mean you want to get back to me, right?" I teased.

"Sure," he laughed. "Goodnight, Rosie. It's late, and I've got an early day tomorrow with Allison."

"How is that working with Allison?" I asked.

"She's a determined lady, but she's good at what she does. And I don't have to worry about her the way I worry about you."

"That must be a relief," I said, sarcastically.

"Look, Rosie, I've got to take this call. It's Allison."

"I love you, too," I said to the air around me.

I looked at the phone in my hand and felt a sadness sweep over me. I needed to understand what was happening in my relationship with Mike. This past year, we had lived in our fresh new love for each other, and we had used it to bond with Isabella and become a family of sorts. The more I thought about our situation, it must have been hard for Mike on several levels. He had a family not of his making, living in houses not his own, and had been pulled away from a life he had been comfortable living. It was apparent, now more than ever, that he loved his work. So if the tables were turned, what would I be willing to sacrifice to keep our relationship going?

There was no question about keeping Isabella in my life. I wanted to be her mother to the end, and I would fight for it. That was a given. Would I fight for Mike if I knew he wasn't happy with the way things were? By not wanting to move our relationship forward, hadn't he already indicated he wasn't happy? Why did things have to be so complicated? I had a lot to think about.

The phone rang again, and when I saw it was Tom, my heart fluttered. I almost didn't answer it but realized I wanted to hear what he had to say.

"Hi there, beautiful," he said, his smooth voice soothing me.

"Hi, Tom. How are things going for you in D.C.?"

"Always busy, always bartering to be done." He cleared his throat. "Rosie, I don't want to be apart from you for two weeks. That's too long a time. I'm coming home at the end of next week. When are you going to Disney World?"

"We leave the day after tomorrow for four days. We should be back by the time you return."

"Perfect timing. And Rosie?"

"Yeah …"

"I intend to get to know you better in all ways. I can't stop thinking about you. I think we've got something good going between us."

I remained silent.

"You feel it too, don't you?" he asked, hope in his voice.

"I do, but how is that going to work out? You have women falling all over you, and I think you'll find me pretty boring after a while."

"I don't believe that at all. Just because women find me attractive doesn't mean I'm interested in them. Those days are over and have been for quite some time. Ask Ana; she'll tell you."

Thinking of my situation with Mike, I said, "I don't know, Tom."

"Let's just enjoy our time together, and if things don't work out, no hard feelings, okay?" he asked in confidence.

I sighed. "Okay. You've got yourself a deal."

"A deal, is it?" he laughed. "I'll call you tomorrow. I want to hear your voice each night just before I close my eyes, my beautiful angel."

I chuckled. "I'm far from an angel, Tom."

"Even better," he mumbled.

My cheeks heated. "Goodnight, Tom."

"Goodnight, love."

I jumped out of bed where I'd been reading to let Sweet Pea out. "What am I doing?" I demanded in a loud voice. She looked at me and winked—even though dogs supposedly aren't able to do so.

THE LOVERS.

CHAPTER 44

The girls were excited as Karen drove us to the airport in Albuquerque. We were meeting Cal and Virginia in Florida. They had already landed and were on their way to the park and the Disney Caribbean Beach Resort located on the property. We'd meet them there in time for dinner and a walk through the park. It would be early to bed and early to rise the next day for a morning of rides and relaxation and swimming in the afternoon.

We hugged Karen goodbye, and Isabella and I kissed Sweet Pea before they pulled away. We waved as we watched them leave.

"Okay, girls, let's get inside."

After we boarded the airplane, the girls sat in the three seats on one side of the aisle while I sat in the aisle seat across from them. Isabella sat in the middle seat and held hands with both Nica and Angela on each side. It was their

247

first plane ride, and I knew they were a bit nervous. I was hoping that by Isabella sitting beside them, they'd relax a bit. I tried to get them from thinking about the flight and concentrate on being at Disney World and the various rides they'd take.

"Did you girls know that I've never been to Disney World either?"

They looked so surprised that I laughed. "Hard to believe, isn't it?"

"What rides do you want to take, Mama?"

"I'm not sure. What rides do you girls want to do?"

Our conversation could be heard among some of the other passengers, and before long, several of them joined in with suggestions of rides to take. It was fun and took the worry away from Nica and Angela's first flight. I was grateful.

Landing in Orlando was quite an experience, what with collecting our bags and finding the correct van to take us to Disney World and the right hotel. If I came again, I would have a limo pick us up. Lesson learned.

When we got to the hotel, we were excited to have Cal and Virginia waiting for us in the lobby. Cal had already checked us in and took us up to our room, next to theirs. I would share the room with the girls so I could keep an eye on them.

After unpacking, we went downstairs to meet Cal and Virginia at the pool cafe. While we sat outside sipping drinks, we reviewed all the information regarding the park and the tours available. The girls took off to walk around the pool.

"You two look so relaxed and happy together," I said, smiling at them.

"We are," responded Cal. "Aren't we, sweetheart?"

"Very much so," Virginia said as she patted his hand.

Cal looked at me. "Is everything okay with you? You look tired."

"Just a lot on my mind," I answered.

"How is Mike doing back in Boston with Allison?" he asked.

I flushed. "Busy. Allison has brought in a lot of work, and Mike's trying to hire a new person to help out."

"That's good, then. Maybe he'll be able to get back to Las Vegas."

"I hope so," I said.

Virginia listened to our conversation. "I have to say that I didn't care for Allison. I can understand if you feel the same way, Rosie."

I chuckled. "You're right about that."

Cal was mulling over a brochure. "Let's have an early dinner right here and then take the trolley tour of the park so that we can get our bearings for tomorrow."

The days seem to fly by, filled with all kinds of rides, junk food, swimming, boat rides on the lake, and various tours. Although it was so much fun, it was exhausting.

It was apparent how much Cal enjoyed his role as grandfather and the one who had made this trip possible for all of us. It had been a wonderful Christmas gift for Isabella, who had asked that he include Nica and Angela, which he'd been happy to do. It was a trip the girls would always remember.

When it was time for us to leave, I knew that both Cal and Virginia were pleased with how this vacation time had turned out. Before heading back to Las Vegas, they would spend a week visiting friends of Virginia's in North Carolina, which would get them out of Nevada's high temperatures.

Mike, always in a hurry lately, had called only once while we were there. It was Tom who called each night. One of the times Tom called, I'd been in the bathroom brushing my teeth. I hollered for Isabella to answer it, and she'd been surprised that it was Tom, not Mike like she'd thought. Even so, she smiled and was pleasant to him. I heard her ask the other girls, "Tom wants to know if you want to go to his ranch and ride the horse again?"

"Yesss," they cried.

When I came into the room, Isabella held the phone out to me with a questioning look. I took it and went out onto the balcony to talk with Tom in private. He was pleased that the girls wanted to come back to the ranch, and he was happy that we'd be home the following day.

After hanging up, I sat outside to enjoy the pretty sunset amid the fading light. With all the twinkling lights in the park, it reminded me of Las Vegas. Isabella slipped out to sit next to me.

"Mama? Is Tom your boyfriend now?"

"He's a friend right now. Does that bother you?"

"A little," she said, honestly. "Are you still mad at Mike? Is it because of Allison?"

I looked at her worried look. "I'm not really mad at Mike. Sometimes we meet others who come into our lives for reasons beyond our control, and then we have to make a choice. Sometimes, it has something to do with karma and past lives."

Isabella frowned. "Mama? I have something to tell you then."

"You do? What is it?"

"When we were at Tom's house to ride the horse, I saw him watching you. When I closed my eyes, I saw you and him together as someone else in the past, like you and me and Grandmother. I could see it, Mama, and there was a baby!"

I was silent, absorbing what she'd said, thinking of my vision I'd had that was similar to hers.

"Does that always happen? Do we always meet again?" Isabella asked, curious.

I pulled her into my lap and hugged her. "I don't know, sweetheart. I do know that being with Tom makes me feel good and safe in a different way than being with Mike does. I'm not saying that it's better; it's just different. I'm lucky to have both Mike and Tom in my life." I sighed. "I don't know how it's going to end up, Isabella. I know you want it to be Mike, but I'm not sure that is what either of us wants."

She sat quietly, her head on my shoulder, although she was big enough to spread beyond my lap. "Do you think that Sammy and I have shared a past lifetime?" she asked, curious.

I laughed and tousled her hair. "I think you've shared *many* lifetimes!"

She giggled. "Me, too."

"Shall we let life unfold for the two of us and see what happens? Will you be okay with that?"

"Yes, Mama," she said as she hugged me tightly. "As long as you and I are together, that's all that matters."

CHAPTER 45

Once again, Karen was there to meet us at the airport when we arrived in Albuquerque. She'd left Sweet Pea at her house so it would be less confusing. The girls chattered on the way to Santa Fe, filling her in on some of what'd taken place.

When we dropped Angela off at her house, Karen and I smiled at seeing her parents and the boys lined up to receive her as if she were royalty. She opened the back car door and ran to them, talking all the way. She was becoming more outgoing and confident, which was a joy to see.

When we arrived home, Isabella and I were about to drag our suitcases out of the trunk when Karen came to stand by us. "Why don't you let Isabella stay with me for a few days? It will give you a nice change from spending all your time with the girls."

I knew Karen was offering me some private time to be with Tom. I looked at Isabella to see what she thought. She nodded her head eagerly. "Yeah, it'd be fun to stay with Auntie Karen and Uncle Coyote. Besides, Sweet Pea is there!"

"Are you sure?" I asked Karen.

"Yes, I'm sure, silly," she answered with a smile.

"Okay, if you're certain." I pulled Isabella into my arms, squeezing her tight. I whispered in her ear. "Have fun, sweetheart. Love you."

"I love you, too, Mama."

It felt funny to walk into the house without Isabella and no dog to greet me. I'd made myself a promise that I wouldn't call Tom, but if he called and wanted to spend some time with me, I would. It had been several days since I'd spoken with Mike and I decided I wasn't going to chase after him, either.

I took my time unpacking, and I began a load of laundry. It was still the afternoon, and I was tired. I decided to take a nap and relax without the noise of the crowds that'd surrounded us for the past four days. It was peaceful without that disturbance, and soon I was asleep.

Dreams filled my mind, and my heart began to pump with foreboding as I envisioned Mike and Tom on the front of the Lovers Card instead of a nude man and woman. They both were reaching out to me, and I was frozen in place, not knowing what I was going to do. Suddenly, I heard a popping noise, and I felt my breath sucked from me. I heard a howling scream that was unbearable to hear. I jarred awake to realize that the cry had come from me. My heart pounded, and I felt a sense of sadness overwhelm me. Coming out of my fog, I heard my cell phone ringing.

I was so lost in my dream that I barely had enough energy to pick it up.

"Hello?"

"Hi there, beautiful," Tom said.

"Hi, Tom. Where are you?" I asked in confusion.

"Right here in Santa Fe. I was hoping I could take you out for dinner."

"What time is it?" I asked.

"Is everything alright?" he asked.

"Yes. I just woke up from a nap, and I'm all confused," I chuckled.

"It's five o'clock. How about I pick you up in an hour and we'll go to a nice little place close by. Or is that too early?"

I sighed. "No, that sounds wonderful."

"Okay, then. See you soon. Can't wait."

I tried to set aside the ache in my heart as I slowly got up to take a shower to be fresh for that night. The warm water flowing over my body helped me awaken, and with that, I became excited to spend time with Tom. I fussed with my hair more than usual, pinning it up on one side. I'd gotten plenty of sunshine in Florida, so my coloring was brighter than expected, so I didn't need any makeup. I put on one of Louie's outfits he'd chosen for me, and when I looked into the mirror, I was happy with the result.

I needn't have worried about what I looked like because when Tom arrived, he took one glance and devoured me with a deep kiss that took my breath away. He held me close and murmured, "My beautiful Rosie."

I felt his nearness and became aware of his sexual response, so I hurried him out the door before anything more intimate could begin.

"C'mon, I'm hungry," I urged.

255

"So am I ... hungry for you," he growled as he pulled me back into another kiss.

"Tom Little Horse, let me go right now. I mean it," I said, slapping away his arm. "I meant it when I said I was hungry."

"Wow, I didn't realize that food was such a priority for you," he chuckled. "I'll have to remember that, my little tigress."

I laughed. "It's just that I haven't eaten since this morning."

"I understand." He eyed me. "I certainly have missed you, my beautiful, feisty lady."

I stopped and looked at Tom. "I've missed you, too," I said sincerely.

"Good," he said with a smile. "C'mon then, let's get you fed."

THE LOVERS.

CHAPTER 46

We sat in a small restaurant tucked away on a side street I'd never been down. That was part of the charm of Santa Fe. There were nooks where treasures were hidden, and this restaurant was one of them. The food was delightful, and the company even more so. Now that Tom and I were more relaxed with each other, we could chat away like long-lost friends while still aware of the sexual tension growing between us.

Tom drew glances from the women around us despite them being there with their own man. He seemed oblivious to their attention, confirming what he'd told me that he wasn't interested in them. There was no doubt about how charming a man Tom could be, and I was as taken with him as I'd ever been with any man. His allure was how he seemed to drink me in, making me feel like I was the only woman worthy of him. It was an odd sensation that I found tempting.

When we finished eating, he reached across the table and held my hand. "What would you like to do now? Would you like an after-dinner coffee or drink? Or would you rather go back to your house for one?"

I searched his eyes and answered honestly, "Let's go home."

"Home it is," he said as he called for the bill with a grin.

I noticed that he left the waitress a large tip, which pleased me for some reason. I liked the idea of him being a generous man.

Back at my house, while I poured us each a glass of Amaretto and soda, Tom stood behind me and wrapped his arms around my waist. He rested his chin on top of my head. "Ah, my beautiful lady, I'm so in love with you. I don't know how it happened, but I'm glad it did."

I felt his hands turn me toward him, and when he bent his head down, I eagerly accepted his deep kiss. I leaned into him, and this time, I couldn't ignore his stiffened manhood. His hands traveled the length of my back and then cupped my behind, lifting me and pulling me closer. His touch thrilled me, and I wanted more. Without a word, he easily picked me up and carried me into the guest bedroom, not wanting to share the bed where I'd laid with Mike. He effortlessly lifted my dress over my head, tossing it onto the floor while I scrambled to undo his belt buckle.

"Here, let me," he said, dropping his pants to the floor. His wanting me was apparent, and I wanted all of him. He kissed me over my bra and panties, and then when I began to moan, he removed them, revealing my nakedness. I was panting by then and had to control myself while he slowly kissed and tasted each of my feminine parts. I moaned and moved toward him.

"Not so fast, my beauty. Let me enjoy you more."

He took his time, and I was nearly desperate for him to go further. I began to plead with him. "Now! I want you now!" I'd never had to beg like that before, and there was a certain stirring in my soul to realize how much I wanted him.

"Okay, baby," he whispered as he entered me with a slow-motion that increased in speed. It was almost painful to have our joining be so beautiful and satisfying as we came close together. I would remember our first time together always. Little did I realize then how much.

We lay together and woke several times to make love again. I couldn't seem to get enough of him. I breathed him in, loving his smell and touch. When morning came, I awoke with Tom lying beside me, studying me.

"You are so beautiful, Rosie."

I felt self-conscious and began to cover myself.

"Oh, no, you don't. I want to kiss every part of you. Just relax and let me do what I want," he pleaded.

I felt myself float away in a sea of unleased pleasure that I'd never experienced before. Mike was an excellent, generous lover, and I loved his touch. But Tom brought out the sensual side of me that demanded more and more of what he offered with his lovemaking.

It turned into a day much like a honeymoon. We spent much of the time making love in and out of the shower, calling for takeout food, and enjoying each other in ways that were new to me. Most surprising of all, I didn't let any thoughts of judgment enter my mind. I simply enjoyed my time with Tom.

Toward the end of the afternoon, Tom suggested, "Let's get dressed and head out to the ranch. I need to check on the animals, and I'll have Ana cook us some food. You'll stay there with me tonight, won't you?"

I nodded, happy with the thought.

Driving onto the ranch, I felt a pang of guilt to realize how happy I felt. A voice inside said, "Everyone deserves to be happy, even you, dummy."

"What are you smiling about?" Tom asked as he grabbed my hand and squeezed it.

"Just happy," I answered.

When we arrived and went inside, I had to smile when I saw the table set and dinner ready for us to pop into the oven. Ana had left a note with cooking instructions and left a thank you to Tom for giving her the following day off. My heart raced with anticipation of what being alone with Tom would bring about.

Once again, while sipping glasses of wine outside on the patio, I was reminded of how easy it had become for me to be with Tom. It was like we'd done this before … just in a different way. I studied him to see if I could see him as the man I'd seen in my earlier vision. There was something about the way he lifted his chin that picked at my memory, and then it was gone.

We ate our dinner leisurely, and then I cleaned up the kitchen while Tom went to his office to take the call that'd come in for him. When he returned, he said, "I have to fly back to Washington. There's a big meeting and vote taking place. We'll still have tonight and tomorrow together before I take the Red Eye back tomorrow night." He came to where I was standing. "I'm disappointed. I was hoping to spend the whole week with you."

Knowing he would be leaving in a few hours made our lovemaking seem more urgent somehow. We spent another night and the next day wrapped in our own needs and wants. The only interruption to our blissful time together was when we noticed an Indian woman emerge from the woods, seemingly on the run. As Tom and I walked toward her, she ran from us and headed back into the park to hide. Tom called out to her in Tewa, but to no avail. She was gone.

"What did you say to that woman, Tom?"

"I told her that the ranch was a safe place."

Later, Tom dropped me off at my house before he continued to Albuquerque to fly back east. He kissed me tenderly. "I love you, my beautiful Rosie."

My eyes filled, and I nodded, too emotional to speak. I was sad to see Tom go but happy to know he planned to be back as soon as he could.

I called Karen to check on Isabella and Sweet Pea. We talked for over an hour. She knew me well enough to understand that, without giving her all the details, my time with Tom had been remarkable.

As I readied myself for bed, I was surprised to see how radiant I looked in the mirror. There was no hiding how happy I felt. Thinking of Tom, I smiled, knowing he was responsible for my glow. As I climbed into bed, my phone rang. Believing it was Tom, I answered without checking the caller ID. "I'm so glad you called!"

"Wow, that's quite a greeting," said Mike, chuckling.

I was stunned. "Hi there, handsome," I forced out.

"Rosie, I've decided to hell with it. I'm taking the weekend off and coming to see my girls."

"You are?" I squeaked. "When?"

"I get in early tomorrow morning, and then I'll have to fly out on Sunday. That'll give us two full days to be together."

"That's wonderful," I said, gathering my thoughts. "Send me your itinerary, and I'll pick you up."

"I'll text it to you right now. I can't wait to see you, Rosie. It's been too long."

"Me too," I mumbled. "See you tomorrow."

I telephoned Karen to update her on the news. "I'll come and get Isabella and Sweet Pea in the morning."

"Are you sure you wouldn't like some privacy time with Mike? I can have them stay another day if you want."

"Yes, I'm positive, Karen. I don't want to do anything to upset Mike, so it's better if we're all together."

"I understand," she said with a sigh.

Do you? I thought unfairly because I didn't understand how I would not hurt someone by being in love with two different men.

CHAPTER 47

Isabella was excited to have Mike visit us. I knew she wanted things back to the way they were before Allison stepped into the picture. She'd said as much to me. We hustled into the airport to meet Mike, Isabella holding Sweet Pea. When I saw Mike at the top of the escalator waiting to come down to the baggage claim area, my heart fluttered. No matter what happened, he was dear to me.

"Howdy, stranger!" I hollered and waved my arms to get his attention.

When he saw me, he smiled and hurried over to where we waited. He placed his overnight bag on the floor and put his arms around Isabella and me, squeezing us tightly. Sweet Pea squirmed for his attention, too. We gathered Mike's bag and headed to the parking garage. We loaded into the car, and I drove. Isabella began to tell Mike all about the trip to Disney World and some of the rides she'd taken.

"Even Grandfather and Virginia went on some rides. You should have been there, Mike! It was so cool."

Mike looked at me. "Cal and Virginia went on rides? That would've been something to see."

"It was, believe me," I chuckled.

"Did you get on the rides, too?" he asked.

"Of course! Not all of them, though, but enough."

Mike smiled. "Sounds like fun."

I turned to him. "How are things back in Boston?"

"Busy, but I needed a break. I'm hoping that we can find the right guy for our next hire."

"What? No more females?" I teased.

Mike shook his head. "Please, one female is enough."

I laughed. "I thought that since Allison is so great, you'd be in the market for another woman in the office."

Mike eyed me. "I'll repeat it… one is enough."

Isabella was quiet in the back, listening to our conversation. Mike turned to her. "What else have you and your sister-friends been up to?"

"Well, let's see. We went to Tom's ranch and rode his horse. That was fun. Mostly though, we have sleepovers at each other's houses. At Nica's house, Grandmother is teaching us all the Indian ways. I'm even learning Tewa."

"Who is Tom? Is he your new boyfriend, Isabella?" asked Mike.

"No, it's …."

I interrupted. "It's Tom Little Horse, Coyote's friend. I think you met him the night of Coyote's bachelor party."

"Him? How did *that* happen?"

"As friends of Karen and Coyote, we were all invited. Tom has a beautiful place where he keeps his Arabian horses. The girls had a great time."

"Well, that's good, I guess. That guy's such a blowhard, though," Mike complained.

"He's very different when he's not out in public," I defended.

Mike was silent.

When we arrived home, Mike was pleased to see the completed garage. He got out of the car and walked around inside it since I hadn't pulled in. "They did an outstanding job. Are you still going ahead with the breezeway?"

"Yes. The contractor will begin that next week."

"Nice. Do you have anything planned for today?" Mike asked.

"No, why?" I asked.

"I thought I'd like to take my ladies out for lunch. Maybe our favorite little place. What do you say?"

"That sounds wonderful to me. Isabella? Are you game?"

"Yes, I wanna go," she said excitedly.

It was nice to sit outside and munch our favorite "Tex-Mex" food. While we were finishing up, we ordered lunch for Grandmother. Then, since Isabella was through eating before us, she left to take it to her.

Mike asked, "Have you been able to help Coyote out?"

"Not much. I agree with him, though, that his nephew was murdered, but I can't come up with anything more than his death was drug-related. He wanted me to go over some of his other files, and when I did, I received a vision. A pretty terrifying one, actually. I saw a bunch of men in a brutal mass killing." I shivered. "I told Coyote to be careful. He says the FBI is taking over, but you know how that goes."

"Were those killings to do with the Scorpions?"

"That's the sense I got," I said, searching his worried eyes.

"You keep yourself away from it all, hear?" he ordered.

"I know," I answered, not wanting to pick a fight about his ordering me around.

"If you're finished, I'll get the bill, and we can head over to say hello to Grandmother and to pick up Isabella."

I nodded. "I'm done."

Mike took my hand as we left the restaurant and headed to the Palace of the Governors. I was glad that he didn't sense my reserve and confusion. I had created an awkward situation by loving two men, and I didn't know what to do. When we reached Grandmother's side, she looked up and smiled.

"Hi, handsome. When did you get back in town?"

Mike reddened at her calling him handsome, although I called him that all the time. "Just here for a few days."

"I think you're timing is impeccable," she smiled, looking at me. "And how are you, my daughter?"

My cheeks heated but, luckily, Mike wasn't paying any attention. Instead, he was being drawn away by Isabella to say hello to Nica, who was at the far end of the line speaking with an older woman there.

"Please don't say a word, Grandmother."

She cackled. "I don't have to; you'll work it out."

We soon left and headed to the grocery store to load up on groceries, much needed after being away and spending time with Tom. "Shall we have Karen and Coyote for dinner tomorrow night?" I asked Mike.

"Great. It'll be good to see them again. How is Karen doing, anyway?"

"Good. Her baby bump is noticeable, and she's over her morning sickness."

"How about we get some steaks then? I'll see if the butcher will cut them for us."

"That 'Sounds like a plan, Stan.' Want me to pick up some of our favorite coconut gelatos?"

"Pick up some pistachio as well. That's Allison's favorite, and it's good."

I said nothing because what could I say? I didn't want to get into a tug of war with Mike since I had shared time with someone outside our relationship as well.

We laughed at Isabella as she studied the variety of frozen pizza, trying to decide which one she wanted. "Why don't we order some freshly made pizza tonight for dinner instead? Is that okay with you, Mike?"

"Sure. Anything is fine as long as it's not Chinese takeout food. I've had a lot of that recently."

"Why so much?" I asked, curious.

"It's easy to pick up for a quick meal when we're on a stakeout."

Looking at the full basket, I asked, "Do we have everything we need? If so, let's go home."

Both Isabella and Mike nodded.

"Okay, then. Let's go check out."

THE LOVERS.

CHAPTER 48

That night after Isabella went to bed with Sweet Pea beside her, Mike and I sat out on the patio and sipped our after-dinner drinks of Amaretto and soda. We sat side by side like we used to.

"A penny for your thoughts," Mike said.

"Just a penny?" I teased.

He chuckled. "What's on your mind?"

"Mike, I want us to take the rest of the summer to think about what we want our relationship to be like come fall," I said earnestly.

"Wow, I didn't expect that. You know that I love you, Rosie, but …."

"I love you too," I interrupted, "but that is not what I'm saying. Let's take the time to consider how we want our relationship to move forward, if at all."

"I know what you'd like, but …"

"Let's not talk about it now," I interrupted again. "I want to enjoy our time together these few days. Then, by the time you're through in Boston and Isabella and I are back in Las Vegas, we'll take a close look at where we stand and where we want to be. Something that works for both of us, okay?"

"Fair enough, I guess," Mike said, hesitantly.

Mike reached for my hand and held onto it. We sat for a while, not saying anything until he suddenly pulled me up from the chair. "Let me show you how much I love you," he growled with lust, propelling me inside the house, toward the bedroom.

It was difficult not to compare Mike's lovemaking to Tom's. Although seemingly similar, it was very different. Mike and I had a compatible love relationship that was very satisfying and comfortable. Tom's lovemaking brought out in me the demanding, never enough, always wanting more sexual energy.

I thought about my earlier vision of myself with the man and the baby. By the look of things in that lifetime, I'd been quite a bit older—almost as if I hadn't found a man worthy of me until he had come into my life. I remembered the look he'd given me, which was so naked, filled with love and lust. I'd been lucky in that lifetime to find the man of my heart. Would I be that lucky again?

I pushed away those thoughts and relaxed in Mike's arms that'd tightened around my waist, making me a part of him as we lay together in bed. I fell asleep without dreams or disturbance of any kind and awoke to see Mike standing at the bureau looking at a scrap of paper. I recognized it. It was the jewelry receipt I'd picked up from his bureau in Las Vegas.

"What is it, Mike?"

"Where did you find this? I've been looking for it."

"Before I left for Santa Fe, you asked me to toss you your keys, and I knocked it off the bureau. We were in a hurry, so I picked it up and stuffed it into my pocket without thinking. I didn't realize I had it until I was here. I've already checked it out with the jewelry store, and the man there said that anytime I want to have my bracelet adjusted to bring it in."

"He wanted to adjust your bracelet?" he asked, surprised.

"Yes, but I wasn't wearing it at the time, so I told him I'd come back. He was very nice."

"Hmm, that's good to know."

We heard knocking on the door. It was Isabella joining us in her morning ritual. Mike crawled back in bed, and I hollered, "C'mon in, Isabella."

She lifted Sweet Pea onto the bed and climbed on top. "This is nice, isn't it, Mama?"

"It is, indeed," I said, aware of what she meant.

"What should we do today?" I asked.

"Angela called last night. She wants a sleepover tonight at her house. Her parents say it's okay with them if it's okay with you."

I chuckled and turned to Mike. "Her parents missed her so much they didn't want to share her with anyone for a few days. So, things must be getting back to normal at her house then." I turned to Isabella. "That's fine with me. Is it okay with you, Mike, since it's your only time here?"

"No, go have fun," he said, tousling her hair.

"Since Karen and Coyote are coming for dinner tonight, they can drop Nica off before they come here," I told Isabella.

"I'll pick up some more charcoal and beer for tonight," Mike offered. "I thought I'd drop in to see if Coyote is available for lunch."

"Okay, I guess I'll do some laundry then. Leave any dirty laundry in the laundry room, and I'll take care of it."

"Anyone for my special pancakes?" Mike asked.

"Yes!" hollered Isabella and me together.

Mike laughed. "Alright. Coming up!"

We all looked at each other and smiled … just like old times.

THE LOVERS.

CHAPTER 49

That night, Karen, Coyote, Mike, and I sat around on the patio, enjoying our drinks and talking. Karen surprised Mike when she placed his hand on her baby bump, and it was touching to watch his facial expression turn to awe as he felt the baby's movements. "Amazing," is all he said.

"Do you want children, Mike?" Karen asked.

He blushed. "It's something to think about, isn't it?" he answered without looking at me.

What the hell did that mean? I asked myself. Why couldn't he have answered simply yes or no? Or even maybe? I bit back any comment, and Karen looked at me with a raised brow.

"What about you, Rosie? Do you want more children?" she asked.

"I never had any brothers and sisters, so yes, I'd like more children."

Mike looked at me but didn't react to what I'd said. Instead, he seemed to become lost in thought. Finally, he spoke. "I hear you all went out to Tom Little Horse's ranch so the girls could ride his horse."

Coyote looked at Karen. "It was just Rosie and me who went with the girls that time. His horses and his whole place is beautiful," she said.

"Rosie says he's not quite the jerk he was that night before your wedding, Coyote."

Coyote chuckled. "He was all that, wasn't he? We grew up together and got into a lot of trouble as kids. We've both come a long way from back then. Tom's an okay guy now. He's got himself into politics in Washington—something I don't envy him for," sighed Coyote.

"Politics is not my cup of tea, either," Mike said.

I rose. "More margaritas, anyone?"

Karen held out her glass of lemonade, although it wasn't completely empty. "I'd like some more, please," she said with a wink, knowing I wanted to change the subject away from Tom.

Mike immediately got up and reached for her glass. "You, Rosie?"

"Yes, please."

It was comfortable for the four of us to be together, relaxed, and stuffed full of tasty food. Our feast ended with a tasty berry pie that Karen had made. It was delicious, and all of us but Coyote had second pieces. Several times I saw Mike check his cell phone until I couldn't stand it any longer.

"Are you expecting a call, Mike?"

He flushed. "Yeah, Allison is supposed to text me whether they arrested the guy we were watching, that's all."

"Wouldn't it be easier if you just called her?" I asked, unhappy.

"It's late back there now. It can wait until tomorrow."

All was quiet until Karen asked innocently enough, "How long are you going to be working in Boston, Mike?"

"Hopefully, I can get out of there in a few weeks," he answered, looking at me. "That's my goal."

"That would be nice," I smiled. Would it? I thought with a flutter of doubt. I sighed. At least by then, we'd know for sure where both Mike and I stood regarding our relationship.

"Well, woman, it's time for you to take a tired man home," Coyote said.

We all rose and headed to the front door. Karen smiled. "This has been great. It's nice to spend time with you again, Mike. When do you leave?"

"Late tomorrow morning. It was just a quick trip to see my girls," Mike responded, putting his arm around my shoulder.

"It's nice you could make it. I'll talk to you tomorrow, Rosie. Thanks for having us," Karen said.

"Goodnight, old man," Mike said to Coyote as he shook his hand goodbye.

Sweet Pea rose from her nap, and I let her out. Together Mike and I cleaned up the mess of our cooking and eating, and then turned off the lights and headed to bed.

We made love again. Because I'd formally requested a separation period, our lovemaking was more intense as we realized we wouldn't be together again for probably a month or, perhaps, never again. I felt torn with that thought and almost said, "To hell with it; I've changed my mind." But I didn't.

I snuggled against Mike and thought about when I first had become aware that he had fallen in love with me. He had been my pretend boyfriend while officially acting as my bodyguard from the dangers of working undercover at the Purple Passion Lounge. At the end of our assignment, he'd come to me and suggested that we take a chance and grow our relationship to see where it would go. Although pleased, I'd been surprised because I thought he was in love with our colleague. That was before Isabella had entered my life. Yet, when she had, he'd made it clear he wanted to be part of our makeshift family. The three of us had had a fantastic first year together, although an eventful one not always to his liking. He hated that I seemed to dig up trouble, and it worried him how many times I'd come close to dying. But something else was going on with him now, and I wasn't sure what it was. Although I was psychic, the answers weren't coming to me. Sometimes as a protection mechanism, they didn't.

When morning came, we lazily stayed in bed, not saying much, until it was time for us to get going or Mike wasn't going to make it to the airport in time. I wrapped my arms around him, "I love you, Mike."

"I love you, my queen. I truly do," he said in a husky voice.

Yet there was a 'but' hanging in the air, or was it just my imagination? My heart felt heavy, but I maintained a positive attitude. "I'm so glad you do," I punched him lightly in the arm playfully.

"Hey!" he laughed and grabbed me, pulling me to him.

It was my turn to squeal as he began to tickle me. Then, we both laughed as Sweet Pea joined in, jumping on us, giving us kisses.

At the airport, we kissed goodbye with no idea what lay ahead for us. I'd have to take it day by day. Isn't that the best way to live, anyhow? I berated myself.

CHAPTER 50

I'd missed a call from Tom the night before, so I was torn whether to call him back. I decided not to. Instead, I called Isabella.

"Hi Sweetheart, are you ready for me to pick you up?"

"Can't I stay here?"

"Not tonight. Let's give Aunt Maria a break, okay?"

"Please, Mama! We're working on a project, and I don't want to miss out."

"Let me talk to Maria then."

"Aunt Maria, Mama wants to talk to you!" she hollered.

"Hi, my dear friend. How is everything there?" I asked.

"All is good. The girls are writing a story and are having a lot of fun with it." She laughed. "Isabella is signaling me for you to let her stay. Is that okay with you?"

"If it's okay with you, it's fine with me."

"How did your visit with Mike go?" she whispered into the phone.

"As well as can be expected. It was good to see him as always, but I have no idea where our relationship stands. We agreed to talk about it at the end of the summer. Hopefully, he should have things tied up in Boston by then."

"Hang in there. It'll work out," encouraged Maria.

"We'll see," I said without conviction. "Tomorrow, the girls can come here, if it's okay with you."

"That sounds nice. I'll plan on it," Maria said.

"Okay then, my dear friend. Over and out," I said, using the term her little boys used.

Maria chuckled. "Yes, over and out."

When I got home, Sweet Pea greeted me, worried that she'd be left behind again. Looking around the house, I saw a mess that comes from people relaxing and living. To get my mind off the two men in my life, I began to clean the house with a vengeance. Before long, the bright afternoon light began to fade, and dusk neared. I had more cleaning left to do when I heard my phone ring. It was from Tom.

"Hi, beautiful, how are you?" he asked in a sexy voice.

My heart thudded in nervous excitement. "I'm fine. How are you and things in Washington?"

"A mess, actually," he chuckled. "Nothing new, though. I'm sorry to miss our call last night. Is everything okay?"

"Yes, everything is fine."

"That's good. I'm going to try to make it back there in a couple of days. I can't wait to see you again," he said in a husky voice.

"I can't wait to see you, too," I responded, surprising myself with its truth.

We talked a bit more about what was going on in Santa Fe, Washington, and the world. Talking to Tom was never boring, so it was no surprise that an hour had passed in a blink of an eye.

"Goodnight, love," Tom said. "Say hello to Isabella."

"Goodnight, Tom Little Horse," I said with a smile in my voice.

Shortly after, I received a text from Mike. "Arrived safely."

Mike wasn't himself. I thought of the one person who might know what was going on with him … Brian. Without hesitating, I tapped in Brian's number. I was surprised that he answered right away.

"Hi, Cowboy, it's me, Rosie."

"Yes, your name came up on the cell," he teased. "Is everything okay?"

"Not really, Brian. What's going on with Mike? What's going on between him and Allison? Be honest with me."

Brian cleared his throat. "What has Mike told you?"

"I want to hear what you have to say, Brian. I'm worried."

"Mike always comes across as the strong, silent type, but the only time I've seen him come out of his shell is when he is with you … and now Allison."

I was speechless; there was no breath left in me to be able to say anything. I felt as if someone had kicked me in the gut.

"Rosie? Are you there?"

I grunted.

"It's not the same as with you and Mike, though. It's just that Allison is all over him, and it's hard for any man to ignore her completely. If it makes you feel any better, he says that she is driving him nuts … and not in a good way."

"As Allison's employer, are you saying that her behavior is okay with you, and you are going to allow it?" I asked in a frosty tone.

"What I'm saying," he said defensively, "is that we are all adults, and given enough time, things will right themselves. You can't force it; you know better than that."

"It sounds as if you're saying to give her enough rope, and she'll hang herself."

"I wouldn't use those words exactly, but pretty much."

"I see. Well, thanks for the update ..."

"Wait," he interrupted. "Hold on. I know that guy pretty well, and I know that he loves you and Isabella. He's just confused right now, okay?"

"Okay? Do I have a choice?" I asked, lashing out in anger.

"Rosie girl, listen to me, please. Don't do anything rash. Let things be for now."

"What are you saying, Brian?"

"Don't give up on him just yet, Rosie."

"Well, thanks for being honest with me."

"One more thing to remember. Mike isn't the only one who loves you. You can count me in on all who do, you know."

That's when my tears began to fall. Barely able to form the words, I choked out, "Goodbye, Brian."

I sat on the couch and sobbed until there were no more tears. How could I even hate Allison? Mike was such a good guy that I couldn't blame her for wanting him in her life. I left the cleaning things out and dragged myself to bed, hoping a good night's sleep would make things seem better in the morning. I was so drained of emotion that I slept like the dead and never heard Mike's call.

CHAPTER 51

The week slipped by. I'd heard from Tom, confirming that he'd be back in Santa Fe the next day. He asked me to join him for dinner at the ranch, and I'd made arrangements for Isabella and Sweet Pea to stay with Maria, who was aware that I was spending time with Tom. There weren't any secrets between us as we'd become sister-friends as well.

It'd been an upsetting week. Things were strained between Mike and me while, at the same time, things were heating up with Tom. A pounding headache was building, and I went to the medicine cabinet to grab some Tylenol to stop it. As I pawed through the vitamins and supplements I usually took daily to find the headache pills, I pulled out a pharmacy bottle that had been pushed back into the corner. When I saw what it was, I could barely breathe. It was my birth control pills. Why were they there? My heart

283

dropped as I realized that since I'd returned to Santa Fe, I had not set up my usual routine for taking any of my pills. I felt hot and flushed. Why hadn't I? It didn't make sense. I was always so careful about everything. I tried to remember the last time I'd taken any of the pills at all. It'd been the last morning I'd been in Las Vegas. I immediately unloaded the medicine cabinet and began to fill my container with my daily pills and supplements. Thank God, it hadn't been that long since I'd been without them.

I was excited to be heading out to the ranch, and when I arrived, Chief barked and then greeted me with enthusiasm. As Tom stepped forward, he took my breath away. I'd forgotten how handsome he was. He smiled and turned to me with softened eyes.

"Hello, beautiful, I've missed you."

I blushed. "Hi, Tom."

He tilted my chin up and kissed me tenderly on my waiting lips before deepening it with passion. "Oh, my God, Rosie, you have no idea how much I've missed you."

"I just might ..." I said with a grin.

Inside, Ana had a pitcher of margaritas waiting for us, but we decided first to see the horses up close. As we stood outside Scout's stall, I felt movement in the corner of the barn and heard whispering. I touched Tom's arm and held my finger across my mouth before pointing to the place where I'd heard the noise. He nodded and led us closer while keeping up a dialogue about the horses. We heard more rustling as we came closer, and when we looked into the empty stall at the end, we jumped back in surprise. Two Indian women looking worn and battered, sat there staring at us in fear.

"What do we have here?" asked Tom in a gentle voice. He switched to Tewa and spoke to them. He seemed shaken to hear what they had to say.

"What is it, Tom?" I asked, worried.

"Women on the run, I'm afraid," he said, shaking his head in disgust. "We'll have to get them into town where it's safe. There's a shelter there somewhere. Can you stay with them while I call Coyote to see what arrangements he can make?"

"Of course." I squatted down beside them and said, "You're going to be safe here." I didn't know if they understood me or not.

Tom returned shortly and spoke to them again in Tewa. He turned to me, "Let's take them up to the house. Ana can feed them, and we'll drive them into town as soon as Coyote has it settled."

The women were shy and embarrassed about their situation but eventually allowed us to usher them up to the house. Ana put together a meal for them in the kitchen, and I watched them eye her food hungrily. Tom handed me a margarita and led me outside onto the patio.

"I hate to see that," he said. "I've seen too much of it in my lifetime."

"I'm so sorry, Tom," I said while putting my arm around his waist. He held me tight against him. "I'd never hurt you, Rosie. I want you to know that."

I knew what he said was the truth. "I know you wouldn't. Why would you even say that?"

"When you come from a background as I had, there's always someone who wants to prove the adage "like father, like son." Always said as if they want it to be true."

"Well, I know better than that. You're a good man, Tom Little Horse."

He bent down and kissed me tenderly. "I love you, Rosie."

Ana came to us. "Why don't I serve your and Rosie's dinner now, Tom? That way, you won't miss out on a meal before you have to go into town."

I knew Ana had heard Tom exclaim his love for me, and I wondered if she approved. When I turned to face her, she smiled at me, happiness on her face.

Coyote called back with the good news that there was room in a safe house for both women. They had a doctor there who would look at their injuries to determine if they'd need a visit to the hospital. We would drop them off at the doctor's office, and he would meet us there and take them to a safe location.

We took Tom's car, and I left mine at his ranch. Without using words, it was understood that Tom would spend the night with me at my house, and together we'd go to his house the next day when I'd pick up my car. Sexual excitement stirred in my body, mingling with my desire to love him completely. Determined to enjoy our time together, I pushed any thoughts of Mike from my mind.

After dropping the women off, we headed to my place. We'd barely gotten through the door when Tom backed me against it and hurriedly began to remove my clothes while I began to remove his. It was a race to the finish, and we laughed at our eagerness. It was a light moment filled with love, lust, and promise.

After reaching a point where it was hard to hold back, Tom lifted me and placed me on the guest bed, where he began his slow, methodical lovemaking that made me scream out in pleasure. It was such a freeing experience, and I couldn't get enough of him.

Afterward, we lay sated in our love for each other. Tom fell asleep while I lay awake, thinking about the two men in my life. The truth was that I'd probably be happy living with either of them since they were such good men in so many ways. And I loved them both … just in different ways. I seemed to be waiting for Mike to decide for both of us what our relationship was going to be. Yet, what did I want? Wasn't it about time I stepped up to claim what would make me happiest? Did I feel obligated to spend my life with Mike since he'd been there for Isabella and me, or was there something more? Was it ever that simple? And Tom had baggage like the rest of us. I needed to know what Mike and Tom wanted in a relationship with *me* and how it fit in with what *I* wanted. Why did life have to be so complicated?

CHAPTER 52

The next morning, I awoke to space where Tom had slept. I heard him on his phone, talking to someone. It sounded like business, and I hoped it wouldn't interfere with our plans today. We were going on another picnic in the Santa Fe National Park.

When he came back into the room, he brushed his hair back with his fingers trying to tame his tousled hair. I didn't think he could do anything that would mess up or take away from his striking good looks. As he walked toward me, I automatically held my arms wide to greet him with my entire body, and the yearning, sensual look he gave me was the same I'd seen in my vision. I was shocked, realizing that it had been Tom in that lifetime, next to me hovering over the bundled baby.

We made love again with an endearing tenderness and something so magical I'd remember it forever. Afterward,

Tom gathered me to him, and I rested my head on his chest, listening to his strong and steady heartbeat. We talked about a future together and the fact that he wanted children. We spoke about Isabella's plight, and he laughed at the idea of how I arranged to have both Maria and me be Isabella's mothers. He declared that she was doing so well because of me. I told him it was more than me who'd assisted. I filled him in on all those who were helping her, including Mike.

He nodded in acknowledgment. "Isabella's a lucky little girl."

"So am I," I declared, kissing him.

"And so am I," he stated. Then he tilted my chin up so that I could look him in the eye. "Rosie, will you marry me?"

I was speechless.

Mistaking my silence, he added, "I've loved you from the first moment I saw you sitting there in that restaurant. I want you to be my wife and the mother of my children. I adore you."

My eyes watered, looking at him. "Will you give me a little time to think about it? I have Isabella to ..."

He gently placed his finger across my lips. "It's okay. Take time to think about it, and let me know as soon as you can."

I nodded. "I love you, Tom Little Horse."

"And I love you, Little Bird."

I didn't even bother to ask Tom why he'd called me that. I didn't think he even realized he had.

We showered together and dressed casually for our outing at the park. When we reached the ranch and entered the kitchen, Ana was standing at the stove, stirring something in a pot, humming a beautiful tune. Once again, we saw that Ana had packed a picnic lunch, sitting on the counter, waiting for us to pick it up. She turned when she heard us. "Oh my, you two are glowing."

Tom kissed her cheek. "What's that quote you used to say—'All good things come to he who waits'?"

"He's waited a long time for you," confirmed Ana, looking at me with love. "I'm happy for you both."

Overcome, I remained quiet.

"Ready, Rosie?" asked Tom, holding his hand out to me. When I felt sudden goosebumps across my body, I hesitated. Tom leaned toward me and grabbed my hand, pulling me with him out the door, leaving a smiling Ana behind.

Before we mounted the mechanical beast, Tom showed me the motorcycle's various parts and how they worked. Hoping to remove my trepidation, he asked whether I wanted to be the driver or the passenger. I let him mount first, then I got on behind him, tightening my arms around him. This time, we slowly made our way to the shady spot of Tom's childhood. Once again, we spread the blanket out together and set up our picnic.

I had to give Ana credit because her picnic lunch was a gourmet's delight. We began with crusty bread, soft cheese, and grapes. Tom handed me a full glass of crisp Riesling wine and poured himself one. He lifted his glass. "Here's to us."

"None, better," I added, and he laughed.

After we had nibbled on our treats, he reached for me. "Let's go down by the water. What do you say?"

"It'll be nice to dangle our feet in it," I said.

As we settled on a log close to the water's edge, Tom took me into his arms and kissed me deeply. "You have me bewitched, Rosie. I can't get enough of you."

"I could say the same about you, my handsome Indian."

He chuckled. "I'm glad to hear it."

Suddenly, I found it hard to breathe. I stood up, and my head swam. I was dizzy and out of balance. Tom rose, alarmed at seeing my state. "What's the matter, Rosie?"

"I don't know. Everything was blank for a minute, and things didn't look familiar." I shook my head and reached out to him to steady myself. "It's passed now; I'm okay."

"Let's clean up and head back to the ranch," Tom said.

We walked to the picnic area. As we were gathering our things, two Indian women came around the bend, startling us. They looked at us in fear. The older one spoke in Tewa to Tom. He nodded and pointed the way down the path we'd taken to arrive here. They hurried along with the older one urging the younger one on, although she seemed to be injured.

"What's going on, Tom?"

He shook his head, upset. "It seems that word has gotten out that my ranch is a safe place for women to get help away from their abusers. I'll call Coyote and see if he'll meet us at the ranch."

"Okay," I mumbled as I bent down with my head between my knees, trying to clear my head of the images of death that were flooding my mind. I felt sick to my stomach, and an overwhelming sadness washed over me.

"Rosie, are you okay?" asked Tom at my side. "What's the matter?"

"Just give me a few minutes, and I'll be fine."

"Okay, I'll pack up while you sit right there on this stump," he ordered.

The underbrush exploded as two men immerged. One of them was the same man Tom had chased away before.

As soon as he saw us, a look of recognition crossed his face. He advanced and angrily demanded, "Where are they?"

"Where are who?" Tom asked.

"What are you, a wise guy? You know who we're talking about. Where are the women?" he slurred.

I stepped forward. "We haven't seen anybody."

"Is that right," he said in a dismissive tone.

"Yes, that's right," I said in defiance.

"Well, I don't believe you, do you White Owl?" he asked the drunken man behind him.

Although both men had been drinking, White Owl was plastered and could barely stand up straight. He was holding a pistol, which worried me when I noticed it. I looked at Tom, who'd seen it as well.

"Look," Tom said, holding his hands in the air in a submissive way. "We're not looking for trouble here. Let us pack up, and we'll be out of here."

"You're not going anywhere," growled the first Indian. "Right, White Owl?"

"Right, Dark Wolf!" he responded, holding his gun higher.

"Hold on, fellas. You don't need any more trouble in your lives right now. Let us go, and things will be fine," implored Tom as he came closer to me. He reached for my hand. He pulled me up, and we began to slowly make our way to the motorcycle, leaving our picnic behind.

My heart was racing. The two Indians were slowly following behind us. As we came close to the bike, the older one lunged forward and grabbed my hair. The sudden force of it flung me to the ground. Tom whipped around and grabbed for him at the same time White Owl squeezed the trigger.

"What the hell did you do that for?" screamed the older Indian. "Let's get the hell out of here."

Tom groaned as he held onto his stomach area with blood leaking out. I went crazy when I saw all the blood. I raced to where the tablecloth lay and ripped it in half. I wadded it up and handed it to Tom to apply pressure on the wound. I looked around, searching for anything that would help Tom. There was nothing.

"Get up, Tom. Let's get you out of here," I ordered, frantic.

I immediately called 911 to report what'd happened and to send an ambulance out to the ranch. I asked the emergency team to call Coyote. Then I grabbed the hand that Tom held out as he tried to get up on his knees. I pulled with all my might. With a grunt, he rose, doubled over.

Everything became in slow motion without thought or feeling. I knew exactly what to do to get the bike going and how to help Tom get up on it. He loosely held onto me with one arm around my waist until I screamed at him, "Tighter, Tom. Hold onto me tighter!" And he did.

I wouldn't have won any prizes for the way I drove the motorcycle, but soon enough, we arrived at the ranch in time to see the ambulance barreling down the road toward us. I screamed. "Help me! Help me, please!"

I drove the bike close to where the ambulance was pulling onto the grass. Coyote had just arrived and was rushing across the lawn toward us. I dropped the bike while I grabbed Tom around the shoulders, pulled him off, and lowered him onto the ground. I hovered over him.

"Tom, can you hear me?"

He moaned and opened his eyes. "I love you, my beautiful Rosie," he panted.

"Hang on; you're going to be alright, Tom," I pleaded.

Coyote immediately came to my side. "What happened, Rosie?"

"He was shot by someone named White Owl. Is he going to be okay?"

The medics surrounded Tom, and Coyote gently pulled me away from them.

"He's going to be alright, isn't it, Coyote?"

Coyote looked to the medics who had surrounded Tom. At the negative shakes of their heads, he said, "It doesn't look good, Rosie."

I pushed aside the medics and squatted down next to Tom, who was barely breathing.

"Yes, Tom Little Horse! Yes, I'll marry you," I exclaimed as I bent down to kiss him. "Can you hear me? I love you!"

Tom blinked tears away. "Good," he whispered hoarsely and smiled. Then, he grimaced and went still.

"Did he pass out?" I asked, searching the faces of the medics. "He's going to be okay, isn't he?"

Embarrassed, the medics turned away, and Coyote reached for me, gathering me in his arms.

"He can't be gone, Coyote. He just can't be. Not now! You have to do something," I wailed, pleading, pulling on him.

"I wish I could," he replied with a sob.

I clambered down on my hands and knees, clutching Coyote's leg. "Please do something, Coyote. I beg of you, please!" I screamed at him as tears slid down both of our faces. Then everything went black after I felt the prick of a needle.

CHAPTER 53

I awoke to Karen sitting beside me, clutching my hand. I was in my bedroom at home, and when I recalled what'd happened, I wept deep, gulping sobs. Karen sat quietly, letting me release some of my anguish. The depth of my sadness was overwhelming me, and I fought it back with my anger.

"What's the point of loving someone only to have them murdered? Why bother to love someone at all? What's the point, Karen?" I demanded, angry. "What the hell?"

"I know you're hurting, Rosie, and I don't blame you for being angry. It's true that you've had to deal with the loss of two men you loved because they were murdered. And that's more than most of us have to endure. But one of your greatest loves is Isabella, and she needs you more than ever right now. She's heard some of your ramblings and is aware of your desire to throw in the towel on life itself. If you want her in your life, you need to show her you do, right now! Are you listening to me?"

I was so surprised by Karen's scolding that I laughed. It surprised her, and then, she too laughed nervously. She'd turned into a strict mother hen, and it was clear that she had no intention of indulging me. Because that was so new, and unlike her, I began to rise to the occasion. I listened as she told me that I'd been kept sedated for two days to calm my state of mind, during which time I'd threatened to end my life to join Tom.

Isabella wanted Grandmother to talk to me, and she and Coyote were on their way now to pick her up to bring her here. More tears fell, and my heart twisted at the realization I'd burdened Isabella with my selfish thoughts. I'd always told her that I wouldn't do anything that would deter me from having her be my daughter. I was a mess, and I needed to pull myself together.

When I heard them enter the house, I sat up in bed and drew my fingers through my hair, trying to give it some shape while Karen went to greet them. The first one to come into my room was Isabella. When she saw me awake, she rushed to my side.

"Oh, Mama! I'm so glad you're awake."

"Come here, my darling daughter. I'm so sorry if I scared you. I'll always be here for you. You know that, right?"

She hesitated a second, "Yes, Mama. Just don't do that again, okay?"

"You've got yourself a deal, my beautiful daughter," I promised as I gathered her into my arms.

"Don't cry, Mama. It's alright."

"I know. I'm just sad."

"I'm sad too," she whispered. "I know you loved Tom."

"Yes, I did ... and still do," I said, planting kisses all over her face until she giggled.

Grandmother came through the door, smiling as she took note of the two of us. Isabella was holding my hand and reached out her other hand for Grandmother to take so that we could be connected. Grandmother looked pleased. "My beautiful daughters."

She studied me for a moment. I felt as if she could see into my soul. "Isabella, will you leave us for a few minutes? I want to talk to Rosie alone."

Immediately, Isabella rose and went out to where Karen and Coyote sat in the kitchen, sipping coffee.

"Grandmother—my mother, I'm glad that you're here," I said as tears fell despite my vow not to share them with her.

She kissed me on the forehead and pushed my hair back away from my face. "Child, life is a bag of tricks. This may be a sad time for you, but out of sadness often comes joy with new beginnings."

"I don't understand what you're saying, Grandmother. I'm finding it hard to think about joy at the moment," I grumbled. She said nothing but nodded her head. "Was it wrong for me to have loved Tom, Grandmother?"

"When has it even been wrong to love, my daughter?" She saw my confusion. "True love is never wrong. Lust without love or manipulating love for one's own benefit is never right. So no, Little Bird, loving Tom wasn't wrong."

"The truth is that given the opportunity, I would love him again."

"Ahh, my daughter. Isn't that what you just did?" she asked with a knowing look.

CHAPTER 54

After nearly a week, I still wasn't my old self. I felt sluggish and not my usual chipper self. Nevertheless, each morning I forced myself up out of bed and put on a smile that was only half there. I made sure to go through the motions of the day so that I wouldn't upset Isabella.

I wanted to go out to Tom's ranch and check on Ana. I knew that she had suffered tremendously with Tom's death because she'd had been a part of his life for many years. For her, it would be as if she lost a son.

It was Maria's turn to have the girls for a sleepover, so after I dropped Isabella at her house, I decided to go out to the ranch. As I did, memories of my time with Tom flowed over me, and I fought tears.

When I arrived, the house was quiet. Ana was nowhere in sight, and even the dog was missing. I smelled something cooking in the oven, and the sliding glass door was open. "Ana?" I called out.

It wasn't until I wandered outside that I saw movement in the barn and headed that way. Goosebumps covered my body. When I got closer to the barn, I could hear voices raised. Fear gripped me as I heard Ana's voice pleading, "Get your hands off me. Leave me alone!"

I stopped and punched in Coyote's number to tell him there was trouble at Tom's ranch, and please come. The dog was barking hysterically. After a yelp, the dog suddenly became quiet. Then I heard muffled whispers and drunken laughter. I sneaked closer to the barn's opened door and waited. Without making a noise, I stepped inside the barn. The darkness of the barn blinded me for a moment, and I was unable to make out who was there. When my vision cleared enough, I saw Ana lying on the barn floor, unconscious, next to Chief. I crept to her side.

"Ana?" I whispered, shaking her.

Suddenly, an arm wrapped around my neck, and I was lifted up and dragged against a body reeking of alcohol. "Lookee here, White Owl. Look who can't stay away from us."

My heart fell. The same two who were responsible for Tom's death. "What have you done to Ana?" I demanded of Dark Wolf.

"I don't tolerate sassiness," he slurred. He pushed me against the outside of Scout's horse stall and then sexually leaned against me. I raised my arm and knocked him across the face with my fist when he began to lower his mouth to mine. "Leave me alone!" I demanded.

He wiped his mouth that was now bleeding, and his eyes hardened. "You bitch."

"Get away from me," I ordered as I tried to push him away. That angered him, and he raised his arm, and with the palm of his hand, he slapped me across the face, jarring me. I was startled and realized I'd have to develop an escape plan fast, or I would be in big trouble. White Owl seemed more interested in drinking his booze than what we were doing, and Ana and the dog were still out cold. I prayed for help. As if to answer my prayers, Scout began to neigh and paw the ground, causing enough racket that we turned to him in alarm. That's when I noticed the shovel just inside the stall. Unexpectedly, without warning, Scout stretched his head over the stall's half-door and bit Dark Wolf on his shoulder, distracting him.

"Holy Shit!" he hollered and jumped around, rubbing his shoulder.

White Owl lumbered forward to see what'd happened, distracting Dark Wolf further, giving me enough time to grab the shovel. I swung the shovel at the two men with all my might, first hitting White Owl and then Dark Wolf in one swipe. The awful sound from the shovel hitting their heads was one that I'd never forget as long as I lived. White Owl fell to the ground and didn't move. Dark Wolf's hit had been slowed by my hitting White Owl first, and he began to rally after a few minutes. I seethed in anger as I looked at the two of them, knowing they were responsible for Tom's death. When I saw the gun lying on the floor that had been knocked from White Owl, I reached for it.

I picked it up and pointed the gun at Dark Wolf. It was the naked fear that crossed his face that made me hesitate from pulling the trigger. Tears rolled down my face. "You bastard."

I raised the gun higher. Dark Wolf began to step back with his hands shielding him.

"Stay right where you are," I ordered.

"Don't shoot me!" he pleaded.

"You deserve to be shot—a man who beats and torments women. Why should you be allowed to live?"

A deep voice interrupted us. "You don't want to do that, Rosie. Give me the gun. The law will take care of him," Coyote said.

I moved the gun away from Coyote's reach. "What makes you so sure he'll get what's coming to him, Coyote? He's just another man who hurts women and never gets more than a scolding, if that. Why not let me handle this right now."

Dark Wolf looked terrified because he sensed I'd like nothing better than to do away with him. Coyote held out his hand to accept the gun from me as tears ran down my face.

"Give me the gun, Rosie. It's what Tom would want you to do," he gently demanded as his eyes softened at my distress.

Hearing that, I handed him the gun and covered my eyes with my hands. "Just get both of them out of my sight," I demanded as I wiped my tears away.

Coyote's deputy cuffed each of them and led them away while Coyote and I stepped to Ana's and Chief's side. Ana sat up and, with one hand, rubbed her head where she'd been hit and, with the other hand, patted the dog, soothing him.

Coyote helped Ana back to the house while I followed with Chief by my side. Then Coyote's cell phone went crazy. As he listened to a call, his face darkened, and disbelief crossed his face.

"What's wrong, Coyote?" I asked, frantic. "It's not Karen, is it?"

"No," he said, shaking his head in dismay. He studied me. "The FBI raided the house where the Scorpions were meeting, and … and you were right, Rosie. It was a blood bath."

"Oh, my God!" I exclaimed.

"The only reason I wasn't with them is that I was called to come here, and I missed their call." He looked amazed. "If you hadn't phoned me to come to Tom's, I would've been in the middle of it."

"You mean you didn't know about the raid?" I asked, confused.

"Typical of the FBI. They must've changed the timing of it without letting me know in advance."

"I'm glad you weren't there, Coyote, and I know Karen will be too."

He nodded, still bewildered by his good luck. "If you ladies are okay, I'm heading into town now."

"Go. We're okay," I urged.

I turned to Ana and pulled her into a hug, and we sobbed together over Tom's death and what'd just occurred. We stayed like that for many minutes. Then we headed back to the house and talked for hours.

Tom had left everything to Ana with the understanding that she sell the ranch and donate the proceeds to the Tesuque Pueblo with specific instructions he'd left. Even with the large mortgage he had on the ranch, it'd still be a nice sum of money along with the value of the two horses. Tom had left Ana the small house he'd previously bought her, and she'd inherit his insurance policy money, so she was financially set for the rest of her life.

"I'm so happy to hear that Tom made sure you'd be okay. He really was a good man, wasn't he?" I asked through new tears.

She nodded, too emotional to speak. Then she rose from her chair. "Stay right there; I have something for you."

She returned, carrying a small velvet box, and handed it to me. "For me?" I asked.

"Yes. Tom was so excited to give it to you. Open it." Inside was a beautiful three karat diamond ring in a beautiful setting.

"Oh, I can't take this," I said, tears forming.

"It's yours, Rosie. Tom would want you to have it. Please, take it." After a few minutes, she patted my hand. "Have it made into a necklace, and his spirit will be with you always."

We talked some more about what Ana intended to do. I left her saying that if she needed my help, I'd be happy to help her. I took the ring, liking the idea of turning it into a pendant, and headed home with a heavy heart.

CHAPTER 55

Another week passed, and I was still feeling sluggish and tired all the time. Karen thought I was depressed, and maybe I was. I'd heard from Mike saying that he'd be out of touch with me for a few days since he was tied up on a case. I didn't argue or fuss. I thought it was already too late to salvage my relationship with him. After all, Brian had made it pretty clear to me that Mike was entranced by Allison.

It was time to think about packing up and heading back to Las Vegas. Knowing that Sammy was back home was making it easier for Isabella to part from her sister-friends. We'd be back in Santa Fe for the Columbus Day weekend so that the girls wouldn't be apart for too long.

I woke up in a dreamy state, thinking about babies. I jolted utterly awake when I realized that I'd missed my period, which had been due several weeks earlier. Good Lord! Was I pregnant?

Before Isabella would be returning from yet another sleepover, I ran my errands. When I returned home, I immediately unloaded the groceries and then dashed into my bathroom to take the pregnancy test. While I sat on the closed toilet seat, waiting for the results, I began to panic. What was I going to do if I was pregnant? Who was the father—Mike or Tom? Would I be willing to raise this child on my own since Tom was no longer here and it looked as if Mike was out of the picture?

I looked at the stick and saw the color had changed to blue—a definite sign of pregnancy. My heart dropped. I took another test, and the results were the same. I thought about the lovemaking that I'd had with the two men in my life. Mike and I didn't worry about protection since I was on the pill, and at the time of our last lovemaking, neither of us knew I hadn't been taking the medication. I thought of the times I'd had with Tom. We'd been careful with Tom using extra protection, but I couldn't be sure we had each time we'd made love since our lovemaking had been so wild. I became determined not to cry about my situation but to continue ahead, and things would work out the way they were supposed to. I didn't even want to talk about it with my sister-friends yet.

We readied the house for our leave during the next few days and said goodbye to our friends. I went alone to say goodbye to Grandmother, who was sitting at her favorite spot at the Palace of the Governors. She watched me approach, and her face lit up, and a broad smile crossed her face.

"Come, my daughter. Sit."

I sat down beside her and took her hands in mine. "We're leaving tomorrow, and I will miss you, Grandmother—my mother."

"I will miss you too. You are troubled, my daughter. What is it you want to tell me?"

"You know, don't you, Grandmother?"

She tilted my chin so our eyes could meet. "Yes, my daughter. The gods have favored you with a child, and you are worried you'll have to explain to everyone how this happened. Am I right?"

"I don't know who the father is, Grandmother."

"Does it matter?"

"Yes," I replied honestly. "Can you tell me who the father is, Grandmother? Do you know?"

She hesitated and stared at me, searching for her words. "Go home and tell Mike that his son is on the way."

"Are you sure, Grandmother? Mike and my relationship has pretty much ended. Brian seems to think that Mike is involved with Allison, and she's almost always there with Mike whenever we talk."

"You might be surprised. The Great One has her own version of the truth, and sometimes it's very different from what we believe."

"Grandmother, I won't tell Mike about the child unless he says he wants to be my life partner. I refuse to *trap* him into a relationship with me."

"Good," she said, patting my hand in approval.

Saying goodbye to Maria and Karen left me feeling lonely. But I was determined to move on with my life with purpose, no matter what happened. Now there would be two children to care for and love.

CHAPTER 56

After Karen dropped us off at the airport in Albuquerque, I sighed. Isabella looked at me in concern. "Are you going to be alright, Mama?"

I smiled and pulled her closer. "Of course. Why wouldn't I be?"

She looked at me, doubt in her eyes. She tilted her head and raised her eyebrows while studying me. "A baby is coming, Mama. I've seen him. And, don't worry, I'm going to help care for him," she stated determinedly.

I looked at her in surprise.

"I've seen him, Mama," she assured me.

"Oh," I said. "I'm amazed that you have."

She laughed. "Even Sammy has seen him," she added.

I grabbed her and held her tight. "I love you, Little One," I said.

She smiled. "I know."

311

Even with Isabella's excitement about the baby, my joy was quickly dampened with thoughts of the precariousness of my rocky relationship with Mike. My heart squeezed at the thought of losing him, and the lyrics of a song I'd heard flowed to me—"What do I have to do to make you love me?" I pushed them aside, knowing I would never force myself on anybody. Things were going to be as they were, no matter what. I hadn't heard from Mike since two days before when he said he'd be back in Las Vegas as soon as he could—said he was sorry, but he couldn't be more definite than that.

When we landed, my stomach was in knots with nerves. Isabella had control of Sweet Pea in her carrier while I had one overhead piece of luggage to handle. We'd pick up our other bags from the regular carousel on the first floor. I was holding onto the railing of the escalator moving downward when I felt Isabella shift beside me. She pointed and said, "Look, Mama!"

At the bottom of the steps stood Mike, looking as handsome as ever with a wide smile. He stood with his arms held wide as we came near.

"What are you doing here?" I asked in surprise before he gathered me into his arms, along with Isabella and Sweet Pea.

"Aren't you glad to see me?" he asked.

"You have no idea," I proclaimed as I looked around. "Where's Allison?"

"Allison? I imagine she's back in Boston, where she belongs."

"Ohhh," I whispered against his shirt.

Mike chuckled. "We have a lot to talk about, don't we?" he said, kissing me lightly. "C'mon, let's get out of here."

Once home, we took the time to unpack and begin to settle in. Isabella received a call from Sammy, inviting her to his house, and we let her go. It left Mike and me some time to talk alone. Seeing his nervousness, I think that he was as anxious as I was to address the issue of our relationship and where each of us wanted it to go.

He took my hand and led me to the couch. Once seated, he turned to me. "I owe you a big apology, Rosie. I wasn't fair to you by not committing to you when I had the opportunity."

As I started to protest, Mike held his hands up, his face red. "No, please let me finish." He held onto my hands and looked intently at me. "Can you find it in your heart to forgive me for my behavior for the time I was in Boston?"

I noticed that he avoided mentioning Allison by name. I paused long enough to make Mike shift in his seat. He squeezed my hands tighter as if to not let me escape until I answered him.

"Mike, when you weren't willing to commit to our relationship, I was devastated. But the act of us not moving forward in our relationship set both of us free to see other people. A test of sorts, I guess." It was my turn to squirm as I looked deep into Mike's eyes. "Outside of our relationship, I spent time with Tom Little Horse, so that you know."

"I thought so. It nearly killed me to realize that it was my doing. If only ...."

"No, Mike, stop right there," I said, holding my hand up in protest. "Please, let's not go down the road of 'if only.' We are where we are now, and we need to make our decision here and now. What do *you* want our relationship to look like going forward?"

"Can you love me again, the way you used to?" he pleaded.

"No," I said, shaking my head. I sat with my thoughts for several minutes. "I want to love you more than that."

Mike took in a deep breath and let it out. "Rosie, here's what I want. I want to go to bed with you at night and wake up with you by my side each morning. I want to love you so much that you'll never have reason to doubt my love. Besides Isabella, I want you to be the mother of our children, and I want to grow old with you. I would be proud to call you my wife," he said with watering eyes that threatened to overflow.

I stared at him, speechless. It was everything I'd wanted to hear.

"What do you say, Rosie?"

"Does ditto say it all?" I asked him, smiling.

"It sure does," he laughed and brushed away my tears.

Then, he enthusiastically pulled me up from the couch where we'd been sitting. He grabbed me and held me tight. "God, Rosie, to think I nearly lost you. I couldn't live with myself if that'd happened. Let's celebrate. I bought a special wine to toast our new beginning."

"About that," I said. "I have something to tell you…."

THANK YOU

Thank you, my beautiful readers, for reading *Death on the Run*. I hope you enjoyed it. If so, please take time to leave an honest review. Your words matter! Your opinion about a book helps others decide whether or not to read it, and we authors are always grateful for your reviews.

The FINAL book of the Death Card Series – *DEATH COMES CALLING* will launch on September 21, 2021, and you won't want to miss out on seeing what happens to Rosie, Mike, Isabella, and everyone. It is available as a pre-order so GRAB IT NOW!

As time passes, Rosie finds herself to be "a woman of a certain age" … and bored. Reviewing her life, she misses her younger years when she was more involved in working with the police to solve cases. So, when Police Chief Roberto calls her to help find a runaway girl, she jumps at the chance.

Working as a mother/daughter team, Isabella and Rosie set out to solve two murders they believe have everything to do with the missing girl. When Joslin unexpectedly gets involved, Rosie doesn't know if she can save her granddaughter in time. Is there any way to stop Death if it comes calling?

If you haven't already, visit www.joanspeck.com to sign up for my newsletter to get free books, enter contests, see what's new and more.

ACKNOWLEDGMENTS

I want to thank Jeanette Johnson, who stepped in to become my proofreader. We know that there are "earth angels," and you are one of them. Thank you!

I'm sincere when I say that I can't do anything regarding my writing without these two beautiful souls:

Kelly Martin. I am blessed to have you in my life. Your creative, artistic talent is without limit. Time after time, you have expanded any idea I may have into something exquisite as you provide me the most beautiful covers, videos, and other artwork. You inspire me, and I love you dearly, my friend.

Jake Naylor. It is hard to put into words how much you mean to me. All you have to offer me and others knows no bounds … you are that gifted. You have a way of adding your touches to make more beautiful whatever I present to you. For years, you have been my rock in creating my websites, layout work, and marketing materials. I'm ever grateful to have you as my gifted friend. You inspire me to be better in all ways. I love you to the heavens and beyond.

BOOKS BY J.S. PECK

THE DEATH CARD SERIES
- Book 1: Death on the Strip
- Book 2: Death at the Lake
- Book 3: Death Returns
- Book 4: Death in the Shadows
- Book 5: Death on the Run

Angels Out of the Dark

BOOKS BY JOAN S. PECK

- The Seven Major Chakras – Keeping it Simple
- A Simple Approach to Living a Successful Life
- What You Need to Know to Live a Spiritual Life
- Prime Threat – Shattering the Power of Addiction

J.S. PECK

Joan was reared in a family of readers in small-town Elmira, New York. Each Sunday afternoon was a special time where each member of her family was able to relax with a good book. "It is when I began reading the Nancy Drew series that I became intrigued with mysteries. To me, the fun of reading mystery books is to become so intrigued by the story it becomes impossible to put the  book down. Many times, a good mystery has caused me to stay up all night to finish it to see if I was able to figure out 'whodunit.' For anyone who is hooked on reading mystery books, there's nothing better than that."

Joan was also raised to be open-minded. She came to the understanding that we are all connected energetically and can communicate with others who have passed on. She brings that idea into her Death Card Series by having the spirit of Rosie's grandmother pop into her life with advice or loving messages. Rosie is portrayed as a psychic, which means she is able to have visions of what is yet to come about.

"I hope you enjoyed reading this book and the entire Death Card Series. If so, please help other readers discover it by leaving a review on Amazon, Goodreads, or Bookbub. I thank you for your kindness."

Joan also writes other books under the name of Joan S. Peck.